THE

TREACHERY OF SISTERS

The Untold Story of Arsinoe and Cleopatra

GAIL COMBS OGLESBY

This book, while based on a true story, is a work of fiction. Though some characters, incidents, and situations are based on the historical record, the work as a whole is a product of the author's imagination.

Copyright © 2024 by Gail Combs Oglesby

All rights reserved, including the right to reproduce this book or portions therof in any form whatsoever. For information contact https://gailoglesby.wordpress.com/

Editing by Alexandrea Dillon
Author photo by Mary Hamilton Photography

Manufactured in the United States of America

Also by Gail Combs Oglesby

The Centenary Chronicles-Tales
of American Women
On the Wings of the Red-Tailed Hawk
Till I Come Home
Her Last Full Measure

*For River whose presence in the world
has brought me so much joy.*

Contents

Chapter 1   Escape from Alexandria 1

Chapter 2   Betrayal 24

Chapter 3   Exile 48

Chapter 4   Outside the Wall 67

Chapter 5   A Beginning and an Ending 85

Chapter 6   To Avoid a War 108

Chapter 7   Run.. 137

Chapter 8   No Time for Pretenders.......................... 160

Chapter 9   Dionysus Incarnate............................. 185

Chapter 10 Power Unleashed..............................211

Chapter 11 Too High a Cost............................... 240

Chapter 12 Another Roman Conquest 266

Epilogue 289

Author's Note 293

Glossary.. 295

About the Author.. 299

CHAPTER ONE

ESCAPE FROM ALEXANDRIA

The granite was cold against my back as I leaned against the wide column, trying to catch my breath. I could hear footsteps running past me. Men shouted, "She must be found! Look everywhere!" If they found me, they would kill me. The tunnel that led out of the palace was just down the corridor. Could I make it? If I hesitated eventually the guards would return. I couldn't stay here. I needed to go now.

"Shhhh… don't make any noise," said the man as he clasped his hand over my mouth.

"Ganymedes! Thank the gods! You found me," I said as I turned to embrace him.

"It was not easy Princess, but we must go before the soldiers come this way. Follow me as quietly as you can," he said as he took my hand and led me behind the sheer curtains billowing in the light breeze and into the door hidden in the wall behind them.

The starkness of the tunnel was an enormous contrast to the

brightness of the palace on the other side of the door. Its walls were decorated with beautiful mosaics encrusted with jewels. It shone in the light like the sun. The colonnaded walkways paraded along the onyx floors with fountains and lush vegetation everywhere you turned. Even this secret door was ebony on the other side to match the decoration on the wall. Very few knew this door even existed. My elder sister Berenice had tried to escape through this tunnel once, but she failed. Father captured her and had her executed. That could certainly be the fate that waited for me as well if my escape were not successful.

The tunnel was dark and dank. It smelled of smoke and stale water. There was a greenish tint to the walls covered with a repugnant feeling liquid and I did my best to walk without touching the walls. It was lit by torches, but Gany doused each one as we passed, plunging the path behind us into darkness. We could hear voices, but they didn't seem to be close, so we kept on moving toward the opening that would take us out to the main street near the market.

The floor started to slope downward, so I knew we were getting close. My brothers and sisters and I used to play in this tunnel when we were children, sneaking out into the market to pretend we were like them, ordinary Egyptians without the burden of royal life. True, being royal has its privileges as my father liked to constantly remind us, but it also had its obligations and scrutiny that was often unwanted. Not to mention the fact that our family had a bad habit of killing each other.

"Almost there, Princess. Watch your head," said Gany as we ducked into the lowest part of the tunnel. They would not catch us now, I realized, and I could not help but breathe a sigh of relief.

I do not know what I would do without Ganymedes. He has been my loyal servant since I was only a child. He had served my older sister Bernice before me but after Father had her executed, he came to serve me, already a eunuch. He was spared because my father did not believe he had been involved in her coup which ousted him from the seat of power in Egypt, forcing him and my half-sister to flee to Turkey. If he had, he would not be standing here now, but instead, he would have been fed to Sobek, the god of the crocodiles. I missed my oldest sister, but the situation I found myself in was partly of her making. She forced Father to align more closely with the Romans, so I did not grieve for her at that moment. When my father King, Ptolemy Auletes, was away in Rome negotiating with Julius Caesar to form an alliance, the citizens revolted against him. Eventually he fled to Turkey with my half-sister Cleopatra. They placed my sister Bernice Epiphaneia, and my mother, Cleopatra Tryphaena, on the throne.

It took Father nearly two years to take his kingdom back from these two Queens of Egypt. My mother sadly died, poisoned perhaps, and Berenice married but she did not have an heir. My father returned with Roman troops and executed her and her husband and reclaimed the throne. I was only eight. When he died, he left my brother Ptolemy XIII who was only twelve, and my half-sister Cleopatra VI who was eighteen as co-rulers. They hated each other. Akin to an asp and a scorpion, they were always vying for the upper hand. It did not take long for my brothers' advisors to convince him to remove our sister so he could rule alone. I felt sorry for him because he was being manipulated by these men and abused by his sister-wife. But what could I do? People looked upon me as a little girl, with no mind for the workings of the palace. They were wrong.

"Wait! I hear something," said Gany, shaking me from my thoughts.

We stood silently, pressing our bodies against the wall to make ourselves as small as we could. I am sure we did not have far to go but if the soldiers came through the tunnel quickly, we might still have been apprehended. If we failed in this effort, we would not get another opportunity. Surely my half-sister would imprison me or more likely, execute me. She was to blame for our situation and more, and yet I feel no pity for her.

Cleopatra brought this on herself, excluding our brother from royal processions and even making coins with only her image and nothing of him. This would have angered anyone, I am sure; it would have angered me. As if the gods had also conspired against her, the Nile barely flooded that first summer and Ptolemy's advisors were quick to blame her. Pompey's son even asked her for help in fighting against Julius Caesar and she gladly offered him grain, soldiers, and ships. However, given that the crops were less forthcoming with little flooding, her move was not received well by the citizens of Alexandria.

My brother dethroned Cleopatra, and she fled to Syria, knowing he would have her killed. Our family has a long history of infighting, mothers fighting children, and husbands killing wives. Since we also only marry within the family, we are basically killing our own bloodline. But that has never stifled the violence or changed our tactics. Our parents were brother and sister who married each other just as Cleopatra is now married to Ptolemy XIII. Since her less than ceremonious departure she had been rallying support for her cause, wanting nothing more than to return to rule in Egypt... preferably without Ptolemy. Skirmishes between his and her forces had been going on for many, many months. But now there was a new complication. It is not just my brother and half-sister who are involved in this dispute. Now Rome has arrived in Alexandria.

Julius Caesar had finally triumphed in the Roman civil war against his old friend Pompey. With the war effectively over, Caesar wanted to capture his enemy and force a reconciliation, so he chased him all the way to Alexandria. Pompey had been a true friend of my father and surely, he thought that he could seek asylum here in the palace in Alexandria. Cleopatra had supported him from her exile as much as she could with her limited means.

Unfortunately, my brother, who was not thinking clearly and who listened too much to others, had Pompey murdered and he presented his severed head to Caesar. He thought that would make him happy, but he was very wrong. Caesar was enraged at him. How dare Ptolemy think he could have a Roman nobleman murdered? He felt it was a gross sign of disrespect, and he demanded that Pompey's remains be gathered and given a proper funeral.

Now in Alexandria, Caesar injected himself into this debacle over who the rightful ruler of Egypt should be. He says my father asked him to arbitrate if the need arose. Even though my brother is on the throne, Caesar is not pleased with him. Even so, he would not dare to openly remove him. When Cleopatra learned that Julius Caesar was coming to Alexandria, she left Syria and slithered back into Egypt hoping she could sway him to intervene on her behalf. I am sure Caesar must know that she had supplied

Pompey, and yet she still thought she could win his support. She has managed to secret herself into the palace and she has spoken to Caesar…some say seduced. Either way, he now supports her cause to be joint rulers again.

With this new development, my brother Ptolemy and I have been confined in the palace for months now. Cleopatra says it is for our safety, but we know it is to keep us imprisoned and prevent us from raising a rebellion. A few days ago, some of our supporters, those who wish Rome were gone, attacked the palace in an attempt to free us. Caesar responded by setting ships on fire in the harbor to draw the rebels away, allowing more Roman troops to get to the palace. But this distraction also gave me an opportunity to flee. If I did not do it now, I may never have gotten another chance. It is only a matter of time before Cleopatra murders all of us to ensure she is the only rightful heir to the throne.

"Wait here. I need to see to a few things. If you must come out, I have made arrangements," said Gany, having finally reached the door to the street.

He slipped through to the other side before I could ask any questions, closing it tightly behind him. Now near-total darkness engulfed me with just a bit of light coming through under the door. I felt the amulet of Osiris hanging around my neck, my fingers tracing the little groves and mounds carved into the bright blue lapis lazuli. Then the voices started echoing through the tunnel, and I could see light coming from torches near the entrance to the palace. They were onto us. The fear was rising in my belly, and it was all I could do to keep my hands from trembling as I grasped the door handle. There was no choice. I opened the door and went through it.

Sunlight blinded me for a moment, and I could barely see what surrounded me. Once my eyes adjusted, I could see that the marketplace was teeming with people running in every direction, scurrying like rats to get out of the way of whatever menace they thought was coming. I covered the lower part of my face and head with my scarf and tried to avoid making any eye contact. There were Roman guards everywhere as well as Egyptian guards from the palace marching through the streets.

Luckily, I was quite small for my age and would probably be mistaken for a child of only ten or eleven, and not a girl of nearly fourteen. I moved to stand across from the tunnel door knowing Gany would come back to this place for me, but before he could, more soldiers came out of the tunnel and flooded into the streets. I knew these men. They had guarded me at the palace. I turned my face toward the wall and looked down at my feet.

"Here, come quickly," said a woman's voice in my ear as she grabbed my hand and pulled me inside a nearby small mud and stone building.

She braced the door with a chair as she held her finger to her lips to let me know silence was necessary. We listened intently with our backs against the door as the voices of the soldiers barked outside, just inches away. My breath was ragged, and I could feel the beads of sweat running down my back. If they found me, surely all would be lost. It took a few minutes, but the angry voices finally faded away and we could breathe.

"Thank you..."

"My name is Nrimeda, Princess Arsinoe," she said with a slight bow.

"How is it that you know who I am?" I asked with trepidation, quickly looking for a way to escape if need be.

"Ganymedes is a friend. He asked me to watch the door in case you were forced to come out. He will be back for you soon. I don't think he thought they would come through the tunnel so quickly."

"Well, you must be the arrangement that Gany spoke of. I am most grateful to you indeed. Thank you, Nrimeda."

She looked to be a woman in her thirties. As I looked around, I realized this small building was her home. The entire thing was about the size of my bedroom in the palace. It was clean and orderly with no sign of children, but perhaps a husband.

"You live here alone?" I asked.

"No, my husband has gone with Ganymedes to gather some supplies. They should return at any moment. Can I get you some wine?" she asked shyly.

"Yes, that would be appreciated."

My throat was parched and the wine, while of poorer quality than I was used to, was most welcome. I sat on the only chair while Nrimeda sat on the edge of the bed. Then there was a knock on the door. My heart leaped into my throat.

"It is them. Not to worry," she said as she quickly removed the chair and slowly opened the door. Gany and another very large man were quickly inside, and she placed the chair against the door again.

"I am sorry I was not back in time, Princess. I hope Nrimeda has made you comfortable," said Gany breathlessly.

"Yes, very. I'm glad to see you though," I said smiling at him.

"This is Usurpria, he is Nrimeda's husband and my help and strength," said Gany as he patted the man on his shoulder.

"Thank you, to you and your wife both for your help," I said warmly.

"It is our duty Princess Arsinoe, and an honor to have you in our home, although I wish it were under better circumstances," he replied with a nod of his head.

"Do you have any word about what is happening at the palace?"

"Yes. Queen Cleopatra sits on the throne, with Julius Caesar at her side. Your brother the Pharaoh is still being held but Cleopatra is enraged by your escape, and she has ordered all the palace guards and what remains of her army to find you."

"Well, that is no surprise. She would slit my throat herself if she had the chance," I said, looking at their anxious faces.

"We need to get you away from here. If you linger, there is no doubt that you will be captured," said Gany.

"There is a small boat waiting to take you south outside the city walls where we have set up an encampment. You will be safe there while we assemble the army behind your cause," added Usurpria.

It is not my cause; not really. It is the cause of our people to drive the Romans back to Rome. My father never should have gone to them. They took Cyprus from his brother, the loss of which led him to take his own life. Caesar has made a show of giving it back to me and my younger brother to buy our compliance, but I would spit in his face if I were near enough. My brother should have had Cleopatra killed. That would have been the wise thing to do. Knowing her and her deviousness she would certainly have dispatched him given the chance, and me too. Now he is a prisoner in his own palace, while I flee, and our dear Cleopatra sits on the throne, as Caesar's puppet. While any Ptolemy with a claim to the throne lives, they are a threat to the other. It is simply the way it is.

"Thank you, Nrimeda. Perhaps our paths will cross again," I said as I prepared to depart.

"I hope so, Princess Arsinoe. It would be a source of happiness for me," she replied.

As Gany, Usurpria, and I boarded the boat I couldn't help but feel wistful. I loved Alexandria. It is the city of my birth and my birthright. It would be impossible to stand by and simply watch it fall into league with the Romans. We are Egyptians. We rule ourselves. If we must fight the Romans, then fight we will. As the sun set, the city was bathed in its last golden glow, and the lights began to fade more and more into the distance. Our boats moved along silently through the water, stopping only occasionally to hide among the reeds when other boats were near. By morning we had arrived in a remote area south of the city. I was surprised at how many people were already assembled there.

"This way, please. We have a place set up for you just here," said Usurpria as he led the way toward a large tent on a hill near the water's edge.

"Thank you all, for getting me safely here. I would like to sleep now for a bit," I said, feeling the weight of what had happened suddenly crashing down on me.

"Of course, Princess. There will always be two guards outside your tent. These are men I trust with my life, and with yours. You need only to call out if you are ever in danger. I will have some food and drink brought to you in case you are hungry. Lira is your servant. She is the daughter of a trusted soldier, and she will be with you always. Get some rest as we have much to do," said Ganymedes as he bowed before leaving me alone in the tent with her.

She was a small girl, about my size. She was rather plain-looking, but her hair was beautiful and full as it rolled off her shoulders. Her tunic was simple but clean and she kept her hands folded in front of her as she looked at the ground. She seemed to be a couple of years younger than I, perhaps just twelve or thirteen. I wondered what she must think about all that was going on around her and of me.

"It is Lira, yes? Could you fetch me some water with which to wash? Are there other clothes I might change into while you wash these?"

"Yes, your Highness. I have water waiting for you just out-side. I will bring it in, and I have placed on the chair, here, a new tunic for you to wear. There is a trunk of clothes waiting for me to unpack and prepare for you which I will do when you awake," she replied with her hands clasped together and her head deeply bowed.

"You will sleep when I sleep?" I asked.

"Yes, my princess. I have been told to always stay with you and to never leave you alone unless you ask me to leave. While you are sleeping on the bed, I will be lying here next to you should you need anything. I have a gong to ring outside the tent to request anything you may need without leaving your side."

"Very good, Lira."

I was grateful for the bowl of water so that I could wash my hands and face. I watched as the layers of dust quickly turned the water into a brownish sludge. The bed was inviting, although small, but the warmth of the blankets was most welcome. The night on the Nile had chilled me to the bone. I could hear Lira lying next to me on the floor quietly saying her prayers, but I was asleep so quickly I did not even hear the end. It was dark when my eyes opened again. I was obliged for the food Gany had brought in. I was ravenous and realized I hadn't eaten in over a day. As I looked around the tent, I noticed a few of my favorite possessions. Gany must have arranged for them to be taken here. My statues of Serapis, Isis, and Ra stood on a small altar, for which I was most grateful. I owed them my prayers for our safe passage, which I planned to do as soon as I had eaten.

"Ah, you are awake, Princess Arsinoe?" asked Gany as he gingerly entered the tent with several more candles which chased away more of the darkness, forcing it into the corners.

"Yes, I slept soundly, and I owe many thanks to Serapis and you for bringing some of my things," I said gratefully.

"I hoped to make you feel less alone here with a few of your possessions to surround you," he said with a smile.

"I am never alone when you are near."

"Your humble servant, my princess," he said with a bow.

"Is General Achillas here?"

"Yes, although some of his troops are still gathering."

We were very lucky to have Achillas with us. He had joined my brother in trying to fight my sisters' return but they had limited success. My brother would not be happy when he learned what I had planned, but as far as I was concerned now, he could no longer be of any help. Achillas would rally his men behind me, and we would try again to remove the vermin scourge that is Rome, and the vile Cleopatra along with it.

"Pasherienptah III is here as well, Princess Arsinoe, for your blessing and crowning which we will do at first light tomorrow. Once we declare you the rightful Queen of Egypt there is no going back. You know it cannot be undone?" said Gany with quite a serious tone.

I sighed deeply, "Yes, I know. To go back now would simply be to face my death. While I am not afraid to do so I would rather know that my death was purposeful and will perhaps free my people from Rome. My brother wants to rule alone, and my sister wants to rule with Caesar, so I have no choice. Egypt is my birthright as much as theirs and I will not go quietly to Cyprus as Caesar wishes and watch Egypt suckle at the teat of the Romans."

"You are very brave Princess Arsinoe. You have always been."

"I owe much to you and Serapis. Make no mistake Gany, you have been like a father to me, and so much more," I said as I kissed him lightly on the cheek.

"I am not worthy of your praise, my queen."

A bit of laughter escaped despite the situation. "Not until tomorrow," I said smiling.

The sun rose across the river in shades of gold and pink shining up into the sky, its rays forming a crown over the water. It was a sign from Horus of his blessing. As I stood on the bank of the river with my soldiers gathered around me, I could not help but feel the power of the moment. My white tunic shone in the sunlight and my gold bracelets and amulets amplified the light. As Pasherienptah went through the ritual, the sun rose higher in the sky, topping the trees until we were all bathed in its warmth and light. I felt a peace settle over me, even though I was signing my death warrant through this action.

"Now in the name of Ra and Serapis, I name you Queen Arsinoe IV, anointed by Isis and Osiris, ruler of all Egypt," proclaimed Pasherienptah.

With that, I turned to face my army, raising my crook and flail toward the sky. One after another, in a wave as far as I could see, the men dropped to one knee with clenched fists over their hearts and their heads bowed. It was an overwhelming sight, and I cleared my throat to speak as loudly as I could. At this moment I was most grateful that my sister had taught me Egyptian as she was learning it. It was the only thing I could be grateful to Cleopatra for, I'm sure.

"I am Arsinoe, the fourth of my name and the rightful Queen of Egypt, one with Isis and blessed by Serapis. With your help, we will remove the stain of Roman blood that taints our throne and our kingdom. We are Egyptians. Our destiny is our own, our fate is our own. With the power of Isis and the strength of men, we will take back what is rightfully mine. What is rightful yours. An Egypt that is ruled by Egyptians! We will chase Julius Caesar back to Rome where he belongs. Now your queen orders you. Rise, pick up your swords, and fight!"

With that, the crowd roared to life cheering and brandishing their swords into the air, calling on the gods and their queen for their favor. My heart swelled as I looked from face to face of these brave men. I knew at that moment that we would prevail. I also knew many of these men would be lost, their faces seen only by the gods until their family joined them in the afterlife. Now the work must begin to plan our attack. There was no time to waste, as to hesitate would be fatal.

"General Achillas, it is an honor to meet you," I said as Gany showed him into my tent. His armor glistened in the sunlight that streamed into the tent.

He immediately dropped to one knee and placed his fist on his heart, just as the soldiers had done earlier. He was a brutish-looking man, with a ruddy and marked complexion. He had the creases and crevices of a man much older than his age. His hands were fat and his fingers short, as was his stature. He was not at all the man I was expecting to see, the one who was brave enough to join with my brother to fight Cleopatra and Rome.

"My queen, I swear to you my undying fealty and that of my troops. We are here to ensure that you will sit on the throne of Egypt," he said as he looked at my feet.

"Rise Achillas, your queen gratefully accepts your fealty and thanks you for it," I replied.

"Yes, my queen," he said as he rose to face me.

His eyes were piercing, and he was looking at me intently. Perhaps he was wondering how it was that he was now taking orders from a mere waif of a girl who called herself the Queen of Egypt. I watched him for a moment, hesitating before I spoke. He waited patiently, respectfully.

"Do you think our cause a just one?"

"Yes, my queen. The throne of Egypt should, as you said, be ruled by Egyptians and not by the interlopers from Rome. I am at your disposal," he said with a gallant sweep of his hand and a slight bow.

"We must attack Caesar at once, from the south where his troops are the weakest. He has concentrated most of his men on the north thinking that an attack will come from the sea," said Gany.

"I have sent scouts to see where the enemy may present the greatest weakness and they seem to support an attack from the sea, and not from the south," replied Achillas.

"No, I am most confident in my sources, and I trust them more than your scouts. We must move in from the south and we must do it quickly before Caesar realizes that Queen Arsinoe has control over most of the Egyptian army," Gany said with a bit of exasperation.

The men looked at me expectantly. I have always trusted Ganymedes and certainly, I would not have come to this place without him. But Achillas oversaw the army. Would he know more than Gany in this case? I did not know and was unsure how to respond but, I knew I could not let them see me as indecisive.

"I agree we must attack quickly, there is no doubt of that. I suggest you each send out your own scouts again and then determine if there is agreement between them. If not, I will make the final decision about the direction the attack will take. Now, see to it at once and return to me when you have more information," I said with a dismissive wave of my hand.

"My queen," said Achillas as he turned quickly and left the tent.

"Arsinoe, are you sure this is wise?" asked Gany.

"You may continue to refer to me by my given name when we are in private. But make no mistake, you are to call me Queen Arsinoe or Pharoah when we are in the company of others."

"Of course, my queen, I meant no disrespect," said Gany as he bowed more deeply than usual.

"None was taken. Yes, I do think this is wise. We cannot afford to alienate Achillas. He is the one to whom the soldiers have rallied. We must tread carefully until we better understand for ourselves if their loyalty could be shifted, perhaps to you?"

"You would place me in charge of the soldiers?" Gany asked with an air of surprise.

"Yes, why would that come as a surprise to you?" I asked with irritation.

"Men are often reluctant to follow those who are… like me, not a true man," he said with an air of resignation.

"Your inability to whore around with the men you lead is of no concern to me. I need someone in charge of the army whom I can trust. Someone I know who will never turn them into a weapon against me. If I say to the soldiers that they will follow you, then they will, but we must not make them suspect that we do not trust Achillas. At least not yet."

"As you say, my queen. If you wish for me to lead this force you need only ask. You know I am sworn to you with my very life, and I will gladly give it in service of your cause," replied Gany as he pounded his fist on his heart.

"I know. Now please, let's see to those scouts. We have no time to waste."

It took four days for the scouts to return and as I suspected Gany had been right. If we had attacked from the sea we would surely have been at a significant disadvantage. Achillas was not happy with the outcome, knowing it made him look weak, but no matter. It would probably be best to dispatch him once we had an opportunity to clear the way for Gany to take control. The first battle with Caesar's forces was a huge success. I made a point of awarding Ganymedes in front of the senior leaders rather than Achillas.

"Gany, we need to remove Achillas when we next encounter enemy forces. I suggest that he be seen to fall in battle, honorable and without cause for suspicion."

"I concur. I will see to it," said Gany without hesitation.

"See that you do. Once he is dead, I will appoint you General of the infantry and chariot forces, keeping General Hemotephe in charge of sea-faring men and ships. Of course, I will continue to oversee all military resources with you and Hemotephe to ensure my orders are carried out," I said. I tried to sound confident, but I could feel myself shaking a bit.

After Gany left I laid down on the bed covering my eyes with my arm. Did I just order a man's death? Were there other options? No, I was confident it was the right thing to do, much as my brother should have done with Cleopatra. I could not risk Achillas having any doubt about our mission. Despite his words, I felt that he could easily be bribed as his allegiance had changed several times over the last year. If he were to turn his forces on me there would be nothing we could do. Lira stood silently in the corner with her head bowed. I wonder if she thinks I am a cruel and heartless leader. Sometimes I pondered whether I should wear the description reluctantly or proudly.

In my heart of hearts, I had prayed to Isis to seek her guidance. It was clear that the person in charge of the military forces must be someone I could trust without reservation. Hemotephe is the cousin of Ganymedes, the son of his mother's brother and they grew up together as siblings after Gany's mother died. As he trusts him with his life, so must I.

While Achillas was fighting what, unbeknownst to him, would be his last battle, Ganymedes took some of the armed forces to take possession of part of the Nile. This will give us control over the canals that bring the lifeblood of water to Alexandria. He has managed to identify the canal that is providing Caesar's water supply for his troops and now he has created a way to force salt water into the cisterns. We hoped that this brackish water would cause the troops to flee, as without clean water they could not survive. If we could force some of his troops to leave, it would give us the upper hand in any future battles. Rome has a mighty army; many say the strongest among all nations. They can never, ever, be underestimated. We must fight with cunning and secrecy in ways they will not expect or be able to respond to effectively.

Word reached me that Achillas was killed in the fighting. We have ensured that he received the rights and burial of a hero, so there would be no question regarding our fondness for him. Ganymedes looks resplendent in his military attire, and it seems as though his fears of acceptance were unwarranted. He has been welcomed warmly as the new leader of our forces. This change brings me great comfort and relief. I was pleased that a meeting of all the leaders had been called.

"My queen, may I present General Hemotephe who leads our fleet, and Vizier Petrus Anneus, the leader of the horse-mounted soldiers and chariots," said Gany as each of the men kneeled in turn and swore their allegiance as they were introduced to me.

"General, Vizier, I thank you for your support of our cause. I am anxious to hear what has been planned for our next attack."

"Unfortunately, our attempt to drive out Roman soldiers by tainting the water has done nothing more than create a distraction for Caesar as he had to attend to it personally. New wells have been dug and so we accomplished little. We have heard that the thirty-seventh legion is traveling by sea toward Alexandria, but they have encountered opposing winds preventing them from making it to shore. They must be short of water by now, having traveled a great distance to get there. I have scouts watching them and the rest of Caesar's fleet as well. He has come with some of his ships to see if they can find water nearby to fill casks and take them out to the men. He sent a few sailors ashore, but we managed to capture them, and they told us where Caesar was on the water. Our plan now is to attack his ships," said Gany.

"Do we have enough ships to do that?"

"We do, my queen," assured Hemotephe.

"So, the three of you are in agreement that this is the best course of action?" I said looking from man to man, their faces absent any expression. I know from my own experience that Gany can be very persuasive, and I would feel more assured if the other men were consenting of their own accord.

"Yes, my queen," replied the Vizier.

"I agree and am confident we can prevail," added Hemotephe.

"We have your blessing?" asked Gany expectantly.

"You do. I will pray to Uat-ur for your safety and your success. Serve me with honor and I will also pray that Ra will ensure your safe passage to the afterlife should you not return."

"Thank you, my queen," said Gany before showing the men from the tent, returning just a few minutes later.

"You are prepared?" I asked with not a small degree of trepidation.

"We are. This will be a great victory for you and for our people," replied Gany confidently as he sheathed and unsheathed his dagger, a nervous habit he had developed.

It occurred to me that perhaps he was not so confident, his body betraying his words. But did I have any other recourse than to trust him? Truly I did not. There is no one else I can turn to whom I can trust like I do Gany, but he lacks experience in military matters. He has indeed been surrounded by these discussions at the palace for many years, but that is different than actually taking men to fight. If he fails, I will fail, and my death will be a certainty. Cleopatra and Caesar will have won, and Egypt will never be the same.

The time seemed to go by slowly waiting for word from the battle. I spent hours in prayer and sacrifice to the gods. There was so much at stake in this battle, so much that could be lost. Not just for me, but for my younger brother too. He and I are the future of our family, and we are Egypt's only hope for keeping Rome at bay. It was hard not to wonder how he was being treated… or more likely, mistreated. He and I had always been close. We were like-minded enjoying many of the same pastimes, but now I regret the times I dodged him when he was being childish. As the hours turned to days, I could not be still. I paced back and forth in my tent till I nearly wore a path in the carpet.

"Your Highness is there anything I can do to ease your mind?" asked Lira with a note of concern.

She had been my only companion since Gany left and we spent our evenings playing senet. Her skill was impressive, and I appreciated that she did not always let me win.

"Get the guard and tell him I'd like to take a walk along the river. Maybe that will calm me."

We walked along the Nile, the lifeblood of Egypt. The river was our ability to feed not just ourselves, but the Romans too.

Each spring the Nile floods, bringing water and fresh soil to our fields, although it has been more modest the last few years than in years past. Birds flew in and out of the water, grabbing at unsuspecting meals that hid just below the surface. Even a few crocodiles splashed up upon the shore to bathe in the sunlight, their tails occasionally swishing to and fro. The sun was blazing, and I appreciated the warmth on my face as I gazed up into the blue sky sending a silent prayer to Hathor for her favor. Suddenly the guard stepped in front of me, pushing me with his arm until my back was against Lira. The three of us stood front to back.

"Your Highness, there is a rider approaching. I cannot tell yet if it is ours," he said as he readied his sword.

Lira and I each pulled out the daggers we wore on our belts. If there was going to be a fight, they would have to deal with all three of us. I could feel my heart beating harder, I wondered if Lira was feeling the same. The rider was coming quickly, and it only took a moment before we realized he was with us, and we could relax. Even still, the guard kept his sword up until the very moment he grabbed the horse's reins.

"Queen Arsinoe, I bring word from General Ganymedes," he said breathlessly as he jumped down from his horse and kneeled at my feet. He had a papyrus in his left hand with his right fist on his heart.

Lira stepped forward, taking the papyrus from him and unfurling it. She read down it quickly, nodded to him and he mounted his horse and turned back toward camp.

"Unfortunately, the word is not good. There was a large battle of ships, but Caesar was victorious. The people of Alexandria tried to retreat but General Ganymedes was able to rally them once again. More ships were brought in and another clash between the Romans and our forces was had, one he was sure he would win. However, the Roman Admiral Euphranor led an even more devastating defeat for us, with heavy losses. There are very few ships left, and all the remaining men are gathering onshore. The Vizier is bringing in chariots and men on foot to reinforce the General's troops, and they intend to now start ground attacks. He will send more word in a few days," concluded Lira as she rolled up the papyrus and waited quietly.

The news was unsettling, to say the least. It made me anxious and worried. My belief has always been that the gods were with us and that we would prevail in this effort. Could I be wrong? I walked closer to the bank of the river, watching the water flowing out to the sea. It progressed along as if led by an unseen force, always moving, never stopping. It took with it anything and anyone who dared to enter. Logs, branches, pieces of boats, bodies of the dead. The river was not just our lifeblood. It was strong, powerful, unstoppable. So must I be.

BETRAYAL

Over the next few months, we had some success. At one point, Caesar was even in jeopardy, having to abandon his purple cloak and armor to avoid drowning in the sea. One of our soldiers managed to recover them, and they were displayed for all to see, a sign of how close we had come to destroying him. But for the most part, we were at a stalemate, with no side winning and no side losing.

"Your Highness, the messenger is here with news from Alexandria," said Lira as she handed me the leather pouch containing various messages and letters.

Most were of no real significance but one from my dear friend Myraiene caught my eye. She was still working in the palace and pretending to be loyal to Cleopatra, but she was as true to me as she had always been. Without her espionage, we would certainly know less about what is happening and what is being planned.

"Oh no, this is the last thing I wanted to hear," I said, trying not to sound like a petulant child, albeit unsuccessfully.

"What is it my queen?" asked Lira.

"That treasonous hemar! My half-sister is with child. The spawn of the vermin Julius Caesar no less. A bastard of both Egypt and Rome is a very dangerous thing. This will give my rival even more reason to strengthen her alliance with Rome, not that she needs any further encouragement," I said with frustration, slamming my fist on the table.

Lira said nothing. She knew me well enough by now to know when it was best to simply stay silent. I understood this was certainly a possibility but now that the reality was here the implications of it made my skin crawl. Caesar would never abandon Cleopatra now. If the child were a boy, it would form an unbreakable bond. In Egypt, women were treated with reverence and given much control over their lives. We could choose who to marry, when to divorce, lend debens, or own a business. We were not seen as inferior and women rulers in Egypt were accepted. Rome was the opposite and so a girl would only be of value to the degree she could be married off to create alliances. A son is something different. A son is a potential successor, and the son of a Pharaoh and a Caesar would be the most powerful man in the world.

"Lira, when is the next dispatch from Ganymedes expected?"

"I do not know, Your Highness. Let me talk with the guard and I will see if we can get an answer to your question," she said as she bowed before stepping outside the tent.

I had grown very fond of this young girl, who was becoming a woman right before my eyes. She was smart, funny, and a good companion especially in these circumstances. She was also much more well educated and read than I had expected which was of great help to me, and she is always anxious to learn more. I antic-ipated the pleasure of raising her to a higher station when we took control of the palace. There were moments, perhaps more than I would like to admit when I wondered if we would prevail in this endeavor. My face was blank. I tried not to show any emotion when reports were brought to me. Only in front of Lira did I let my feelings be known.

"There is a rider expected anytime now Your Highness."

"Good, tell the guard to inform me as soon as he is sighted," I replied.

Gany's reports seemed to come less and less frequently and so I often felt as if I was trying to steer a ship in the dark sea where there is no lighthouse. Which direction should we go? What should we do? This is where my years failed me. My lack of experience in the art of war meant I had to rely on others, and I knew not how to evaluate their skills. If they lost an encounter is that their fault or simply Montu the god of war influencing the outcome for which they should not be blamed? The afternoon faded to evening as I spent the day reading, thankful for the many scrolls that had been brought for me. Language, art, and history. I poured over them all, expanding my knowledge and my mind.

Cleopatra is very learned and that works to her advantage. I knew I must read and study as much as I could if I was to be of any value in our efforts to unseat her. Even the history and cul-ture of the Romans were of interest to me as they may give me insight into how Caesar thought. I suspect he was fully in charge of the military by now and so it was his strategy that we needed to understand rather than hers. The torches had been lit before the rider finally arrived.

"Your Highness, I have word from the battle," said the rider as he knelt at my feet, and I motioned for Lira to take the papyrus.

"Read it," I commanded as I tried to hide my shaking hands.

"Attacks on Caesar's troops have been successful at holding back the enemy, but no new progress has been made by either side. Citizens of Alexandria are weary of the fighting. They are calling on Caesar to return Ptolemy to the throne to rule with Cleopatra. They want to bring an end to hostilities and are calling for your surrender or capture. This is a dangerous time; you must be on your guard. I will try to return to you in the next few days. It is signed by General Ganymedes three days ago."

"Send a message to him at once. See if he can convince Caesar to release my brother under the guise of negotiating a ceasefire. I believe if we can free him from the palace, he will join me and strengthen our position. In the meantime, I think it best if we move the encampment as soon as possible. Too many people know where I am. Send it at once and tell the guards to begin preparations. We will leave at dawn," I said decisively.

Gany and I had talked about this possibility and so I knew where he wanted me to go but I dare not say more in the message in case our rider was intercepted. We wouldn't have time to take everything with us. We must take only what we need so we will not be weighed down. Ra will bring the sun again in just a few hours so time is precious.

"Lira, burn all messages that have come from our leaders. We cannot risk information getting back to Caesar should this encampment be found. Choose the most important items to take with us and leave behind that which we can do without."

"Yes, my Queen," she replied as she began pulling the trunks into the center of the room while also making a pile of items to be burned.

The night was filled with the sounds of soldiers yelling instructions and the crackling of large fires. No one would be sleeping tonight. Sadly, I would have to leave the papyrus I have been reading, but there was no choice, although I will not have them burned. It will change nothing if they are found. Lira is packing our clothing, but she has stopped now, staring into the trunk as if looking for an answer to an unasked question.

"Lira, what is it?"

"Your Highness, I think we should exchange our clothes before we depart," she said finally breaking her stare to look at me intently.

"Why?"

"In case we encounter Caesar's soldiers along the way, they will take me and perhaps leave you, so that you could flee," she said with all seriousness.

It was a reasonable plan. We were about the same size and hair color. No one who knew me well would be deceived, but a soldier who does not would only assume I am the Queen by my attire and demeanor.

"We will have to change your hair and eyes too. It is a good plan. Come sit here and let me do it for you," I said motioning toward the chair.

Had this been another time, another moment, we would have laughed playfully about our attempt at deception, but this was deadly serious. I worked quickly, changing her hairstyle to emulate the one I usually wore. Then she worked to take down my hair so that it was more like hers. Once wearing my tunic, with my amulets and arm cuffs, she made a very passable version of me.

"It is time my Queen," said the guard as he lifted the flap of the tent.

I started to go first but then realized Lira needed to go and I must follow her. The guards did not seem to notice our ploy and considering they saw us daily it was quite a good sign. As I walked behind her toward the barge it struck me as very odd. Since coming here, I have walked behind no one. I would have to work very hard to remind myself of the place I now held, at least until we were safely in our new camp. Once on the barge, Lira sat in my chair, and I sat on the cushion at her feet. It was chilly but no blanket was offered to me, only to her. She did her best to position herself so that the blanket provided me with some warmth, but it was not nearly enough, and I shivered in the dampness of the early dawn. The sun would be up soon enough and then it would be warm. I kept reminding myself that dawn was soon, trying to keep my teeth from chattering.

We both spoke little throughout the journey knowing that might be the one thing that would give us away. If the guards became aware, then they might not be so convincing if we encountered any problems. It was interesting to see the river from this different vantage point, my eyes just above the level of the water. The reeds seemed so much bigger and majestic with their large plumes, the birds taller, the water darker. Once the sun was high in the sky it was indeed warm, too warm. I longed for the canopy's shade but that was just impossible. Thankfully the day was uneventful and as the sun was just starting to reach the horizon, we pulled the barge up to the bank of the river. I was glad to stand up and stretch my legs.

The path was rather muddy which seemed strange given that there had been no rain for many days, this being the dry time of year. It would only be wet if many men had gone this way who had walked through the water at the edge of the bank as we had just done. My blood ran cold. Others had been up this path before us, and not too long ago. Was it Gany? I doubt my message about our move had reached him yet but as he knew this was the place we would go, perhaps he had others already here in anticipation should that time come. We walked along for a few more minutes before coming to a clearing where there were a couple of tents, and a few horses tethered to a tree. The soldier at the front of the line shouted something to the other men before drawing his sword. I didn't understand all of what he said but one thing became instantly clear… the Romans were here. We had been betrayed.

"Hide, Your Highness," said one of the soldiers while pushing Lira back down the path and into the bushes. She grabbed my arm and pulled me with her, and we huddled together as the sound of bronze swords, cursing, screaming, and calling out to the gods filled the air. My heart was pounding as we tried to make ourselves smaller and smaller, and I could hear Lira whispering prayers to Sekhmet, the goddess of war and battle for her protection, which we surely needed at this moment. It was over in just a few moments, and it took no time at all for the Roman soldiers to find us.

"Well, it is good to see you again," said a man's voice. I thought I recognized it as he grabbed Lira by the arm and pulled her up and onto the path.

"You would be well advised to remove your hands from me at once!" she retorted, struggling to pull away from him.

"Oh, I don't think you are in any position to tell us what we can and cannot do," said the man as he brought his dagger up to her chin.

I dare not look up at him, or any of them, keeping my eyes on the ground hoping they would not recognize me.

"You will release me at once. I am the rightful Queen of Egypt, and I will not be treated in this way," snapped Lira.

The man just laughed as he half dragged her, half walked her toward one of the tents. Another man grabbed my arm, and we followed behind. I said nothing and looked at no one.

"Caesar wants her alive," said one of the soldiers with a low growl that sounded more like it belonged to an animal than a man.

"She will be alive when we get to Alexandria, but she might wish she was with Osiris instead by the time we get there," he replied with a laugh.

They opened the tent flap and thrust us inside, both of us falling onto the dirt floor. There was a small carpet in the corner, a table, one chair, and nothing else. Not even a blanket, torch, or water bucket was present.

"My queen are you hurt?" whispered Lira as she helped me up.

"No, are you?" I asked as I brushed the dirt off my tunic and pulled the brambles out of my hair.

"No, just a scrape on my leg from one of the bushes but it is not bleeding badly."

"Let me see," I said as she sat down on the chair so I could lift her gown.

"That needs to be washed," I said looking up at her.

I felt like we were no longer playing a charade. Instead, we were simply two women trying to survive and I was afraid that might be harder than we imagined. While the soldiers might not rape her, a royal of Egypt, there would be nothing to deter them from assaulting me. I have not yet known a man and the thought that my first encounter might be with a Roman soldier made me feel sick in the pit of my belly. But I could not dwell on it, I needed to tend to the cut on Lira's leg.

"Let me see if I can get some water to get this cleaned up. Sit here quietly I will return as quickly as I can."

"Your Highness, you can't! It's not safe. Someone may recognize you. I will be fine… please just stay here," said Lira as she held onto my arm, almost in tears.

"No, it will be fine. I cannot afford for you to become sick and die. If you do, then I will surely be sold off as a slave rather than taken back to Alexandria. So please, let me do this. I will return quickly," I whispered. I freed myself from her grasp and darted out of the tent before she could protest again.

There were a couple of soldiers standing near a fire and while they looked up at me, they seemed disinterested and made no move toward me. There was a shaduf nearby and I picked it up and walked over toward the soldiers, trying to step around the blood-soaked dirt. The bodies of our fallen soldiers were piled up waiting to be burned.

"I need water for the Queen," I said in a voice barely above a whisper.

"The Queen is in Alexandria, and I am sure she has all the water she needs," came the reply followed by a great deal of laughter and spitting on the ground.

"If you wish to return the Queen to Caesar alive as you have been bidden, you will get me water, now," I said as handed the vessel to the closest soldier before turning on my heels to return to the tent.

I could hear them laughing but no matter. They could ridicule us all they wished as long as they came with water. Some food would be good too, but I did not expect too much. To my surprise they did come, with water and bread, setting it on the table without a word. We looked at each other wide-eyed before suddenly breaking out in peals of laughter.

"Shhh, not so loud," I said as we both tried to regain our composure.

I don't know why that was such a source of merriment at that moment. Perhaps the feeling that we had succeeded when failure was the more likely outcome. Or perhaps, it was just the sense of relief in having the two things we needed most. Never would I have imagined that just water and stale bread would bring me such a feeling of relief.

"Let me do that, my Queen," said Lira as I started to bathe her leg.

"It will be easier for me to see it clearly. I do not mind," I replied.

"When do you think we will leave for Alexandria?" she asked just as I was drying off her leg with the bottom of her gown.

"I don't think they will want to stay here long. There are few of them and they risk our men coming to rescue us."

"How did they know to find us here? In this place?" she asked, looking puzzled.

"Ah, that is a good question. It means that someone who knew we might come here has betrayed us. I did not mention this place in my message, so it had to have come from someone close to me. Only a few of our men knew of this place, and even fewer that we were on the move and would arrive here within a short time. We can trust no one now," I said with a resigned sigh.

Several days passed at the campsite. We did not leave the tent unless it was necessary hoping that the soldiers would leave us alone if we kept to ourselves. Fortunately for us, other than to bring us water, bread, and a little meat, they did. We could hear them talking about us at night. They also discussed Cleopatra and what was transpiring in the capital. Caesar had made himself at home in Alexandria and strutted around the grounds of the palace as if he were the ruler, they say. We could hear them laughing and making fun of Cleopatra and her subservience to that man. It gave me hope that Alexandria and Egypt's citizens would continue to rise in my defense. But it was also possible that Caesar would simply have me murdered as soon as we returned, not willing to take a chance that others would come to my aid. It was no matter; it would be as the gods wished it to be and I was not afraid to go to the afterlife secure in the knowledge that I had done the right thing.

It was time. At first light we were dragged down to the boat with some of the soldiers while others rode off toward Alexandria. The soldiers continued to believe that Lira was the Queen of Egypt and that I was her servant. However, once we reach Alexandria the deception would be harder to maintain. I did not fully know what that would mean for either of us. It would take two more days and nights to finally reach the city. Once we arrived, I was shocked to see its deterioration. This was not the Alexandria I remembered; everything was in shambles.

The constant conflicts over the last years had taken their toll, and the beautiful city I visited in my dreams was run down and decaying from lack of attention. Scorched earth and buildings littered the landscape from the many fires. Smoke lingered over the city like a pale specter, snaking its way in and out of the buildings and alleyways. Once on the shore, we were loaded into the prisoner cage which was being pulled by two donkeys. They intended to embarrass and humiliate us, but little did they know I felt nothing in response to the jeers of the Roman soldiers. I cared only about my people, who stood quietly and watched. Even if they were supporters, they dared not reveal their loyalty within earshot of the Roman soldiers.

When we arrived at the palace, Roman soldiers stood on either side of us with shields and swords at the ready as we made our way up the stairs. But there was no need. No one was coming to rescue us... at least not today. While Gany had been successful in getting my brother released and he had joined our troops as I had hoped, I heard one of the guards say that he had drowned when his boat capsized as he tried to cross the Nile. Gany was our only hope now. If left alone we might be able to leave through the tunnel once again, assuming it had not been closed since my first escape. I was in awe of Lira's composure and courage. She looked every bit the Queen of Egypt, a few Egyptians who dared even rendered their tribute as we walked past. I knew though the closer we got to the throne room, the closer we came to death. I was sure of it.

As we walked along the colonnade it felt odd to be back in the palace, my home. I wondered if my room was as I had left it or has someone else had taken up residence in it. As we approached the throne room the heat in my cheeks began to rise. Was it fear, or was it just excitement? I was not sure myself, but I knew in my heart that this charade was likely to end soon. The room was relatively full. The sea of people parted to make way for us as we were led toward the front of the room where Cleopatra and Caesar sat side by side on the dais. I did not see any sign of my younger brother. The guard stopped me about twenty feet from the throne at the edge of the crowd, but Lira continued to the bottom of the steps. Her head was held high, and she showed no fear and certainly no deference to those who now sat in judgment before her. She was certainly doing her part to convince people that she was Queen Arsinoe, but I doubted my sister would be fooled.

"Arsinoe, how happy I am that you have returned to us," said Cleopatra snidely as she smiled at Lira.

"I had little choice," she replied.

Cleopatra sat up straighter in her chair and looked at her intently, studying her features and clothes.

"You have changed my sister. Perhaps all this time spent living in a tent and eating nothing but stale bread?" she said as the crowd laughed.

Lira wisely did not respond. She knew the less she spoke, the better. Around me, I began to hear a few whispers. People were talking about her appearance. Caesar leaned over and whispered something to my sister, who then stood and motioned for Lira to come closer. As she stepped on the bottom step Cleopatra began to laugh until she was laughing hysterically. Eventually, others joined in, although I am sure they had no idea why she was laughing. Suddenly she stopped.

"This is not my sister. I do not know who this woman is," she spat angrily as she sat back down.

"Kneel before Queen Cleopatra!" admonished Caesar as the soldier pushed Lira to the floor onto her knees.

"I do not understand, Your Highness. This is the woman who arrived at the place where we were told your sister would be. She said she was the Queen of Egypt," said the soldier, clearly flustered.

"Who are you? What is your name?" demanded Caesar as a soldier pulled Lira's hair back, forcing her to look up at him.

My hands were sweating. I could hear my heart pounding, reverberating in my head. As I looked around, I realized that the soldier who had led me into the room had moved closer to the throne. No one was watching me. If I was careful, I might be able to blend into the crowd and slip away as they left. If I did, what would happen to Lira? She was prepared to give her life for mine. She had made that clear when we first embarked on this plan. She would expect me to escape if I could.

"I am no one. My name is Lira. I met a woman who paid me to wear her clothes. She told me to go with the men accompanying her to the place where your men found me. She did not tell me her name. I simply did as she asked."

"But you told these soldiers you were the Queen of Egypt?" asked Cleopatra.

"That is what the woman paid me to say," she replied.

If I hadn't been so frightened, I would have found this exchange most comical indeed. The soldiers looked at each other in disbelief and began pointing fingers to deflect the blame for this grave error onto each other. In the confusion and raised voices I moved farther and farther into the crowd, trying to keep my eyes on the ground.

"Was this woman alone when you found her?" asked Caesar.

"No, my Emperor. She was with a small group of Egyptian soldiers and a servant girl. The soldiers were all killed during our efforts to seize the Queen, I mean, this woman, who we believed was the Queen," he said.

"Where is the girl who was with her?"

I stood perfectly still. Trying to flee would be futile. My best hope was that the soldiers would simply not be able to pick me out of the crowd.

"She is here," said the soldier who had brought me in. Then he looked around in panic, suddenly realizing I was no longer standing next to him.

Everyone started backing up toward the outer edges of the room and I moved with them until my back was against the outside wall. The soldiers began going through the crowd looking at all the women who were there. I crouched behind the man in front of me pretending to tie my sandal, but then the boot of a Roman soldier came into view.

"Stand up," he barked at me.

Reluctantly I stood and he grabbed my arm pulling me out of the crowd.

"Here she is," he said as he pulled me up to where Lira was still kneeling, and he put me on my knees next to her.

"I am sorry, my queen," she whispered to me.

"Do not be. You have been a loyal servant and a friend, and I thank you," I whispered back as I stood up.

"Cleopatra, the years have not been kind to you, I am sorry to say," I said as I glared at her with my hands on my hips.

The crowd gasped behind me and even a few dared to laugh but not loudly.

"Arsinoe, it is you! And dressed fittingly as a servant girl," she said as she leaned back on the throne.

"Where are my brothers?"

"It is of no concern to you but Ptolemy, our youngest brother, is here in the palace under my protection. Our older brother, Ptolemy XIII was sent to negotiate your surrender, but the gods were not with him. Maybe you heard that he drowned in a terrible accident as he was trying to cross the Nile?"

"I'm sure the Nile took him with your help," I retorted.

"You would be wise to watch your tongue," replied Caesar, my sister unable to deny my accusation herself.

"I am the rightful Queen of Egypt, Queen Arsinoe VI, one with Isis. Your alliance with Rome is the very epitome of treason. You have brought shame upon the legacy that our father left to us, and I will not be a party to it. I will stand with Egypt and Egyptians against you for as long as I breathe. In the name of Sekhmet and Ra, I curse you and your bastard offspring. I will have my vengeance on you either in this life or the next," I replied, my voice steady and strong.

"Enough!" yelled Caesar as he pounded his fist on the arm of the chair. "Take her to a cell. Take them both," he said with a wave of his hand.

There were loud murmurs in the crowd, but no one spoke out against the order. Lira and I were unceremoniously dragged out of the throne room and down to the prison cells in the catacombs below the palace. I had never been down here. My father always said it was not a place to go unless you intended to never return to the land of the living above. No one could escape from this place without help. At that point, I did not know how much help I might be able to muster. Ganymedes and his men were our only hope. Surely word would reach him that I had been captured but how long that might take I did not know. More importantly, I did not know how long we had. Now that I was the only real threat to my sister's rein, I had no doubt she would have me killed.

We sat on the floor leaning against the wall. The straw was full of fleas. Rats and mice scurried along the shadows at the edges of the walls. An overwhelming stench of human waste and death hung in the air and burned our throats just through the act of breathing. This was by far the lowest point in my life. Lira's too, I expected.

"I am sorry, my queen, that our deceit did not work. I was hopeful that you would be able to get away before it was discovered," Lira said quietly.

"You were so brave and so confident. You did everything you could, truly," I said as I reached over and squeezed her hand.

"My life is yours, my queen. Use it to your benefit while you are alive, and then I will serve you in the afterlife as your faithful servant," she replied with a sadness in her voice.

"We need to find a way to get out of here," I said rather loudly as if my words might be heard by one of the gods.

"Queen Arsinoe?" a man's voice said from somewhere nearby.

"Yes. Who is there?"

"It is Usurpria, Your Highness. I am in a cell here in the back. I cannot see you, but I can hear you if you speak loudly."

We rose and went up to the cell bars, craning our necks to see if we could identify where he was.

"How long have you been here?" I replied.

"About three days, I think. The soldiers captured me when I was trying to get a message to one of our spies here in the palace."

"Does Ganymedes know you are here?" I asked hopefully.

There was no response.

"Usurpria?"

"Yes, Your Highness I am here. I am aggrieved to tell you that Ganymedes was killed a few days before I was captured. The Vizier has taken over and he must be the one who betrayed you. Most of our soldiers have left. They've given up on the fight. They are tired. We have just a small band of men still dedicated to your cause. The Pharaoh, your brother, tried to rally more support, but he drowned. I do not believe accidentally."

Seldom have I ever cried in my life, and not since I was a young child. My father always said that tears were a sign of weakness, a display of emotion that served no one. I did not cry when he died, but I cried now. Not just for Gany who was more like a father to me than my father had been, but for my country. It was clear now that all was lost. Caesar would continue to tighten his grip on the throat of our country, squeezing out of us the deben and food that he needed for Rome. He cared nothing for us, only the bounty of our homeland. I heard during our days with the Roman soldiers that his child with Cleopatra is a boy they have named Caesarion. He could certainly be the one to unite Egypt and Rome under one ruler. I'm sure that is what my sister would want, but it tears at my very heart to think about it.

"Thank you Usurpria. I am sure you and Ganymedes did

all that you could, and I know that you will be rewarded in the afterlife for your loyalty and sacrifice. Does Nrimeda know you are here?"

"She died, Your Highness, some months ago from a sickness," he replied quietly.

"I will pray to Isis and Osiris for you to join your wife in your next life and that you will both be rewarded for your loyalty," I said, with a smile he could not see.

We did not hear his voice again. Just two days later, without warning, the soldiers came for us. We were being taken to Rome. Caesar was planning a triumph, a parade, and I was to be displayed as a kind of battle trophy. I was his prize for securing Egypt. The humiliation endured by Lira here was nothing compared to the degradation I would suffer in Rome. But I refuse to take my own life, for once I am gone, they have truly won. As long as I had breath, I had hope.

The journey to Rome was long. The roads were choked with dust. By the time we arrived we were covered in dirt and our own eliminations as were we never allowed out of the prisoner cage. While I was grateful to have Lira with me, I also felt guilt that she was being forced to endure this horror because of me. She never complained and was only concerned for my comfort, but never her own. As we rattled through the streets of Rome people threw rotten fruit at us as they jeered and laughed. It was almost a relief to reach our cell in the Roman jail near the Senate. Having been in the cage for so long we could barely stand when they opened the door and had to be lifted out. As we stood in chains waiting for them to take us inside, a litter that bore Cleopatra and her son went by to the elation of cheering crowds. I could not even bear to look at her. I could only hope she could not see me.

The cell was cold and damp, but it was a relief from the hot sun we had endured for several days. Even better, there was water which we used to bathe. Lira gave me her gown, standing naked while she washed mine. It was not much improved, but I was grateful for her attempt to make me more comfortable and presentable. I did not doubt that I would be brought in front of Caesar and the Senate to be sentenced as is the custom here. The idea that I would appear in front of these men in this condition was humiliating.

I needed to remember that I was more than my appearance. I was made by the gods of khet. My physical being, ba, my persona, and most importantly my ka and ib, my essence and heart. There was nothing the Romans could do to touch that. When I joined my family in the afterlife, I would be unblemished and would do justice to my royal lineage. The Ptolemies have ruled Egypt for hundreds of years, but it saddened me terribly that this may now be coming to an end. I did not think Cleopatra would be well received when her time came to join us.

We sat in this putrid cell for what seemed like an eternity but surely it was only a few days. It was hard to gauge the night from the day as so little light made its way down in the darkness. The worst part of being here was not the darkness but rather the vermin. The straw was scratchy, and things crawled in and out of it. We constantly kept brushing them away. Lira had even grabbed a rat by its tail, flinging it out of the cell just as it was poised to bite. Finally, the guards came for me, but it seemed that Lira was not coming with me. I hoped that meant they might let her go. Either way, I knew I would not see her in this life again.

"My queen, I will pray for your safe travels. I will pray that Osiris welcomes you to the underworld and that the forty-two judges will not be harsh with you."

"Thank you, Lira, for everything. You are the closest thing I have had to a true friend, and I would not have managed this long without you. It is my sincere hope that you will be released and that you can find your way back to Egypt and to your family… or that your journey will be swift. I will see you again in the afterlife," I said as I embraced her.

She started to cry, which I had not expected. It brought to me my own tears which I quickly wiped away. I could not let these men see me crying or see me as weak. As I walked with the Roman soldiers through the building I marveled at the many beautiful statues and mosaics. For just a moment, I saw the Romans in a favorable light. Perhaps they were not entirely barbaric after all. When we arrived in what I assumed was their throne room, I expected to see Cleopatra, but there was no sign of her. Only Caesar sat on a large chair. Men, who I assumed were from the Senate, were standing around him.

The soldier stopped a few feet from Caesar and pushed me down to my knees.

"Can this be the Queen of Egypt? This is just a mere waif of a girl," said one of the men laughing.

"Caesar, I thought you said this girl was dangerous. Since when are you afraid of children?" said another.

"She is more devious than she looks. She was able to raise an army against Queen Cleopatra who is the rightful heir to the throne per her father's wishes," said Caesar, attempting to strike a more serious tone.

"She doesn't look like she could raise an army of mice," said another they referred to as Cassius.

I had been worried that my bedraggled and dirty appearance would put me at a disadvantage with these men, but it may be to my benefit. My small stature can't hurt either, which has become even smaller after several weeks with little food. I did my best to make myself look even less intimidating kneeling here on the floor.

"I intend to put this woman to death for treason unless the Senate can tell me why I should not."

"My Emperor, the people of Rome have seen this poor urchin paraded through the streets. While they may revel in pelting her with rotten fruit, I don't believe they would support the execution of a child. We are Romans. The Egyptians may kill their children, but we do not do that here," said Cassius.

"Here, here," chimed in several others.

I kept my head down. Was it even possible that they would let me go? I didn't see how they could. Would they keep me imprisoned until I died without Caesar's direct action? I thought I would prefer to be executed now rather than endure that. I raised my head to look at these men standing there in judgment of me.

"I have no remorse for my actions. The throne of Egypt is my birthright. Should my sister, Queen Cleopatra, die then I am the rightful heir. With no Ptolemy on the throne of Egypt, the country could fall into civil war. Certainly, that cannot be good for Rome," I said quietly.

"Well, she may only be a child but a rather clever one as she makes a valid observation," said the man standing next to Cassius called Brutus.

"I will not return her to Egypt where she can continue to undermine the Queen," said Caesar angrily.

"Then send her to exile somewhere else. Somewhere that she can be held by those friendly to the Roman empire and where she will be available to you in the future should she be needed," said another man who was standing in the back.

"I agree. If something were to befall Cleopatra, we could perhaps assume control of Egypt by placing this girl on the throne there. Then without shedding so much as a single drop of blood, Egypt would be ours. Their granaries and seaports would be of great value to Rome," noted another tall man standing near the window.

"The Temple of Artemis?" asked Cassius.

"It is a good solution; she can be held there, and no one need know. Besides, in a few months, her name will be forgotten. She can live out her days there while causing no harm. Better this plan than inciting people to rebel against you for executing a child. If she becomes a problem in the future she can always be dealt with then," said Brutus.

I couldn't believe what I was hearing. They were going to let me live, thinking I would go quietly to Ephesus and live my life as though I were no one. Part of me wanted to laugh, part of me wanted to cry. These men looked upon me as a child unworthy of their attention. I wasn't even worth the risk of executing. Caesar looked at me thoughtfully. He reminded me of my father in some ways. They had been aligned once as he helped my father to return to the throne and oust Berenice. Perhaps he would look upon me with kindness because of it. He was hard to read. His face was expressionless as the others waited for him to respond.

"Yes, I think that is a good outcome, for all," replied Caesar at last.

The men murmured their ascent as one of the guards pulled me to my feet. I looked at Caesar as he spoke directly to me for the first time.

"See this as the gift from the gods that it is, Princess Arsinoe. Devote yourself to quiet study at the temple and do nothing to further antagonize your sister. Do you understand?"

I nodded, and with that and a wave of Caesar's hand, the guards escorted me back to the cell to await my departure to Ephesus. I could hear the men's laughter echoing through the halls as I was dragged away, and it made me smile. They were making a mistake in underestimating me. I hoped they lived long enough to regret it.

Chapter Three

EXILE

The sea spray felt good on my face. The sun warmed my skin. Slowly the seawater healed my many sores and cuts... and my spirit, too. We had been on the water for several days, and finally land was beginning to come into view in the distance. I looked over at Lira and smiled. I couldn't believe we were here. It took some convincing for Caesar to send me into exile rather than execute me, but eventually, he decided it would be best. I asked for Lira to come with me, and they simply agreed, probably thinking it wise she not be able to tell anyone what was being done. If she were with me, no tales could be told. I was so grateful to have her, given that I was now headed to a place where I knew no one and had not been since I was a child.

Everyone knew of the Temple of Artemis. It was dedicated to the goddess of that name, although the Romans called her Diana. It was the most beautiful temple in the world, a place of quiet contemplation and learning. Scholars come from near and far to visit the Library of Celsus and despite this being exile, I was looking forward to reading more. Given the requirement that I stay on the temple grounds I would clearly have plenty of time to read, as there would be little else to do, and I still had much to learn if I was going to get the throne of Egypt back.

While Caesar may have been successful at getting me out of Egypt, he could never take Egypt out of me. My heart and ka will always be one with my homeland. My father had come here for sanctuary when my sister Berenice revolted against him and fomented a rebellion. He loved his time here and the people were generous to him. He formed many strong alliances and friendships. I am hoping that some of those friends may be willing to help me defend the honor of Egypt and take back what is mine. Finally, the boat pulled up to the wharf and we tied off as we gathered up our things. We didn't have much in the way of possessions. A bit of an embarrassment to be sure, but nothing to be done now.

"Take my hand, Arsinoe," said Lira as she reached down to me in the boat to pull me up onto the wharf.

It sounds so odd to hear her call me by my given name, but part of the agreement I made with Caesar was that I would not use my titles. I could not be called princess or queen, just Arsinoe.

"I am so grateful we are finally here. I am grateful that you are with me," I said as I pulled myself up onto the wharf.

"Forever your humble servant," she replied with a slight wink.

"Princess Arsinoe," a man called out as he waved and walked toward us, moving quickly.

I immediately froze, terrified that the Roman guards who were delivering us to our exile would report this infraction back to Caesar.

"Here," I said, waving my hand in the air in reply.

"Princess, I am very happy you have arrived. My name is Bennu," replied the man with a slight bow.

"I am honored to meet you Bennu, but please, just call me Arsinoe, if you would," I said as I acknowledged his gesture of respect.

"Of course, I understand," he said clearly flustered and probably somewhat confused, but all would be known in time.

"Bennu is an Egyptian name, is it not?"

"Yes Prin... Arsinoe. I came here with your father many years ago and he asked me to stay on when he returned to Alexandria. I have maintained a small villa here for your family ever since in case there was a need to return," came the reply.

A young man with Bennu took our meager bags and he hurried ahead of us along the wharf. Bennu took note of how little we had brought with us, and I felt rather humiliated. He did not say anything about it for which I was grateful. How was it that just six months ago I was the Queen of Egypt and now I had few worldly possessions and no standing in my own country?

"I am very happy to see you Arsinoe. I have not seen you since you were a very young child, although I wish it were under better circumstances," said Bennu as we walked side by side along the wharf with Lira following quietly behind.

"Thank you Bennu. I'm afraid I do not remember having visited here before. Can I assume that Julius Caesar has informed you of my circumstances in this exile?" I asked, glancing over to gauge the reaction in his eyes.

"Yes. I received a communication from Faberius the secretary of Caesar telling me that you and your companion would be coming. They were aware that your father had been in my villa when he was here years ago. They asked if I would open my door to you, which I am honored to do. But there was not much more information provided. I understand your sister Cleopatra is now on the throne with his support?"

"Half-sister," I replied as if somehow reminding people we did not share the same mother made her climbing into bed with the Roman less appalling, or at least less of a reflection on me and my father.

"Yes, of course, my apologies," he replied.

"No need to apologize. So where is this villa, Bennu? Is it in a place where we will be... safe?" I inquired.

"Yes, my Prin... sorry this will take some getting used to. Yes, Arsinoe. It is in the Temple complex, and it is considered sacred ground. You will be safe there. No one would dare to come for you while you are under the protection of the goddess. The same cannot be said if you are outside the complex," he said with a serious tone.

Would they come for me? Maybe not right away, especially if they just saw me as a girl without power and means. Still, once word got out that I was trying to reclaim my birthright I did not doubt that Caesar would indeed ensure I was murdered where I stood. The walk was a pleasant one and the city was a cacophony of voices, clothing, colors of skin, and architecture. It was wonderful to feel this freedom, to walk where I pleased, even if it was only for a few fleeting moments.

It made me smile thinking that my father would have walked this same road as he made his way to the house that he had shared with Bennu. Finally, after many twists and turns, we reached the temple complex. It was truly humbling in its magnificence. The marble shone brightly in the sun reflecting its rays back into the clouds, sparkling in the air like so many fine jewels. Its many decorated columns and doors were magnificent and took my breath away. It was truly a fitting tribute to its namesake, Artemis. We had many beautiful buildings in Alexandria, but this was certainly one of the most beautiful sights I had ever seen.

"It is beautiful," said Lira wistfully as she stood next to me gazing up at the structure that now stood before us.

"Indeed, for most the first glimpse of it is an overwhelming experience. Visitors come from all over to see it, and many weep as they are touched deeply by its magnificence," said Bennu.

"We are going to live here?" said Lira with more than a bit of trepidation.

"No, not in the temple proper. We will walk partway through the main temple, and then back out to an area of small houses and villas. It is outside the temple but within its outer walls where many live who care for the temple. I have lived there now for many years, and I often work in the library. Like everyone who is part of the temple, I help with entertaining important visitors as well," replied Bennu.

"I don't know if I have properly thanked you for welcoming us into your home," I said suddenly realizing I was beholden to this man for our care.

"It is my honor Arsinoe. Your father was always kind to me when he and Cleopatra were here, and I have sworn to him that I would always be here for your family. I'm sure he never imagined this... situation," he said matter-of-factly.

"And Cleopatra, what did you think of her?"

"She was very devoted to your father I think, but also it was obvious that some of that devotion was intended to ingratiate herself into your father's favor so that he would look kindly upon her at the time of his passing," replied Bennu.

"You are a very astute man, Bennu," I said with a wink.

"I think it best we speak candidly and openly of these things between ourselves in private. I would never of course do anything to tarnish your father's memory or the standing of Egypt. But like many who once called Egypt home, I do not agree with what Caesar has done with your sister's acquiescence and collusion."

I looked at him thoughtfully. He appeared to be a man of about fifty years perhaps, of medium stature with a neatly trimmed beard and modest but well-made clothing and shoes. His eyes were kind, a bright brown that reflected the slightest amount of past pain or sorrow. I realized I knew nothing about him. I supposed we had nothing but time to get to know one another, and I found myself looking forward to it. This man would be vital to me for as long as I stayed here, however long or short that might be.

"Here we are," he said finally as he opened the door to one of the villas off the side courtyard.

It was a lovely home. It was certainly not on par with the palace in Egypt, but it was well-appointed. Many beautiful statues and faience decorated the interior. The rooms were welcoming, and it felt like a home. I wondered if Bennu had a wife and children. I had not even thought to ask.

"Bennu, you live here alone?" I asked.

"There are two of my family here with me. One is my cousin Cente. The other is her husband, Amon, who took your bags at the harbor. They help me to run the house and look after our guests, but they are family rather than servants. My wife and my daughter died from a sickness some years ago. I have never been able to see my way clear to finding another wife," he said with a shrug.

"I am very sorry for your loss Bennu. I hope that Sekhmet will bring to your heart her healing powers," I said sincerely.

"Thank you, Princess."

I didn't bother to correct him. Within the walls of this house, there was no harm in saying it I supposed. Perhaps it was good that all in this household understood my true position. Still, I wondered how Bennu kept up this villa and his family with what must be little or no income from his work in the temple.

"This will be your room Arsinoe, and there is a smaller room behind here for you Lira. Cente has purchased some things for you that she thought you might need, and she will be happy to go to the market for anything else you may want. Lira, she has also bought a few things for you which are in your room," said Bennu gesturing to the small doorway to the right of the bed.

The room was nicely furnished and big enough for a large bed, as well as several small couches and a beautiful dressing table where there were several small pots. It was an inviting and comfortable space although much smaller than my room in the palace had been. On the bed were several garments, a few pairs of shoes, and even some necklaces and bracelets. Suddenly, I felt very embarrassed, realizing I had no deben of my own.

"Bennu, I appreciate your generosity, but I must tell you…" I said haltingly.

"No, no need my Princess. I understand. Your father had planned a long time ago in case any of his children should need to find sanctuary here. There is more than enough for your care, and that of your companion," said Bennu with a little bow.

I breathed a sigh of relief. At least I would not have to grovel, or the gods forbid, find work to support myself. That meant I could focus on the future. Perhaps Father even left enough deben for me to raise an army to try to take back my birthright. But I mustn't get ahead of myself. Bennu seemed like he was sympathetic to my plight, but would he be willing to go that far? I would have to tread slowly on this Roman soil.

"Thank you, Bennu, for all of your kindness, and please thank Cente for me as well" I said with a smile.

"Of course, it is our pleasure. Now I will leave you to wash and change. I will have Cente bring you some wine and fruit. Water is just there. You are free to wander the house and grounds but do not go out through the garden into the streets. Once outside the wall, you are no longer under the protection of the goddess Artemis and your safety can no longer be assured."

"I understand," I said solemnly.

"If you are up to it, we shall dine together?"

"Of course, it would be my pleasure," I replied.

With that, Lira and I were alone for the first time in many days. I plopped down on the bed and lay back feeling the softness of the bedding and the plushness of the pillows. A far cry from the Roman prison cell and shackles that we were in just a few weeks ago. I sighed and patted the bed next to me.

"Come lay down here next to me," I said to Lira who happily complied.

"Oh, this is lovely," she said, exhaling loudly.

"It surely is," I said as I reached over and grabbed her hand.

"You know Lira, you are more than a servant; you are probably the one and only true friend that I have ever had, and I want to thank you for all that you have done for me."

"My queen, you need not thank me. It is my honor and duty to serve you, and I am most humbled to be called your friend," she said as she squeezed my hand.

Although unintended, we quickly fell asleep together on the large bed, exhausted from our travels. Once we woke, we indulged in baths and reveled in clean clothes that, while of ordinary fabric, were well made. There was also a beautiful collar necklace made with many blue and white faience beads, as well as an amulet of the goddess within whose walls we had found our safety. Lira also had an amulet and we both had lovely bracelets and combs for our hair. A little kohl around my eyes and a red paste on my lips and I felt like myself for the first time in a long time. Perhaps since I first fled the palace.

Once we were dressed, we wandered around the house a bit, exploring the rooms. The villa was lovely with several beautiful courtyards overflowing with lush greenery and brilliant flowering plants. In one there was even a small fountain that reminded me a bit of one we had at the palace. You could still see the touches of a woman here and there, and on the wall in one of the corridors was a drawing of a woman and a small girl. I could only assume they were Bennu's wife and daughter.

I looked at it, fixated on the face of the girl who looked to be about seven or eight. She seemed to stare at me intently from the fresco. There was sadness in her eyes, a window to her soul. I wondered if she knew what the gods had in store for her and that her trip to the afterlife would come much sooner than she probably imagined. Finally, we found a charming room decorated with tiles of blue and white with a large table and chairs in the center. There was a woman in her late twenties and the man we had seen earlier bringing platters of food to the table. There were also carafes of wine and water. On the table were beautifully crafted glasses of silver and plates of terra cotta.

"Good evening," I said smiling.

"Ah," said the woman, somewhat startled as she turned, wiping her hands on her apron.

"I am Arsinoe, and this is my companion Lira," I said.

"Yes, of course, Princess Arsinoe. It is my pleasure to meet you. I am Cente, and this is my husband Amon," she replied as they both made a little bow in my direction. "I came to your room earlier, but you were both asleep and I did not want to wake you," she said shyly.

"Oh, thank you. My apologies that we did not meet then but as you can imagine we were quite tired indeed," I replied.

"Of course," she said with a bow before heading back to what I assumed was the kitchen.

"I'm so happy to see that you will both join us," said Bennu as he entered from a doorway off to the right from a room I assumed was where he slept.

"Thank you for welcoming us with such a lovely meal," I said as we sat down at the table. Amon poured the wine as Cente returned from the kitchen with two large platters and another young man followed behind her with two more. We all settled into seats with me at one end and Bennu at the other. Everything smelled wonderful and suddenly I found that I was quite hungry indeed.

"I trust all is well and that you found everything that you needed?" asked Bennu as a platter of meat made its way around the table.

"Indeed, and we slept a bit. I already feel very refreshed," I said with a smile.

"The clothes and shoes were to your liking?" asked Cente.

"They are lovely. The shoes are a bit big, perhaps something a little bit smaller?"

"Certainly, I will see to it first thing in the morning," she replied.

For hours we talked about what has transpired these many months, everyone chiming in with questions and Lira and I doing our best to answer them all. It was an unusual evening for me but one I enjoyed very much. Perhaps this is what real families did… how they behaved, how they ate and drank. For a minute I wondered what it would be like to be average, without the weight of history and expectations on your shoulders. To be a girl who lives a simpler life, a husband, a child, and no worries about whether at some unsuspecting moment, you would be murdered. Ah well, that was not my destiny. Being the Queen of Egypt was. But for a moment, just one moment, it felt good to just be no one of any particular importance.

The months crept up on me. It seemed like we had just arrived yesterday, but it had been nearly four months already. We spent weeks just learning our way around the temple and the grounds, each day bringing something more stunningly beautiful than the day before. There seem to be no words to describe this place in its true magnificence. The people I met have also been very welcoming. Within the temple, I was not afraid for people to know who I was. Within these walls, I felt safe and protected. Lira and I wandered without fear. Some of the men and women who have occasionally joined us for dinner had also voiced concern about Cleopatra's reign, and this made me hopeful that I may be able to rally support against her.

As wonderful as the temple complex was, there was con-sternation for me whenever I saw others going out through the gate and into town. It was a constant reminder for me that I was not like everyone else. I was a bird in a gilded cage, but a cage, nonetheless. Even Lira was allowed to go into town to retrieve the things I needed, although she tried her best to downplay that privilege. Once the sun had gone down and the temple was quiet, and the visitors gone, we walked the courtyard in the cool evening breeze just the two of us. It had become a ritual of sorts and my favorite time of day. We talked about what was happening in the temple, the news from town, and of course the news from Alexandria.

"Cleopatra was with child again, but it appears the child did not survive," said Lira as we sat on the steps of the Temple, watching the sunset over the city.

"Caesar's child?"

"Yes, so it appears, but Meskhenet has not blessed her this time," Lira replied.

"I am not surprised. Her alliance both in and out of bed with the Roman is treason. She deserves no support from the gods," I said bluntly.

"Sadly, there is also word that your younger brother has died from a sickness some time ago."

"Ah, that saddens me terribly, but it also does not come as a surprise. Cleopatra never wanted to share the throne with anyone. More likely he was poisoned rather than dying from a sickness. She would not risk him coming of an age at which he would be equipped to fight her," I said shaking me head.

"Surely the gods will be welcoming to him, and he will be fairly judged."

"A boy, he was just a little boy…"

"Forgive me if I am overstepping but have you spoken with Bennu to see if he would support an effort to try and rally an army against her?"

"No, I have not, but you are right to ask. I have been complacent these last few months and that cannot continue. Now is the time to focus on winning back the throne and freeing my people from the heinous behavior of my half-sister," I said as the last rays of the sun vanished into a pink glow that filled the sky. The air was crisp and invigorated me.

We talked for a bit more before we returned to the villa, and I went at once to find Bennu who was in the library.

"Ah, Arsinoe, how was your walk?" asked Bennu as he looked up from the scroll he was reading.

"It was especially peaceful this evening. The sunset was glorious in its beauty and so I know the gods were smiling upon us," I replied. "May I sit?"

"Of course," said Bennu gesturing to the chair next to him.

"I want to thank you again for your kindness and generosity to us these past few months. I am not sure where we would be were it not for you and your family," I said sincerely.

"It was my honor to help your father and sister when they came here in exile and I am pleased to do the same for you, although I wish I did not have to do so. Your father was saddened by your older sister's betrayal. It brought him a great deal of pain," said Bennu.

"He could have just exiled her instead of executing her, but he chose not to do that. Why?" I asked.

"Because he knew it would not stop. She would continue to whittle away at his grasp on the throne, much as you and your brothers and sister have done to each other over the past few years."

His words made me grimace and I realized he was right. I was no better than Berenice or Ptolemy or any of them. We had all been fighting each other. Even I once thought it would have been right for my brother to have Cleopatra killed before she could find a way to escape. She did exactly what any of us could have predicted. She returned and fought for control, just as I wished to do... as any of us would have done. The difference was that she did it with Rome's help.

"As much as I hate what Cleopatra is doing, I wonder if Egypt has suffered enough. Maybe it is time we let the people have some peace, even if that peace comes at the expense of accepting more Roman interference," I said. It was more of a question than a statement.

"Ah, peace. It is always fleeting it seems, as if the gods have destined us to fight among ourselves for their entertainment. People in power want to stay in power. People who are abused by those in power want to fight back against that abuse. It seems as if it is a never-ending cycle just as the sun and moon rise each day."

"Does that mean you think peace will never come?" I asked sadly.

"No, I don't think we are destined to fight endlessly. I hope the gods take pity on us at some point in the future and impart more wisdom to the men and women who control such things."

"I need to ask you about…" I hesitated.

"Speak freely, Arsinoe. We are friends and I want you to ask what you will," said Bennu as a slight smile formed on his lips.

"I need to have an honest conversation with you about my resources. I need to understand what beneficence my father may have provided in case I want to…" once again my voice trailed off as if I somehow could not come to terms with what I needed to say.

"Ah, I have been anticipating this conversation. You want to know if your father left enough deben for you to raise an army?" asked Bennu.

Bennu was direct and spoke plainly, characteristics I admired in him very much and appreciated a great deal at that moment.

"Yes. That is indeed what I wish to know."

Bennu set down his scroll he had been reading and rose, walking toward the table where he picked up a large ornately decorated box which he brought over and handed to me.

"What is this?"

"Inside you will find a letter from your father. You will see the box is still sealed with his mark. He did not know which of his children, or perhaps their children, may come here to open this box. My promise to him was that I would keep it in the event one of them did. But he also instructed me not to give it unless the question you have proposed had been asked of me. I will leave you to read it in private," he said with a slight bow before he left me alone, the box on my lap.

I could feel my heart pounding in my chest. A letter in my father's own hand? Intended for whom? I doubted he ever thought it would be me, his youngest daughter, sitting there now. Surely, he assumed it would be one of his sons or maybe even one of their sons. I pried up the latch which broke the seal. The box opened with a creak, and I gently blew the dust away. Inside was a small scroll as well as a velvet bag tied at the top. I removed them both before setting the box on the floor by my feet. The blue velvet bag contained a handful of precious stones, including several large emeralds, which were clearly worth a great deal. I put those back in the bag and carefully set them back in the box.

My hands shook a bit as I took a deep breath trying to steady my nerves. Now, for the scroll.

"My child, I thank the gods that you are alive and with my dear friend Bennu as I am sure you would not be here had you not prevailed against significant odds. If you are here, it also means that you have lost the throne of Egypt. Know that I have also felt the weight and agony of this moment and survived it. My fear has long been that my progeny would continue to fight each other for the right to rule, much as my own child Berenice has done to me. It was my hope that you would all find a way to rule together. Should that not be the case I have made provisions for you to raise an army to try to regain the throne. Carefully consider this before you go against one of our own, whether this is driven by your own need for power and control or if

it is in the best interest of Egypt. If you decide to fight, then fight to the death for your birthright, especially if it is against an interloper. But should you decide not to fight know that neither I nor the gods will curse you. Fate is in control and sometimes we simply must accept it. Whatever you decide to do, Osiris and I will still welcome you to the afterlife with no harsh judgment. Now, it is up to you I can guide you no more. You must follow your heart, follow the gods, do what is right, and do what you must."

Why the tears were slowly streaming down my face I did not really know. Perhaps it was simply that at that moment I was missing my father's presence and guidance. Maybe it's just that I wished I were not here, facing the challenge. I was just into my eighteenth year by a few months and yet, many years of my life have already been spent in war.

"Arsinoe," Bennu said quietly.

I hadn't realized he had returned, and I quickly wiped the tears from my face. I sat up straight in my chair and pushed the hair out of my eyes.

"Yes? Please, come sit with me," I replied, my voice catching in my throat.

"I am sorry. I did not mean to interrupt," he said.

"No, no. I am grateful you came back, and I also so very much appreciate the support you gave to my father. It was clear in his letter he saw you as a trusted friend."

"You pay me great homage with your words, and I am humbled. I hope your father saw me as a friend and someone he could trust. I hope you do as well," replied Bennu, his eyes moist with tears of his own.

"Of course. I am most grateful to you and to your family for everything you have done. Having read my father's letter I know what I am to do, but first I must understand. How much deben has my father left in your keeping?"

"He left with me fifty deben a year to maintain the house and my family. In addition, he has left nearly ten thousand deben should anyone come to me in need of them. There are also Roman gold coins and the bag of jewels. It was all to be donated to the Temple as an offering for the god's favor should no one from his family return," Bennu replied.

"Where is it kept? Do you have access to it?"

"Yes, there is a secret place inside the temple where it is hidden. I monitor it carefully to ensure that it is safe and protected. Only one other person knows of this to ensure that Rome would not try to seize the money. We have maintained the utmost secrecy, princess," whispered Bennu as he glanced around the room.

That, along with the value of the gems that were in the purse, might be enough. It would be a good start at least.

"You are going to fight?" asked Bennu.

"Yes, I am. Do you think that is the wrong thing to do?" I asked hesitantly.

"It is not for me to say. The gods do not speak to me as they do to you, as they did to your father. You are of royal blood; the Ptolemy dynasty has been chosen by the gods and it is your calling. They descended from the royal family of Macedonia before becoming the leaders of Egypt. The first Ptolemy ruler was a consort to Alexander the Great and a strong and powerful leader in his own right. Your history is a rich and storied one. Your destiny is ruled by Horus. But know this… I was sworn to help your father, and I will swear my allegiance to you without hesitation," he said as he pounded his chest with his closed fist.

"Thank you, Bennu. Your support and loyalty are most welcome, and I thank you. I want to respect you and your family and certainly would not want to cause you any kind of pain or suffering because of my actions."

"My family knows my heart. They will support you as I do. You need not fear, but I do very much appreciate your thoughtfulness. We are here to serve you, all of us."

After Bennu left me, I could not help but feel frightened. The hair on the back of my neck was standing up, my palms were moist, and my breathing was ragged. What was I thinking? I was just a girl; Pompey could not even prevail against Caesar, and he had Roman soldiers at his command. I had already lost this fight once. Did I really think I could defeat him now? It seemed that my father's wish was clear. But still…

While Rome had always been involved in Egyptian affairs to some degree before, this unholy alliance between Rome and Cleopatra is a betrayal in every way. My father said an interloper was a reason to fight, and Rome was certainly that. It seemed the way was clear; I must find a way to set aside any trepidation I might have. My destiny had been written by the gods long before they breathed life into this body. I needed to fight to take back the throne of Egypt, no matter the cost.

Chapter Four

OUTSIDE THE WALL

For the next few months, Bennu and I worked to create a council of advisors and supporters of my cause. We met in secret every week as we planned our next steps. These men, all of Egyptian descent, were risking their lives and those of their families to meet like this. We did our best to hide the purpose of our gathering, and we were cautious with our words spoken to others outside our circle. Masduse, Darius, Amon, Ziyad, Bennu, Lira, and I had come to trust each other these past few months and the conversation flowed as freely as the wine. Before we tried to rally more support, we had to be clear about what needed to happen since once it became known I was trying again to raise an army, Caesar would come for me. He would come for us all.

"Princess, we have not discussed this at length, but I think it might be worth considering whether or not we should approach Cyprus for their help," said Darius questioningly.

My gaze settled on him. I am infatuated with Darius, despite myself, and I hang on his every word. He was one of the most handsome men I had ever seen. His dark curly hair hung down to his shoulders and he was always pushing it out of his eyes. Those eyes. A greenish blue like the Aegean Sea with long lashes that nearly touched his eyebrows. He was not tall, only a hand-width taller than me. But he was muscular and strong, and when I watched him wield his sword in practice it was with a strength I had never seen.

When he looked at me, I could feel my heart flutter and my loins stir. Even at this age, I still had not known a man, but I often thought of lying with him. But I am a queen. So unlike Cleopatra who lowers herself to mate with the Roman, I will save myself for the one who will rule with me.

There are no brothers left for me to marry. The shrew has seen to that. But surely there would be someone I could find to rule with me and to provide children who would see the Ptolemy dynasty continue. If not, Caesarion would likely be the ruler. I would not stand for that… not for a day, not even for a moment.

"Princess?"

I suddenly realized I had been lost in my thoughts. Everyone was staring at me waiting for a reply.

"My apologies, I was thinking about what you said," I replied, shaking my head as if to clear the cobwebs. I smiled at Darius while feeling my cheeks turning bright red.

"Who sits as the leader there now? A Roman, no doubt," asked Ziyad.

"Yes, I believe his name is Lucius. His father is a friend of Cassius who is no admirer of Julius Caesar. We may be able to persuade him to join us," said Masduse as he looked around the table trying to gauge the others response.

"When Caesar was trying to placate me and my younger brother, he gave us Cyprus to rule over, probably thinking we would leave Alexandria, go there, and leave Cleopatra alone. Truly it was not his to give. The Romans had taken it from my father's brother, so it was ours to begin with."

"Well, maybe we would find a sympathetic ear and men who would join the cause. I doubt they like having the Romans there any more than Alexandria does," added Bennu.

"So Bennu, would you go and talk to Lucius?" I asked.

"I think you should go," replied Darius.

There was an audible gasp from Lira, but the men managed to maintain their composure.

"She cannot leave the temple. It's not safe!" replied Lira with a great deal of panic.

It's true. I have not left the temple in nearly a year; I've forgotten what life is like beyond these walls. I allow myself to look out the gate, but I never go beyond it. Never.

"If we are going to have any chance of convincing the Cyprians to join us, I think they must hear from you directly, my princess," Darius said looking at me.

"No, it's not safe. If we lose her, we lose Egypt," replied Lira as she took my hand in hers. "You cannot go! You cannot."

The others were quiet, seemingly in deep contemplation. My heart was pounding at the very thought of leaving the temple. I knew I must not allow myself to be swayed by my affection for Darius. If someone else had suggested it, I would probably have discounted it immediately.

"I think Darius is right," said Masduse at last.

"Agreed," added Ziyad.

I looked at Bennu. His opinion mattered more to me than any of the others. If he believed it was necessary, and more importantly possible, then I would go myself if it was the right thing to do. We all waited patiently until he finally spoke.

"Princess, your safety, your very life has been placed in my care. I take that responsibility most fervently. I pray each morning and night to the gods for your health and safety. But I also owe you my loyalty and support as your father asked of me. If getting back the crown of Egypt is important enough for you to risk your life, then you must go. If it is not, I doubt we can convince others to risk theirs."

Small beads of sweat were running down my forehead and I wiped them away before they could sting my eyes. He was right of course. If I was not willing to risk it all, then why should others do so on my behalf? I looked at Lira. I could see she was holding back tears, but I also knew she would do whatever I asked without hesitation.

"You are right. I need to go to Cyprus myself."

Lira was visibly upset, and I reached over to squeeze her hand. Her friendship meant a great deal to me. It was not my intention to cause her pain, but we all must do what is necessary. Even me.

"Now to figure out how to do that while ensuring we can get you safely back to the temple. It will not be easy. I'm sure that Caesar has spies among the citizens who live just outside the gates. I suspect they visit the temple and are rewarded for reporting on your movements. But if we can get Cyprus on our side, and with those who support you here, we could have a real chance of taking on Cleopatra," said Masduse.

"I think I have an idea," I replied with a mischievous smile. It had worked to a degree before. Perhaps it could work again.

For weeks we spent every waking hour covering all the details lest anything be overlooked. Ziyad was already possessed of a large sailing vessel, and he occasionally went to Cyprus to trade so no one would think it odd if he were to make that trip now. The only unusual aspect would be a woman aboard the ship, so it was clear I would have to leave the temple and sail as a young man. Darius would also come to act as my older brother to keep me safe. But still, people might quickly become suspicious if they did not see me for the several months it would take to make the trip.

Once again, Lira would become Princess Arsinoe. She would be tasked with dressing as me, making our nightly trips to the courtyard. Cente would play the role of Lira. If she stayed inside the temple grounds when she appeared as me, she should be safe. She just needed to be seen by others so that no one would report my disappearance to Caesar. Her company will be missed dearly, but we had no choice. She would have to take on this role again, one which she played so expertly before. We had both gotten taller since then, but still, we were very close to the same size. Even our skin tone and hair color were very similar. It is a deception Bennu is confident we can get away with.

The night before we were to leave, Lira and I took our usual walk in the evening to the courtyard. This time she was dressed as me and I was dressed as a simple house girl. When we returned to the villa, she would tightly braid my hair so I could hide it under a small turban. Then the girl would be gone, and a young boy would stand in her place.

"Are you scared?" asked Lira as we sat on the steps watching the setting sun.

"No. After the time we spent in a Roman prison I don't think there is much that can scare me anymore," I replied with a wry smile.

"It makes my skin crawl just thinking of it," she replied with a shudder.

"I am looking forward to gazing upon the sea again. It will be wonderful to feel the spray of the water on my face and see anything other than these walls... as beautiful as they may be," I said wistfully.

"I have prepared a small trunk for you. In it are your finest clothes and best jewels to wear when you go to meet with Lucius. He needs to know he speaks to the Queen of Egypt, and I want you to very much look the part. I wish I could be there to help you dress and do your hair, but Darius has promised to find a woman to help when you arrive."

"Thank you, Lira. I will miss you. We have not been apart even a single day for many years now. It will be strange to know you are not nearby," I replied as I put my arm around her shoulders and pulled her close to me.

"Princess, I do not think..."

"Ah yes you are right," I replied as I removed my arm.

Lira often mentioned that she felt like she was being followed and watched so even here on the steps at this hour we must be careful.

"I know you can be persuasive, and I will pray to Amon, Isis, and Osiris for your well-being and success each morning and night till you return. And of course, you have Darius to look after you," said Lira with a smile.

"Is it that obvious?"

"Only to me," she replied with a glint in her eye.

"I must confess the idea of spending several months at sea with him both thrills me and frightens me," I said with a girlish laugh.

"You are a queen, but you are also a woman. Must you choose between the two?" she asked.

"Rightly or wrongly, it seems that is my burden. Perhaps because of Cleopatra's wanton behavior I hold my chastity close to my heart and hope that the gods will find a way for me to, someday, be both," I replied as the last of the sun slid down slipped from our view.

Lira did not reply.

"We should go. There is still much to do," I said as I rose and extended my hand to Lira to help her.

"If you do not return, I will see you in the afterlife where I will continue to serve you," she said as she squeezed my hand before letting it go.

I slept little that night, knowing that tomorrow I would walk out the temple's front doors and back out into the world. The morning sun was barely above the horizon when I finished dressing. Cente had brought some food to my room, but I had no desire for it. Lira was still sleeping, and I decided not to wake her. We said our goodbyes last night. I slipped quietly into the corridor. As I passed the drawing of Bennu's wife and daughter, I stopped. I took a moment to look again into their eyes as if searching for something, an answer to a question I didn't even know to ask.

"They are lovely, aren't they?" said Bennu from behind me.

"Oh, you startled me," I said, gasping.

"I am sorry my Princess," he replied with a little bow.

"Yes, they are lovely. I've never asked. What were their names?"

"My wife, Aziz, and my daughter, Feme."

"Feme means love does it not?"

"Yes. It seemed so fitting when she was born. We loved her more than life itself and we would have done anything for her. I can see why the gods were anxious to have her with them. She was truly the embodiment of love, and I look forward to the day I see her again," said Bennu.

"It is my hope she welcomes you with open arms," I said as I embraced him.

"Thank you. I pray to Osiris every night that when the time comes, we will all be together again. Losing a child is a pain that tears at the heart every day. The pain does dull with time, but it never goes away. It only becomes a part of you… a part of everything you do in your life."

"I am sorry Bennu. I cannot imagine what it is like to endure that kind of loss. Was there nothing that could be done?"

"No. Many in the city were ill, and despite my prayers and the prayers of my wife's family and our many offerings, they still left us. I am thankful that Aziz went to the river before Feme so that she was there to help her cross. I would not have wanted her to be afraid that she was alone in her journey," said Bennu, his voice cracking with emotion.

I embraced him again, holding him tightly to me. I could feel sorrow emanating through his very skin. Clearly, I must remember to pray for him more often.

"Are you ready, my princess?" he said. He wiped away what I am sure was a tear that had trickled down his face.

"Yes. I will leave you now and go to meet Darius in the temple as we had planned. Can I pass for a boy?"

"Hmm, come here," he said as he led me toward one of the beautiful palms that sat near the fountain. He reached into the pot and pinched some dirt rubbing it between his hands before gently putting some on my nose and cheeks. "There, much better."

As I walked through the temple I wondered if I would return. Would this be the last time I marveled at its beauty and wonder? If it were, I would die knowing I had done all that I could to reclaim the throne, protect my people, and be judged favorably by the gods. The morning crowds were just starting to arrive, and I marveled at how easily I blended in. No one paid me any attention. Most of the wealthier visitors looked through me as if I were not even there. While it was an odd feeling, it reassured me that my appearance was as we had hoped. Arriving at the designated meeting place, I waited patiently for Darius, scanning the crowds for his face. Finally, he came into view, and I was much relieved.

"So, what do you think?" I asked when he got closer.

"I think you should speak as little as possible when others are around," he said with a laugh. "Otherwise, I doubt that Caesar himself could pick you out of a crowd."

"Ah yes, Lira and I have experienced this issue before," I said smiling.

"And don't smile too much. It makes your eyes sparkle and look more beautiful than they already are," he whispered in my ear.

The feeling of his breath on my neck made my knees weak and for a moment I thought I might collapse on the floor. He thought my eyes were beautiful.

This was going to be a long two-month journey.

"Ready?"

"Yes," I replied with as much conviction as I could muster.

We walked silently next to each other toward the front of the temple. Darius nodded his greeting at those we encountered who he knew. As we walked down the steps and continued across the grass to the gate, I could feel my heart pounding. The gate was open as it always was this time of day, and the crowds flowed freely in and out. Just a few more steps and suddenly… I was in the street. Somehow the noise of the crowds of people had been muffled by the walls of the temple. I was taken aback by the sounds of the raised voices, the carts rattling over the stones, and even music coming from somewhere. It always seemed quiet to me at the temple and the noise of the street outside was a bit of a surprise. But I reveled in it.

I wanted to stop and stare and take it all in, but Darius took my elbow and kept me moving through the crowd. There were so many people pushing against each other as they passed through the streets. I realized it would be nothing for someone to stab me and then just disappear into the crowd. Darius must have felt me stiffen up.

"You are safe with me Amin. No one is noticing you and Lira will do her part. Do not be afraid," he said quietly.

Amin. It was the name we had chosen for me to be called, and it was going to take some getting used to. As we walked to the wharf, I could feel myself relax more and more. He was right, no one noticed me at all. We were almost on the ship. There were a few Roman soldiers at the port, but they paid us no mind. When Ziyad's ship came into view it was a relief. Still, even on the ship, we must be careful as no one else knew my identity and we all agreed it was best to keep it that way.

"Good morning," cried Ziyad, waving as we approached.

"Good morning," replied Darius.

I tried my best not to smile but my relief was palpable.

"Amin! It is nice to see you outside the temple," said Ziyad.

I nodded as Darius helped me onto the ship. Ziyad used his body to screen his assistance from the view of others.

"Thank you, Ziyad. It is beyond my comprehension that I am truly here," I said in a voice barely above a whisper.

"Ah, the voice, of course," he said with a hearty laugh.

"I've told Amin to talk as little as possible in the company of others," replied Darius looking at me with a serious stare.

"Yes, I think that is best. I've been able to make a private cabin of sorts for the two of you. I'm sorry, Amin, but to put you in there alone would raise a great deal of suspicion. You and Darius will have to occupy it together."

My heart leaped into my throat. How would I ever manage two months of lying near this man when just the feel of his breath on my neck aroused me? I dug my fingernails into the palm of my hand causing enough pain to distract my mind. While the men loaded the supplies, I sat up on the bow watching the bales and casks coming and going from the other ships. There were so many languages I did not recognize, and skin tones from light brown to very black and every shade in between. It felt so wonderful to be able to see the horizon across the sea. The world felt so big. The sky was bluer, the breeze was fresher, and the dampness in the air was a refreshing respite from the growing heat of the day.

"Amin, would you like some bread or cheese? I also have a bit of wine," said Darius.

I nodded, greedily accepting his offering. I ate with a vigor I had not felt in a long time. If only I could travel as myself, as Arsinoe, Queen of Egypt, this moment would be perfect. But I was grateful just to be doing something, anything to advance my cause.

"Are you still hungry? Do you need something else?"

"No, thank you, Darius," I whispered as I wiped my mouth with the back of my hand.

He smiled. I felt so safe with him. Even though I knew my attraction to him must be tempered I was grateful he was with me. The men were getting ready to cast off the lines and Darius had me stand next to him pretending to work as best I could so as not to draw the attention of anyone on the wharf who might be watching. While I was still small for my age, a boy of my size would be expected to pull and coil ropes. I did the best I could. Before I knew it, the bow of the ship had turned toward the open sea, and we began moving away from the dock. In only a few minutes we were too far out for me to be noticed, and I went back to my perch on the bow.

Darius and Ziyad told the other men that I was not well and so they seemed to accept that I could do little work. They also kept their distance in case my illness was something they might wish to avoid. I stayed in this spot until the sun had nearly disappeared. I just couldn't bring myself to go into the confines of the ship. This freedom was just what my ka needed, and I prayed to Uat-Ur, the god of the sea, for our safe passage. Finally, the swaying of the ship nearly put me to sleep, and it could be avoided no more. I was going to have to go below. Darius was not there when I reached the little area that Ziyad had created for us, and I was grateful for the privacy as I removed my turban and washed my face.

There was a clean tunic laid out on the bed. One bed. It was big enough for both of us, but just barely. After I changed, I climbed in and moved as far over as I could, turning my face to the cool wood of the ship. Before I knew it, I was asleep.

If Darius came in during the night I did not hear him. The bed next to me was still cool to the touch when I awoke in the morning. I languished for a few minutes enjoying the gentle rise and fall of the ship. The sea has always been a respite for me. My mother used to say I was part fish, always wanting to be in and around the water. As I child I loved to play on the banks of the Nile, throwing stones and digging in the mud. My love of the water would serve me well for these next few weeks. Finally, I forced myself from the bed and donned the disguise that I would be forced to wear for the trip. The clothes I did not mind. They were comfortable and easy to wear, but the turban made my head hurt and I missed the feeling of the wind through my hair.

"So, you finally decided to join us," I heard from behind me as I popped my head up through the hatch.

Darius was sitting on a cask near the back of the ship whittling away at a piece of wood with a small knife. The sun was much higher in the sky than I thought it would be. I must have been more tired than I realized.

"Good morning," I said quietly but with a genuine smile.

"More like afternoon if you ask me. Ra is in the sky already and Khonus will not be far behind. You slept well I take it?"

"Better than I have in some time. Perhaps it is the sea or maybe because I am no longer a prisoner," I replied as I leaned on the railing at the back of the ship.

The water was a beautiful green that roiled behind us as the white foam of the waves marked our progress. Save for another ship quite some distance away there was nothing else to see… no land, no birds, just the open water. The breeze smelled fresh and new as if the day held all the promise that was possible, and it could hold no more.

"Did you come to the cabin to sleep?" I asked.

"I did. A pallet on the floor next to the bed served me well, my princess," he said, not making eye contact with me.

"Amin," I said, playfully poking his arm with my finger.

"No one is near us. We cannot be heard," he replied, poking me back.

"True, but we should probably be consistent so that mistakes are not made," I said matter-of-factly.

"Yes Amin," he replied with a little nod of his head.

"Why did you sleep on the floor?"

He looked at me intently. His eyes matched the color of the water churning behind him and his wavy locks were, for a change, off his face making his eyes even more striking. How one man could be so blessed by the gods I did not know.

"It would be presumptuous of me to assume you would be comfortable with me lying next to you, and I did not want to wake you," he said finally.

"Darius, we have weeks to go and weeks to return to the

temple. You cannot sleep on the floor all that time. I will not have it. We can share the bed, I insist," I replied feeling the heat rising in my cheeks.

Did he know how I felt about him? How could he not? I felt like it was written all over my face. My body ached for him to hold me in his arms.

"I cannot," he replied.

I was visibly taken aback by his words. Was he saying that he was repulsed by the idea of lying next to me?

"Why not?"

"You are a Princess, a future Queen of Egypt. I am your humble and loyal servant, but I am also a man. Lying next to you alone in the night, I do not know if I could… trust myself," he said candidly.

I breathed deeply, filling my lungs with air and letting it slowly escape as my mind formulated a response.

"Darius, it is true that I am of royal blood, but you are not just my servant. You are a friend, and for this trip, you are my protector. Having said that, the dilemma you speak of is one I know well and understand."

"What are you saying, Arsinoe?"

"If things were different… if we were in a different time or place, we would be free to be together, to act on these feelings of desire we have for each other. But we both know that we cannot. We will have to simply push our feelings aside. I would be horribly worried about your well-being if you were to spend these weeks lying on the damp floor," I said trying to sound mature and in control, which belied the butterflies I could feel in my belly.

"Have you been with a man before?"

"No, and my commitment to my cause, the cause of the Egyptian people, prevents me from doing so in a carnal way now. Tell me you understand this, Darius?"

"I do, and I would never do anything to disrespect you or take advantage of you in any way. You have my word," he replied as he put his right fist over his heart.

"Good. Then going forward we will share the bed, yes?"

"Amin, go and find us some bread, would you?" he said good-naturedly.

The days grew into weeks, and we fell into a comfortable rhythm. Darius taught me to fish, and I enjoyed joining the others as we worked to catch our food for the day. At night, we spent hours and hours playing senet. Ziyad would often join us in the cabin where we could talk as we played, strategizing the words that would need to be said when we reached Cyprus. He also taught me how to play another game with stones. The evenings were often filled with laughter. This was a freedom I had not known in a very long time. I felt as if I were growing into myself, into the person I was supposed to be before all of this. Before Cleopatra destroyed the world as I knew it and took away from me the life I was supposed to have.

I took on the task of salting the fish and preparing many of the meals, as repetitive as they were, I did my best to make them at least palatable. The meals were an improvement over those made by the man called Winersta who had done the meals early on. The small crew welcomed the improvement, and it also prevented them from asking why I did not do more of the heavy labor. I'm sure that they could all see that, whether I was a man or woman, I was slight in body and unable to do many of the things they did easily.

Cleopatra would surely laugh at my situation if she could see me now. Cleaning and cooking were things we always had others to do for us. Now I must do these things not just for myself, but for others too! All though she may find humor in this, if I were to be successful in Cyprus, an army at her door would force her from the throne of Egypt. That would be no laughing matter indeed. My every waking thought was of nothing else. Even in my dreams I often saw myself sitting on the throne as the Queen of Egypt at last.

Missing my dear friend Lira was not something I had anticipated. She had become like family to me. In many ways, she was better than family as she had no expectations, demands, or hidden agendas. She is the one person to whom I could say what I was thinking and feeling, and she never judged me harshly. She would say if she disagreed, or she might offer another perspective, but always with a gentle tone. I thought of the Temple as being so small and confining, but after a few weeks on this ship, it felt even smaller than being confined to the temple grounds. I often wished for our evening walk and to sit on the steps watching the sunset. Wistful is not an emotion I indulged in often, but it seemed appropriate.

As promised, Darius would come to bed every evening sometime after I would retire. I would always lay with my back to him and him with his back to me, but I would often relax until our bodies were touching. His warmth was a comfort, and his regular breathing would lull me back to sleep if I awoke. I had not felt this safe, and dare I say, loved, in a very long time. It was unspoken between us, but we knew. We both knew whenever we looked at each other that what we felt for each other was love. There was no other name to call it.

How this would end, neither of us could predict. Only the gods would know. If Cyprus would not come to my aid, then perhaps the cause was lost. What would my life be like if I were not Queen of Egypt? A life with Darius perhaps? Children playing and laughing, not afraid of who might be waiting for them in the shadows. It sounded idyllic, wonderful even, but I could not help but hope I would never know.

A BEGINNING AND AN ENDING

"It won't be long now," said Darius, pointing up at a seagull flying overhead.

"You think so?" I replied hopefully.

"Yes. These birds will fly only so far from land. I would say in another couple of days we will begin to see land on the horizon."

My emotions were conflicted. I couldn't wait to get to Cyprus to see if Lucius would help us, but it also meant the journey was coming to an end. My nights lying with Darius would be over, at least for the time being. He was right. Only two short days later, land appeared just as he had predicted. We all gathered on the deck to say our prayers to Amon, Isis, and Osiris for our safe passage and fair winds. We had been very fortunate having encountered no rough seas and no Roman ships who might want to board and inspect our cargo. Ziyad, Darius, and I agreed it would be best to go ashore as Amin instead of as Princess Arsinoe.

There was a place we planned to stay for a few days. Ziyad has used it before, and from there we would send Darius as an emissary to speak to Lucius to arrange a meeting. If he refused, this would all have been for naught. But I couldn't think about that. I must focus on being successful. I must be the epitome of confidence and project only a royal air. If he doubted my ability to rule, he would likely not be willing to support my cause. Truth be told, as much as I was anxious to speak with Lucius, I was also looking forward to taking my hair down and becoming a woman again after so many weeks as a man. In the privacy of our cabin, I did my best to wash my braids without removing them as there was no one onboard who could help me to braid them again. If my hair began to creep out from underneath my turban it would raise a great deal of suspicion.

Once again on my perch at the bow of the ship, I could see the wharf and other ships and as before, the constant movement of goods from the ship to the shore. Many of the men wore only white loincloths, their bronze skin covered in sweat glistened in the sun. It was a marvel that they could carry such weight, and their strength was fully on display as they hoisted the heavy bales onto their shoulders to carry them to waiting carts. The breeze smelled different now as it picked up the odor of flowers, trees, and even food cooking. It was a welcome change. As we inched closer, the voices began to carry across the water. They were yelling out for help and direction. In all my years I had never been at sea for so long and I confess I was looking forward to setting foot on dry land again. My trunk was packed and ready to be taken ashore so that I could complete my transition back to Princess Arsinoe.

"Are you ready?" Darius whispered into my ear.

"If the gods will bless me and you will be with me, then yes. I am ready. No matter the outcome, we must try. If we fail here, our odds of success are slim," I replied as I leaned slightly into his chest.

If he had wrapped his arms around me and reassured me, it would have been a perfect moment, but he could not. I was sure he was thinking it, just as I was.

"I need to help with the mooring. Stay here and I will return for you as soon as I am done," he said before turning away.

Despite myself, I shivered slightly in the cool breeze. The sun was warm on my arms and face, but without Darius behind me, I cooled. The warmth he brought when he was close dissipated, just as the sun's heat dissipates when Ra goes to the underworld at the end of each day. We were finally moored, and the men were opening all the hatches. They began the process of bringing up our stored goods of grain and papyrus. We would bring copper back to Ephesus, as it is plentiful here.

"Amin, come here!" I heard Ziyad yell as he waited by the gangplank. Darius was on the dock already.

I scurried over to him, trying to contain my excitement at the thought of finally going ashore.

"Yes, Ziyad," I said with a slight bow expected of a younger man toward one his senior and the captain of the vessel.

"I need you to help Darius. Go ashore," he said pointing to him as he stood there expectantly.

"Thank you, Ziyad, for everything."

In a voice barely above a whisper, he replied, "You will be the Queen of Egypt again. The gods have told me so in my prayers. I will always be your humble servant," he said.

I desired to embrace him to show him how thankful I was for the risk he had taken bringing me on this journey, but that would have to wait till we were in private.

"Yes, right away," I responded in my best Amin voice with a bit of a wink, before hurrying down the roughhewn board to the dock.

Once on land, I realized my legs felt a bit strange. It was odd not to feel constant movement underneath me.

"Easy there," said Darius as he took my elbow and steadied me.

There were so many people around us I dared not speak. I nodded at him, afraid to even smile as he had once warned me against doing. Complacency had become my companion these last weeks but once again I must be on guard, lest I spoil the mission before it had even begun. What Julius Caesar would do if he were to learn that I traveled to Cyprus was anyone's guess, but it was my hope we could sustain the veil of secrecy we had worked so hard to create a bit longer.

"Just stay close behind me. We are going to the place where Ziyad will meet us later," said Darius as we made our way down the crowded street. Carts and donkeys were everywhere, with people jostling to make their way to the markets that lined the streets. Children were running and laughing as their mothers tried to keep them in line. A little girl fell right in front of me and began to cry, just as a cart headed right toward her.

"Oh, no. No, you are alright. Stand up before you get stepped on," I said without thinking as I snatched her out of the path of the oncoming cart.

The little girl looked at me as she gulped back her tears. I brushed off her tunic and her skinned knees as best I could.

"Omenia, what are you doing? Come here," a woman said angrily. I assumed this must be her mother as she rushed over to us and grabbed her hand.

"The nice lady helped me," she said looking up at her mother.

The woman looked at me for a moment, staring into my eyes as if by that alone she could tell that underneath this disguise, we were alike. She also seemed to instantly understand my need for secrecy.

"Thank you, young man, for helping my daughter," she said before turning away quickly, her child in tow as she continued up the street.

The little girl turned back to look at me as her mother dragged her away. She waved before they stopped at the stall of a fruit seller a short distance away.

I couldn't help but smile until I realized that Darius was nowhere in sight. He must not have realized that I had stopped. My heart began to pound as my eyes searched the crowd in all directions for his face, but he was not to be found. Tears were welling up in my eyes, but I brushed them away. They would do me no good now. Should I try to go back to the ship? We had already made so many twists and turns. I was not sure I knew the way, but could I risk asking for directions? I moved over to the side of the road and leaned against a stone building. For a moment it reminded me of when I escaped the palace through the tunnel, and I had to enter the market without Gany. Nrimeda was there to rescue me as Gany had planned, but now there was no one. I knew no one and had no idea where to turn.

"Do you need some help?" said the woman.

It was her, the woman with the little girl. She had seen me

standing here, clearly in distress, and she came back to see what was wrong. As I looked into the woman's eyes, her little girl who held tightly to her hand reached out and grabbed mine with the other.

"You helped me. Now we can help you," she said politely.

Cold sweat was running down my back and my palms were sweaty as I felt the little girl's hand in mine.

"What is your name?" asked the woman.

"Amin," I whispered.

"Are you lost?"

"I was with my brother, but we were separated when I…"

"When you stopped to help Omenia?"

I nodded. Should I ask her to show me the way to the dock? The panic within me was rising. What had I done? Would stopping to help this little girl be my undoing and cost me the throne?

"Amin, Amin! Where have you been?" chided Darius as he suddenly appeared from the crowd, pulling me into an embrace.

The relief I felt was overwhelming. I wanted nothing more than to collapse and let him carry me the rest of the way, safe in his arms.

"It is my fault. Well, it was my daughter's fault. Amin stopped to help her when she fell. If he had not, she could have easily been hurt by a passing cart," said the woman.

Darius looked at the woman and the little girl, his eyes now wide with surprise…and fear. Did she realize I was not a boy? Would she tell one of the many Roman guards wandering the streets? He looked around, gauging whether we should try to run and if so in what direction, when the woman put her hand on his arm.

"You need not worry. I am grateful my child is safe, and you have reunited. I wish you and your… brother a good day," she said with a slight bow.

"I thought you were a girl," said Omenia rather loudly as she let go of my hand.

"No, Amin is a boy. That is why he wears a turban," replied her mother.

"Thank you," replied Darius.

"May the gods bless you, my child," whispered the woman before she and Omenia disappeared into the crowd once again.

We walked hurriedly and in silence toward our destination. I was most grateful when the gate to a small villa closed behind us, and we were safely inside.

"I am sorry," I said finally.

"Princess, you owe me no apology. You did what any person would have done, certainly anyone as kindhearted as you. It seems it did no harm, and I made sure the woman did not follow us. Even if she says something to one of the Romans, which I doubt she will, they will not find you now," he said reassuringly.

We stepped inside the lovely villa to be greeted by a tall thin man and a very pretty woman who appeared to be the age of his daughter rather than his wife.

"Greetings Princess Arsinoe. Welcome to our humble home. It is our sincere pleasure to have you here with us. I am called Stonius, and this is my daughter Bithsea," said the man with a deep bow which his daughter emulated.

"Thank you for your kindness and your shelter. We require both," I replied with a smile.

"Also, a bath," said Darius with a laugh.

"Of course, princess. My daughter will show you to your room and assist you as I am sure you are anxious to bathe and change as well."

"This way, princess," said Bithsea, gesturing to the hallway on the left.

We walked together silently down the long hall which was decorated with beautiful frescos and gilded statues. It was clear that Stonius was a man of some means and presumably our entrée to meet with Lucius. Bithsea opened the door into a beautiful room decorated in shades of green and blue that was filled with fresh plants and flowers. At one end, stairs led down to a large bath where a young girl was pouring oil and dropping fresh flowers into the water.

"Bithsea, could you help me get these braids out of my hair?" I asked as I peeled off the turban.

"Of course, princess. We are here to serve you in whatever way we can. Sit here and I will help you," she said as she pulled up a small seat.

She made quick work of removing the braids. The sensation of having my hair brushed after all these weeks was one I could hardly put into words. Peeling off my clothes, I walked into the bath, relishing the feel of the water on my dry and dirty skin. The young girl took my clothes away to be washed and Bithsea removed from my trunk the things I had brought with me. She also opened a cabinet that held additional tunics and shoes for me to put on when I was finished. The water was neither cold nor hot, simply warm and soothing. The oils were soaked up into my skin in a matter of moments. When she returned, the young girl joined me in the bath, washing my hair and scrubbing the dirt from my back, feet, and legs. Soon there was a film of dirt on top of the water. I stood on the steps while Bithsea rinsed my hair and body, ensuring none of the grime remained.

She wrapped me in a soft linen cloth which covered me from head to toe as she squeezed the water out of my hair. It had grown so much during the journey; it was down nearly to my waist. It was once again a delight to have her brush through it. A few clips would hold it back off my face, but it felt good to feel it on my shoulders and back once again. I would not wear the decorated tunic I brought with me, but instead something simpler, saving it for my meeting with Lucius.

The clothes she provided were lovely. The material was of fine quality and felt elegant and smooth against my skin. Bithsea helped with my cuffs and a beautiful blue-green amulet of Osiris on a gold chain. I must remember to thank Stonius for his generosity, but for now, I was hungry and looking forward to fruit and fresh meat which we had not eaten for weeks. Oh, and wine. After this day I was in desperate need of wine and plenty of it.

"If you are ready, my princess, my father, and the others are waiting for you in the atrium," said Bithsea just as I was putting the finishing touches on my eyes with the kohl stick.

"Of course," I replied, rising from the seat to follow her out of the room.

The villa was much larger than I had first realized. As we walked to the atrium, we passed several young men and women carrying platters of food and shadufs of water and wine. We paused at the entry to the atrium, and I saw there were four or five men and two women in addition to Ziyad and Darius. I steadied myself with a deep breath, smoothed out my tunic, and lifted my head. I smiled just as everyone turned in my direction.

"May I present Princess Arsinoe, the future and rightful Queen of Egypt," said Darius as he rushed to my side, taking my arm to lead me into the room.

"Who are these people?" I whispered while still trying to smile.

"They are your supporters, but do not worry. I must say you look beautiful. No jewel in the world could outshine your beauty," he whispered back.

"Princess, you look much refreshed," said Stonius as he replaced Darius at my side. "Let me introduce you to the people who have gathered here to meet you and support you in your efforts."

One by one we went around the room as he introduced me to each of the people who had gathered. Visernus the Elder and his wife Toemaya, Petrus and his wife Isiries, and several other men, all from the ruling council of Cyprus under Lucius. I was stunned. Frankly, I did not have expectations as to how much or little support we might receive. The fact that these important men were here I assumed was a good sign. Based on how these people were dressed and how they spoke, I could see that they were people of means. It takes a great deal of money to raise an army. Many men will come to a cause simply for the coin they can earn, but they will abandon it just as quickly if the coin runs dry.

Once we were settled at the table, we enjoyed significant amounts of wonderfully delicious food, and the wine was flowing freely before the serious conversation began.

"Princess Arsinoe, I must say I have been a follower of your escapades for several years now since you first tried to unseat your sister Cleopatra from the throne some time ago," said Visernus as he lifted his glass in a toast to me. "Her half-sister," said Darius before I had a chance to.

"I'm honored, Visernus. The Ptolemy's have had a long and prosperous relationship with Cyprus for many, many years. It is my hope that when Egypt is removed from Rome's clutches, we will again," I responded, raising my own glass in his direction.

"You failed to break the bond between Caesar and Cleopatra when you tried before, and now they have a child together. What makes you think you can be successful now?" asked Isiries bluntly.

I put down my glass and cleared my throat. This was a moment much anticipated and rehearsed. This was the chance to make my case, although I did not expect it to happen so quickly.

"Your question is valid," I replied. Everything in the room became quiet. The stillness was stifling as everyone looked at me expectantly, waiting for my reply. The male servant had even stopped pouring wine. As everyone looked at me, I made a point of looking each one in the eye, one after the other till I settled on Isiries. She seemed to regard me with a bit of disdain, or perhaps it was just apprehension. After all, she and her husband were putting themselves at risk to be here with me. Seemingly, she did not seem to feel the risk was worth it.

"My father and his younger brother, the former King of Cyprus, instilled in me a deep love of my country and yours. He saw Egypt and Cyprus as one united under Ptolemy rule. While I did not know my father well, he was in exile for many years when I was young, he still had a significant impact on me. He taught all his children to have a deep love for Egypt and its people. We are one with each other, and with the gods and it was so... until Rome broke us apart, taking Cyprus from us and now controlling Egypt through Cleopatra. To be a subject of Rome is to be lessened and weakened. We will not have our fates controlled by Caesar rather than ourselves and our gods. I, for one, do not wish to be held in such a state. My birthright, given to me by hundreds of years of Pharaohs, is the throne of Egypt. It is my wish to rule my homeland with the wisdom of the ages and the grace of the gods. You are right, we failed before, but only when we were betrayed by a man whom we thought we could trust."

"You speak very passionately Princess, and I admire you, but as Isiries says you did fail before," noted Visernus.

"We nearly had Caesar; his death was imminent. He should have drowned in the sea, and he would have had he not shed his cloak and breastplate. This time… this time we will not make the mistake again of trusting those who are not true believers in my cause, and of me. I am anointed by Osiris. We will prevail in our cause. The throne of Egypt will be returned to its rightful glory and to an Egyptian who is faithful and without reproach. It will return to the Ptolemy dynasty. It will return to all Egyptians who despise the Romans, it will return… to me. And Cyprus will join us and rise to its glory once again."

"Here, here," came the cries as all the men and women stood and raised their glasses in my direction. Their cheers rang through the air. Darius was beaming at me with an admiration I had not seen in his eyes before.

"To Queen Arsinoe IV! The rightful ruler of Egypt," said Petrus.

"To the queen," came the hearty response as everyone drained their glasses.

Isiries still seemed subdued in her support, but I paid it no mind, the overall tone was supportive and that was enough. The conversation continued over sweets, and I ate heartily. I was cherishing this moment with a newfound sense of confidence and clarity. Over the course of the last few weeks, I had played this moment over and over in my mind. It seemed that I had said what was needed, at least for those gathered here. The true test was to come when I spoke to Lucius.

Over the next week, Darius, Petrus, and Stonius called upon the palace to see about arranging an opportunity for me to come and meet with Lucius. While I tried to be patient, my anxiety was rising daily. What would I do if he would not see me? But I need not have worried. Darius was very persuasive, and Petrus was a distant relative of the ruler, well-known to him, and was respected as an advisor. As the day arrived, I could hardly contain my restlessness, and the appointed time could not come soon enough. Bithsea had helped me to dress and arrange my hair. Looking at myself in the mirror, I saw a woman looking back at me, no longer a girl.

My tunic was of the finest linen, and I had brought with me all the finest jewels that I had been able to assemble. One vibrant blue sapphire that had been left by my father was of particular brilliance. It hung from my neck on a long, beautiful gold chain. Bithsea deftly arranged my hair, partly braided while some still hung down my back, nearly to my waist. She had taken pains to dress it with palm oil and my hair shimmered as if it were a part of the sun itself, the light reflecting off my long black locks.

"It is time, my queen," said Darius as he entered my room.

"I am ready," I said to my reflection.

"You look beautiful, Arsinoe. He will not be able to resist you. No man in his right mind could," he replied.

"What would I do without you to flatter me?"

"I hope that you shall never know. I am your humble servant for as long as you will have me," he said sincerely.

"You are coming with me?"

"Yes, Lucius has sent a litter for you. I will ride alongside, ensuring your safety until we arrive at the palace. Then, the guards will take you to see Lucius. I will be nearby. Do not fear, you will be safe," he said as he pounded his breastplate with his closed fist.

In his finest tunic and military regalia, he was even more handsome. It was difficult to concentrate on the task that lay ahead. While Darius was not of royal blood, he was from a renowned and respected family, and he had served Ephesus well in many of its battles. He would make a fine husband for any woman, and I was sure he would also be a wonderful father. It would wound me to my core to see him with someone else, but I knew there was no choice. The throne would be my priority. While I would have him as my husband without hesitation, I did not think that the Egyptian people would be so welcoming.

"Arsinoe?"

I shook my head, bringing myself back to the moment. This daydreaming of Darius and a life with him had once again distracted me. It must stop.

"Yes, I am sorry. We should go," I said rather curtly.

"This way," he said, gesturing toward the garden at the side of the villa.

There was a litter waiting, and Darius helped me to climb inside before pulling some of the curtains. The men then lifted it to their shoulders as Darius mounted a beautiful black stallion. Stonius opened a gate leading out to the street. Several other men on horseback led the way. I pulled the curtains closed but I could see out through the cloth a little, but not enough to make out any details as we wound our way through the streets. I could hear the clatter of the horses' hooves on the rocky path, and I could tell that Darius was on his mount next to me. When I dared to peek out between the cloths, I could see him with one hand on the reins and the other on the hilt of his sword.

There were many people in the streets as we jostled along. I could hear their voices talking about the everyday things as people do, rushing to get meat for a meal and to fetch their children from school. It seemed so ordinary, and no one paid me any attention. Perhaps a litter being escorted by palace guards occurred more often than one might think.

It seemed it was only a few minutes before the litter was being set down again and I waited patiently as Darius had instructed. Finally, the curtains parted, and I could see I was in another garden, this one much more elaborate than the one in Stonius' villa. Large statues of the gods were in every corner of the courtyard and there were fountains and pools of water surrounded by lush greenery of every size and shape. Some bloomed with flowers that were the size of my hand in colors of red, pink, and white and their perfume filled the air. There were guards at each of the archways leading in and out of the garden and a young man offered his hand to help me from the litter.

"Please follow me," said the boy, never looking up at my face, keeping his eyes focused on the ground.

We walked through one of the archways into a long colonnade

where Darius was waiting with the two men who had come on horseback to get me. He nodded in my direction but did not follow. The other two men fell in behind me and for a moment I felt panic rising in my throat as I realized Darius was not coming with me. I glanced back at him as we started walking down the hallway, and he smiled broadly. It reassured me some. The only sounds were the gentle clinking of the metal on the guards' uniforms and the soft padding of the boy's feet.

"In here," said the boy as he opened a large wooden door. I went inside the men who had led me here now standing on either side of the doorway.

It was a library filled from floor to ceiling with scrolls. There were several reading tables with writing instruments and what appeared to be blank papyrus. The door closed behind me with a loud thud.

I looked around but there seemed to be no one in the room. Perhaps I was just to wait here before I was taken to wherever Lucius would be. The shelves of scrolls were an inviting sight, and it would have been wonderful to simply sit and read for hours. My hand gently stroked the wooden ends of the scrolls as I wandered around the room. Each shelf was labeled with the names of all the great philosophers, generals, and scholars. They marked the writer of the scrolls contained within.

"Do you like to read?" A man's voice shattered the silence and startled me so much that I let out an involuntary gasp as I turned toward the doorway.

"Oh, forgive me. I did not mean to frighten you," said the man apologetically as he came in to the room through the garden.

"No need to apologize. I was simply caught by surprise. Yes, I do like to read. I was very fortunate to grow up with a large library and a family who encouraged reading. It has been a solace for me in times of uncertainty," I replied with a wry smile.

"For me as well. When I cannot sleep or have a weight on my heart I often come here and find something to amuse or enlighten me. Sometimes I also find that I have fallen asleep with a scroll in hand," he replied smiling.

"You are very fortunate to have access to such a wonderful cache of information. So, this palace is your home?"

"Yes, for a few years now, and I do appreciate the position I am in and the access it provides. You are here to see Lucius, I take it?" he asked, cocking his head to one side.

"Indeed, a young man showed me to this room. If I am disturbing you, I could wait outside," I said, gesturing to the door.

"No, no need. Please have a seat here. There is a pleasant breeze, and it looks as if there is some wine here. May I pour you a glass? There is also some fruit, bread, and cheese if you are hungry."

"Yes, thank you," I replied as I settled into a plush chaise near an archway that led to a smaller version of the garden I had seen earlier.

"So why would a young, beautiful, and clearly important woman be here alone to speak to Lucius? Do you have business to discuss with him or is it something else?" he said with a hint of a smile.

Normally I would be more cautious but somehow this man made me feel at ease. Surely others in the palace must know I was coming. Maybe I could use this as an opportunity to learn more about Lucius that I might use to my benefit when I did meet him.

"I am here to ask for his help to get back my throne, the throne of Egypt."

"Ah, you must be Arsinoe. I heard that you were coming. But your sister Cleopatra is on the throne, is she not? Caesar exiled you to the Temple of Artemis. Why would you risk your very life to make this journey?"

"Cleopatra has defiled herself with the Roman and betrayed the people of Egypt. We deserve to be led by an Egyptian who is above reproach, and who has the best interest of its people at the fore. The Ptolemy family has ruled Egypt for hundreds of years without Roman interference."

"Yes, and here in Cyprus as well. Your great-uncle was a wonderful ruler, and we were saddened when he took his life. But surely you must understand that Lucius was appointed by Julius Caesar himself. Why would he turn on him to help you?"

"Because like Egypt, Cyprus is being shackled by Rome. Would it not be better for Cyprus to return to its former glory, with the support of Egypt?"

He leaned back onto the chaise he had perched on opposite me and closed his eyes. I did not know what to do. Was he thinking or did my question upset him in some way? I suddenly realized I did not even know this man's name and perhaps I had just sabotaged my meeting with Lucius. Was this man someone close to him?

"Lucius is, I hear, a man very much interested in getting independence from Rome for Cyprus. Although, as you and I both know, this would not be an easy task. He does have the support of Cassius and others in the Senate, but the Roman army is without a doubt the strongest and most experienced in the world. Do you really think that Egypt's army could be successful against them?"

"Yes, I do. We were nearly successful against them before and everything I have heard tells me that there is no affection for Cleopatra within their ranks. They will turn on her and the Romans if they are given the chance."

"And what would you propose to do with Cleopatra if you were able to unseat her? Would you exile her as Julius Caesar did to you?"

"No."

The man looked at me, a bit of surprise in his eyes

"Caesar was a fool to give in to pressure from the Senate to not execute me. He should have anticipated that at some point I would try again to regain the throne. My half-sister showed no mercy to our brothers, and I would show none to her," I replied pragmatically.

"Well, you seem sincere in your desire to rule Egypt again. It will be interesting to see how Lucius responds to your plea for help from Cyprus. Now, if you will excuse me," he said as he unexpectedly rose from the chaise and went back out the door I had entered earlier.

A large sigh escaped as I lay back on the chaise. What did I do? Why would I trust this man with such important information? A wave of disappointment washed over me. How could I have been so reckless? What would I tell Darius and the others about my failure? I would never be able to face them. Several hours passed and the sun was starting to get low in the sky. Perhaps I was being held captive here before being turned over to the Roman guards. Surely, they would take me back to Rome to be executed. There would be no reprieve this time. Then there was a light knock at the door. I sat up, smoothing out my tunic and pushing the hair away from my face.

"Yes?" I asked confidently.

The door opened and the young boy I had seen earlier reappeared.

"Come with me, please?" he asked, once again keeping his eyes on the ground.

We walked for what seemed like a long distance before we turned and entered a large room that was filled with people. There were men mostly, but I did notice a few women toward the front of the room.

"Princess Arsinoe of Egypt," said the boy in a voice much bigger than one might have expected for his size.

The crowd parted and at the front of the room, I could see a small dais much like the one we had in the palace in Egypt. On it sat a large ornately carved chair polished to a sheen. Standing in front of the chair the man I had spoken to in the library. I assumed he would be announcing Lucius once I reached the front of the room.

All eyes were on me, and I could feel small beads of sweat running down the side of my face. The man motioned for me to come forward. As I walked through the crowd, I could feel the stares of every person in the room. Piercing stares, from faces that seemed to be devoid of any emotion. It reminded me of being brought in front of Cleopatra when Lira and I tried to deceive her. *Stand up straight, don't show any fear,* I kept saying to myself. Now nearly at the dais, the man stepped back and sat down in the chair and the crowd turned to face the front of the room once again.

"Princess Arsinoe, welcome to Cyprus. I trust you had a pleasant voyage. I am Lucius of Erstile, the appointed Governor of Cyprus," he said with a sly smile and a slight nod.

I wanted to laugh and cry. The man I had spoken to earlier in the library was Lucius himself. Was he planning on humiliating me here, in front of all these people?

"It was uneventful, which is all that one can ask from Tefnut. Thank you for the warm welcome and for agreeing to speak to me," I replied with a hesitating smile of my own.

"My pleasure, I can assure you," he replied.

I was a bit bewildered. Was I to speak now in front of all these people to make my case for Cyprus to join our cause? I did not see how I could. It would be only a matter of days before someone in this crowd got word back to Rome. I would be signing my own death warrant.

"Curricle, could you clear the room please," he said motioning to a man standing to his right.

The man made a little bow toward Lucius, then toward me, before he began shooing the people from the room as if they were so many sheep. They shuffled silently out of the room and down the hall. I waited quietly, looking only at Lucius, until everyone was gone save two guards standing behind the dais. Presumably, they never left him alone with anyone.

"I think you owe me an explanation," I said angrily.

"My apologies, princess. It was not my initial intention to deceive you. It just simply occurred. You seemed so at ease I felt perhaps it was better to talk in that way rather than with the formality that can come when people enter this room."

"But you could have told me who you were before you left?"

"That is true. I could have, but I was unexpectedly summoned away, and I did not have time to reveal myself to you," he replied.

"I saw no one summon you," I said rather skeptically.

"No, I am sure you did not. It is done through a whistle that sounds very much like a bird. I heard it from the garden which summoned me without revealing to you, or anyone I may be in conversation with, that I am needed elsewhere."

"So, are you going to help me?" I asked bluntly.

"No, I was not planning to do so. While I do not doubt your conviction in your cause and the people of Egypt, I am afraid I do not have faith that the Egyptian army can defeat Caesar, especially since he and Cleopatra now share a child. That will only strengthen his bond with Egypt. Frankly, I believe that Caesar now fancies himself ruler of both Rome and Egypt, despite what your sister may believe, and there are men now in both Alexandria and Rome who want to encourage that belief. Ruling both countries makes him the most powerful man in the world. Some might say he already was, but now there would be no question. There is, however, an issue you had not considered."

"And what might that be?"

"The people of Rome do not like Cleopatra any more than you do. She is vilified in the Senate and people speak of her power over Caesar as if it were sorcery of some kind. The Egyptian whore they call her, and worse, although not in Caesar's presence. Much like in Egypt, the people of Rome are very much concerned about maintaining the status they believe they possess by being Roman. They do not like the idea of a future ruler of Rome being of mixed blood if you will. Caesar's infatuation, or whatever you may call it, is seen as a distraction that takes his focus off Rome, where they believe it should be," he said bluntly.

"Well, they see her as she is then, which is as it should be. But how does that serve me? It is not like I can use the Roman Senate's disdain for her to my advantage in some way."

"It is not just their concerns about Cleopatra. There is more," replied Lucius. "He has disrespected the Senate and made many believe he wishes to be dictator for life, which goes against everything the Republic stands for."

"Still, I do not see how that helps my cause," I said with enormous frustration, throwing my hands up in the air and shrugging my shoulders.

"Well, as it turns out, it was an advantage that has unexpectedly helped you with no intercession from you at all. This news I received late this afternoon has forced me to rethink my position."

"I am sorry. I do not understand," I replied looking at him with utter confusion.

"I was summoned away because an urgent messenger arrived at the palace while we were in the library. It brought news from Rome."

"What kind of news?" I asked.

"Julius Caesar has been murdered by members of the Roman Senate."

CHAPTER SIX

TO AVOID A WAR

I instantly collapsed falling forward onto the stairs. My legs were shaking, and my knees were weak. I felt as if I were choking to death, a weight bearing down on my chest, unable to breath. Did that mean I was no longer a prisoner?

"Please, Arsinoe, breathe," said Lucius as he leaned over me with concern etched into his face and eyes.

Finally, I croaked out, "He is dead? You are certain?"

"Yes, Queen Arsinoe, I am certain. Together we will put you back on the throne of Egypt."

The blood was draining from my head, and I could hear a buzzing in my ears like the sound of a small insect. Queen. He called me queen.

"Here, drink this," he said as he handed me a glass of wine that the man who had appeared from behind a curtain handed to him.

The entire glass was drained before I managed to regain my composure, and he helped me sit up.

"So, now you are going to support me in my cause to regain the throne?"

"I am. With Julius Caesar gone, I doubt Cleopatra will have any of the support from Rome she has been enjoying while he was alive. It will be a much easier task than it would have been before, and it is an opportunity for Cyprus to declare its independence from Rome as well. We can support each other in this cause, yes?"

"Indeed, we can," I said as I looked up at him, smiling my relief nearly palpable.

My anger toward him earlier had dissipated. Now, I felt nothing but thankfulness and joy. Without Caesar to defend her, Cleopatra would not be nearly as formidable. I wondered if she knew yet. If she knew the father of her child, the man who helped her take the throne of Egypt from our brother and me, was no more.

"Will Rome help me in my fight against her?"

"No. No, there is no possibility that they will intervene in that way. The Senate will be glad to have her no longer as a distraction, but they will not come to your aide against her.

"But what of the little bastard Caesarion? Will they want to protect him so he might someday take his father's place?" I asked.

"It appears he will have no birthright left to him by his father. Marc Antony, who has been Caesar's help and stay, summoned the Senate to ensure that the assassins would not be punished, but that enraged the lower classes who highly venerated Caesar. There has been some rioting, but it seems that Caesar had let his wishes be known in a document naming Gaius Octavius, his grandnephew, as his sole heir. Octavius was left the title of Caesar as well as his wealth.

I couldn't help but laugh. Cleopatra's plan to sit on the thrones of both Egypt and Rome had failed and her son was left with no claim on the Roman seat of power.

"You are amused by these developments," observed Lucius as he cocked his head in my direction.

"Probably more than I should be, may the gods forgive me, but it is a source of great amusement to me that her plans have come to nothing."

"She still sits on the throne of Egypt, and that is far from nothing. If it were, you would not wish to claim it so desperately," he replied rather scornfully.

"You are right. Now we must focus our efforts on getting the throne back. Do you think I am now free to come and go as I please?"

Lucius looked at me thoughtfully for a moment before responding.

"No, I do not think that would be wise. Many will not yet know what has happened in Rome. It will take some time for the news to spread. Also, there are some both here and in Ephesus who are loyal to the Pharaoh, and they will recognize the danger you present to her. We should get you safely back to the Temple. Then we can plan our next move," said Lucius with a very serious tone.

I stood and walked over to the archway that led out to a courtyard. It was a beautiful palace. The courtyards overflowed with beautiful greenery, flowers, and fountains. The sound of the water reminded me of my home, my palace, in Egypt. The smell of the flowers was intoxicating and rivaled the very best of perfumes. The fragrance was both soothing and exhilarating. I breathed in the air, pulling it deep into my chest. A thought kept running through my mind. To be honest, it was not a new idea. It had been there for some time in my thoughts but was unspoken to anyone. Not even Darius, in the privacy of our little cabin on the boat, had heard my idea. Was it safe now to give voice to what I was thinking?

"What it is, my queen?" asked Lucius as he came and stood next to me, the two of us shoulder to shoulder, staring out upon the succulent landscape.

"What if there was a way to take back the throne of Egypt with very little blood spilled?" I asked quietly as I continued to gaze out on the gardens.

"I'm listening," replied Lucius.

"Instead of waging a full-scale war, why not just sneak into the palace and kill Cleopatra? As the only remaining Ptolemy with a claim to the throne, it becomes mine."

"She is heavily guarded, and she will be even more so now that Caesar is dead."

"True, but I know that palace like no one else. I'm sure I could get two or three men in there with me. We don't have to worry about getting back out. I know there are citizens loyal to me on the inside. I receive reports from them from time to time," I added.

"That is a very dangerous move on your part, but as you say, if you are successful, a coup is much cleaner and quicker than a war. But if you fail, all will be lost."

I turned to face him. My cheeks were warm, and I could feel a bit of fear rising from my belly. I forced myself to push it down. Bennu had said once that if I were not willing to die for this cause, I should not expect others to do so.

"It is a chance I am willing to take," I said solemnly.

The days turned quickly into weeks as we prepared to travel to Alexandria rather than back to Ephesus to carry out my plan. Lucius arranged for a large ship to take us, and this time I did not have to pretend to be a boy. We were simply like any other ship coming to Egypt to trade. Lucius had sworn his loyalty to me, and he was confident there was no risk to me while on the crossing. Once in Alexandria, however, I would once again become Amin to slip into the palace. Lucius has sent word to Bennu to begin preparing for war in the event the coup is not successful, but I tried not to think about that. We must prevail. It was our best and most reliable option. A full-scale war could go either way, and I despite Lucius assurances no one could not predict how Rome would react.

"The ship is nearly ready, my queen," said Darius as he sat down next to me on the bed. I had maps of Alexandria, and the palace spread out all around me. Over the last few days, Darius, Lucius's friend Gallenus, and I had studied them over and over, making sure we all knew the layout of the palace. Any mistake would surely be fatal and our voyage to the underworld could start much sooner than we would like.

I smiled at him. I had missed his company these last weeks as he spent much of his time at the dock preparing the ship for our voyage. He was very much against my plan, at least at first. But, when I agreed that he could be one of the two men to go with me, he seemed resigned to the fact that our coup attempt was going to happen, whether he agreed with my plan or not.

"Good. I am anxious to get to Alexandria, to be home," I said with a smile.

"I have not been in Alexandria in many years. I wish my return were under better circumstances, but when we have you safely back on the throne, Alexandria will also become my home once again."

"You will stay?"

"It is beyond my capacity to leave you now, Arsinoe. My heart and allegiance are fully yours and although I know that we can never be together as husband and wife, I will still stand by your side until you travel to the river. Even then, I will sail with you," he said quietly.

My hand caressed his cheek, feeling the smoothness of his skin and the roughness of his beard as I searched his face for that light that drew me to him. When my gaze settled upon his eyes, it was like a beacon in the darkness. He was like the lighthouse at Alexandria. He kept me from being tossed up onto the rocky shore where the sea would have had me splintered into a thousand shards. I leaned forward and lightly touched my lips to his. I could feel the heat passing between us. My heart told me this affection between us was innocent, but that was a lie I told myself and told him. I wanted to believe that the kiss meant little to me, when in fact it meant much, much more.

"I know you are afraid for me, but with you there and with the help of Gallenus and Osiris on our side, I do not know how we can fail," I replied.

"Do not underestimate your half-sister. She will be well-guarded, and it has been some time since you were last in the palace. Things may have changed," he said frankly.

"I know, but no matter what we encounter I am confident we can reach her. When we do there will be no mercy shown to her.

She has shown none to me or our brothers who I am sure have both died by her hand," I said angrily.

"Gallenus has a darkness about him. He is, I am told by others, a man who will quietly and swiftly dispatch Cleopatra without hesitation."

"If the gods are with us, I can only pray it will be so."

"I will return in the morning to get you. We will leave at first light," said Darius as he stood to go.

"Thank you, for all that you have done, but most importantly for believing in me and trusting in what I say," I said as I lightly took his hand in mine.

He brought my hand to his lips, kissing it gently, and I felt my heart quicken as always. Truly, could I continue to resist my desire for him?

"My queen, I am your humble and devoted servant," he said with a slight bow before he turned to go.

After the formalities of our goodbyes, I found myself once again in a litter being carried through the streets. While we agreed that I did not need to hide myself on the ship, the curtains were still drawn so as not to bring too much attention. It was not clear to any of us what Rome's response, really Octavian's response, would be should he find out what we were planning. Perhaps they would have no interest in intervening, but we did not wish to fan any flames, so we kept my presence in Cyprus quiet, at least for now. Lucius would do nothing to raise suspicions with his overseer until we were sure I had regained the throne of Egypt. Then we could bring the Egyptian army's resources to his aid, as I was sure Rome would protest. First Egypt, then Cyprus.

Till then, Lucius must be seen as loyal to Rome. As we jostled along the road, the breeze lightly blew the curtains in and out, providing occasional glimpses of the street. For a moment I even thought I saw Omenia, the little girl I had stopped to help in the street when I first arrived. I wondered if she would recognize me not dressed as a boy, and the thought made me smile. The little one had been certain I was a girl, like her, and only her mother's insistence that I was a boy made her doubt her observations. Children, in their innocence, seem to be able to see beyond the superficial to what we truly are.

Darius was waiting, as promised, and he helped me out of the litter and up the gangway. The men were lined up on each side, bowing their heads as I passed by, which was a far cry from my voyage here. As I did on Ziyad's boat, I stood at the bow as we eased out of the harbor while the men cast off the final lines. As we turned away from Cyprus, I wondered for a moment if I would ever see it again. While I did my best to convey my confidence about our planned mission, in my heart I had doubts. Evading all the guards would be a formidable task and one that may end with all our deaths. I would at least take some comfort in knowing that Darius would be with me in the afterlife and that Lira would join me as soon as she learned I had crossed the river.

I reflected for a moment on how fortunate I was to have those who have been so devoted to me and my cause. This time, I had a cabin to myself, but Darius and Gallenus came regularly to discuss our strategy. We spent time going over and over the maps I had drawn out, discussing our approach. We needed Gallenus, but he made me squirm. There is something about the man, a darkness as Darius had said, that disturbs me. Often, I saw him on the deck where he seemed to be constantly sharpening a long and curved blade that he carried on his belt. It was a blade so sharp it would slash through a throat in an instant, nearly removing the victim's head.

Today is a day best spent below deck. The sea was angry, the sky was dark, and the waves crashed against the ship with enormous force. We all feared for our lives. I spent every moment praying to Tefnut for our safety. The voices above suddenly called out in alarm. Someone had been washed overboard into the sea. Quickly I climbed the ladder and opened the hatch. The waves were washing over the ship, leaving white foam on the deck. The men were being tossed to and fro as if they were mere children. Water splashed down the hatch and I closed it quickly behind me. A few men were struggling to steer the vessel while the rest of the men were at the side of the ship, trying to rescue the man who had fallen overboard. I looked around to find Darius and as I searched each of the faces a terrifying realization came over me. It was him. It was Darius who had fallen overboard. I rushed to the side of the ship where the men were working to save him.

"Darius!" I screamed out against the sound of the wind and waves.

I could see him hanging on to the end of a rope, sometimes fully engulfed in the water, sometimes with his head bobbing out of the dark foamy waves.

"Pull! Pull him up!" I yelled as I grabbed the rope, trying to help.

It felt like we were trying to pull up much more than a mere man due to the force of the water pulling against us. I closed my eyes and prayed to Osiris, to Isis, to Tefnut the god of the sea. I could not... I would not lose this man.

"Now! Pull harder!" roared the man leaning over the railing.

The ship leaned toward where Darius hung off the rope, then suddenly they had him by the arm. They jerked him upward as hard as they could with one strong motion.

Darius and his rescuers fell onto the deck in a tangle of ropes as everyone tried their best to keep their footing lest anyone else find themselves in the waves. Darius was panting, doing his best to catch his breath.

"Down, get down," he barked out hoarsely, pointing at the hatch.

"I will, but you must come too!" I screamed back over the howling wind, the sea stinging my face and eyes.

He nodded, and the man who had pulled him up helped to get him to the open hatch, but he was hard hit by a wave, knocking him off his feet. He fell into the opening landing on the deck below. I quickly scrambled down the ladder after him.

"Thank you," I said to the man who had helped saved him before he closed the hatch, the water still seeping down the stairs.

Darius lay at the bottom of the ladder now, a small amount of blood oozing out of a cut on his head. He seemed confused, and his speech made no sense. The ship was still rolling violently but I did my best to drag him into my cabin so that I could tend to his wound. It seemed like hours went by before the noise of the storm faded and the ship began to settle. I had been sitting on the floor with Darius' head in my lap the whole time, waiting, hoping he would wake up. He continued to sleep, only making the occasional mutter.

"Queen Arsinoe are you safe?" asked Gallenus as peeked his head around the door of the cabin.

"I am, but Darius…" I said, my voice quavering, tears ready to flow.

"Let me help you," he said as he lifted Darius off the floor and onto the bed. His strength surprised even me, but I was tremendously grateful for it.

Darius moaned as Gallenus laid him on the bed. His eyes did not open. I struggled to get to my feet after hours of sitting in one place, but I finally managed to get upright. I rinsed out the cloth I had been using in the bowl.

"Be still, my love. You are safe," I said as I wiped his brow.

Gallenus looked at me with surprise. He seemingly had not picked up on our feelings for each other, but there could be no mistake now. It could not be unsaid. We would have to hope that this knowledge did not change our mission and that Gallenus kept this to himself. I hoped he would not use the information to manipulate us in any way.

"Owwww," said Darius as he raised her arm toward the wound on his head.

"No, no. Do not touch it. You will be fine," I said as I grabbed his hand.

"What…" said Darius with a breathy moan.

"You were washed overboard, but Octanerus and a couple of the other men were able to get a rope to you. Eventually, they were able to pull you back on board. The Queen has been tending to you here in her cabin for the last few hours, but the storm has passed now, and the sea is calm. We lost one man to the depths and there is minor damage to the ship, but we are repairing it now," replied Gallenus.

"Yes, I remember. Arsinoe, on the deck?"

"I came up to help when I heard the men yelling."

Unexpectedly he reached over and grabbed my arm, more tightly than I expected. So hard, in fact, that it almost hurt. He coughed and cleared his throat.

"Do not ever do that again, risk yourself for me. Promise me," he said, his eyes still closed but his hand firmly on my arm. His voice was gravelly and coarse.

"I am the queen. I will do as I wish. You will not tell me how I can and cannot behave, toward you or any man," I retorted as I pulled my arm from his grasp.

Gallenus was snorting, trying his best to stifle a laugh behind me, until I turned to glare at him. Then he went silent.

"Fetch me some wine for Darius at once," I said curtly.

"Of course," he said with a slight bow before exiting the cabin.

Darius tried to sit up, but it clearly aggravated the pain in his head, so he lay back down with a low moan.

One of the other men appeared with wine, and it did seem to refresh him, but I thought it best he continued to lie down.

"Are you angry with me?" I asked finally.

"Yes," he said, turning to look at me, his eyes watery and red. Several dark bruises were forming on his face, arms, and hands.

"You needed my help," I replied in my own defense.

"No, I needed you to stay safely inside this ship. You could have cost me my life, as I am sure that every man would have abandoned me to help you if the need had arisen. In the future, your safety is always paramount. Nothing and no one are more important. Without you, the rest of us are nothing, with no purpose or no meaning to our lives."

"Truly I am sorry. I did not realize how dangerous things

were on deck. I simply… reacted when I thought you might be in trouble," I said sheepishly.

"Your care for me is most appreciated, but please do not let it happen again," he said with a slight smile and a grimace.

"Are you in pain?"

"Just a bit. It will be fine. Nothing a bit more wine cannot address."

It took more than a bit of wine and several more days before Darius was up and about again. I prayed relentlessly for his recovery and Isis answered me, even if it took longer than I would have liked. We were only a few days from Alexandria. If Darius was not at his best, we may very well have to delay our attempt against Cleopatra. Once again, I was to don the mask of Amin, and Darius was doing his best to braid my hair. It was so long that it kept falling out under his unskilled hands.

"We need to cut it. There is no way your hair is going to stay inside this turban," said Darius with exasperation.

"Then cut it. My hair will grow again, but if we are discovered, my hair will not matter," I said as I handed him the small knife I always wore on my belt.

"Please forgive me, Isis," he said as he began to hack off large sections of my hair just below my ears. I cringed as the pieces fluttered down onto the deck around me. Despite my bravado, I felt the loss of my hair intently. I would have to cover my head, but if I could do so with the neme, the crown of the Pharaohs, it would have all been worth it.

Tomorrow we would arrive in Alexandria, and the anticipation of being home was almost more than I could bear. As sleep continued to elude me, I finally decided to seek the fresh air of the upper deck. Khonsu was high and bright in the heavens, illuminating the sky and outshining the stars. A few wisps of white clouds sailed past her, moving quickly as if they were trying to avoid being captured and taken to the underworld when Ra rose again. The breeze felt wonderful on my face even if I could no longer enjoy the feeling of my hair blowing in it as the turban was already tightly wound on my head. I pulled my linen wrap around me. The air was also a bit cooler than we had experienced for the last few days.

The few men working the ship paid me no mind as I stood at the bow gazing out into the distance. The journey had been a perilous one and it nearly ended in tragedy. It was not going to get any easier. It was going to take every bit of cunning we could muster and many gold coins to get us to the room where we would find Cleopatra asleep. In a matter of days, I could be sitting on the throne of Egypt. It was hard to imagine it, and yet I could think about little else. It consumed me like the locusts consume a field. As I gazed across the sea, I began to sense a change. It was small at first barely perceptible, just a pinpoint of light. Then a little more, and soon I realized we were there. Alexandria lay on the horizon. The lighthouse would guide me home.

We had agreed we would wait till the sun was low in the sky before getting off the ship so that we could blend into the crowd of dock workers headed to their homes at the end of the day. It was all I could do not to leap from the ship and run down the street. It felt so wonderful to be home, to be in Egypt again. The voices, the clothes, and the smells coming from the market stalls made me feel comforted and secure. I hadn't realized how much I had missed it. My soul was quenched, and I felt whole again, for the first time in many years.

The day went by agonizingly slowly. Impatiently, I watched the shore as I paced back and forth on the deck. My home was right there, in front of me, yet it still felt so far away. Everyone else had been on and off the ship except for me and my envy was growing within me with each passing moment. The sun moved so slowly across the sky that at one point I thought perhaps it had even stopped!

"We should go now," said Gallenus unexpectedly as he wrapped the tail of his turban around the lower half of his face. I leaped to my feet; it was finally time. Darius and I did the same before we prepared to follow him down the gangplank and off the ship.

"Stay close to me. No stopping to help little girls, eh?" said Darius under his breath.

I jabbed him playfully in the side, but I could see this was not a laughing matter to him. Suddenly, I was embarrassed by my childish gesture in such serious circumstances. A few steps down the wooden plank and there I was on the ground, in Egypt again. An overwhelming desire to kneel and pray to thank the gods overcame me but I knew to do so would be to draw too much attention. I said my prayers silently as we walked. We blended into the swell of workers headed back to their homes after a day's work. No one paid us any mind, which was exactly as we had hoped. This time, I held discreetly onto the hem of Darius's sleeve. I was not going to risk getting separated again. We walked for some time, till the crowds were beginning to thin, with the light of day fading into shades of gold and purple in the sky. Oddly, it reminded me of the cloak that Julius Caesar had once worn. It was a strange thought to cross my mind at this moment. Or perhaps it was an omen from the gods to tell me that soon I too would be wearing the robes of the ruler.

Finally, we reached a modest-looking building. Gallenus motioned for us to stay back a bit, up against the wall, while he knocked on the wooden door. No one answered. He knocked again and the door creaked open just a bit, a shaft of light spilling out onto the street. We could not hear what was being said, but Gallenus seemed to be in an animated conversation with someone inside. These arrangements had been made by Lucius and for a moment I was concerned. I had been betrayed before by men I thought I could trust. Could it be happening again? Could Lucius have had me brought here just to turn me over to Cleopatra in exchange for some favor?

"Darius," I whispered.

"I know what you must be thinking but be patient. No one will harm you while I live," he murmured.

In his hand, I could see he was holding his knife turned up into his sleeve so that Gallenus could not see it. It was clear that even Darius had his doubts. Let us hope we were both wrong. At last, the door opened widely and Gallenus gestured for us to go inside. Darius went first and I followed closely behind him, keeping in my character of Amin lest we find ourselves not among friends. It was a modest room with a couple of small beds, a table with four chairs, and a small altar to the god Ptah. The owner of this house must be a craftsman or some sort of building planner.

"Welcome," said the smaller of the two men. "I am Obersius,

and this is my brother Watenatie," he added, as they both offered a little bow, not directed toward anyone in particular.

"I am Gallenus. This is Darius, and of course, Queen Arsinoe."

"We are your humble servants, my queen. We are very happy to have you back in Egypt where you belong," said Watenatie, his clenched fist over his heart as he nodded in my direction.

Darius pushed me gently out from behind him where I had been hiding in his shadow and I unwrapped my face.

"Thank you, Watenatie, and Obersius for allowing us into your home," I said quietly.

"I have not seen you since you were a little girl," said Obersius.

"I'm sorry I do not remember you. Should I?"

"No, of course you would not. I worked for your father when I was a very young man. I designed much of the palace with the help of my brother. We oversaw the building of some of the later phases and the addition of the central gardens and fountains. I used to see you running through the palace playfully as little children do," said Obersius with a timid smile.

"The thought of that gives me great pleasure. Are you still working in the palace?" I asked.

"Yes, we work on maintaining and repairing things as the palace may need. We are there a few days each week," said Watenatie.

Lucius' plan now made a great deal of sense. This was our way into the palace.

"So, you understand why we are here?" asked Darius.

"Yes, we do, and you have our full support. We have told no one that you were coming as Lucius requested. We know maintaining secrecy is vital to your plan," replied Obersius.

"Is the palace much as it was when I left?" I asked hesitantly.

"There have been a few changes, including sealing up the tunnel through which you previously escaped, but not to worry. Cleopatra had another tunnel made that goes directly to her quarters in the event she needed to leave the palace unseen. It goes directly to the Nile. You can take a boat to the entrance and then you will be able to go through that tunnel and directly into her rooms."

I looked from face to face, stunned by this news. Not only did we have a way to get into the palace, but it would take us directly to where we needed to go. Happy tears were streaming down my face. I could not believe the gods had favored us so.

"It is not quite as easy as that sounds," said Gallenus.

"What do you mean?" asked Darius.

"There are soldiers stationed at the entrance and at the door where the tunnel comes into the palace, I am told."

"Yes, that is so," nodded Watenatie in agreement.

"But you still think this is the best way in?" I asked skeptically.

"It is, my queen," replied Obersius.

"Since Caesar's passing, the Pharaoh has kept a full garrison of soldiers stationed around the palace. The path of least resistance will be the tunnel. I am sure of it," added Watenatie.

For the rest of the evening, we talked about how best to approach the tunnel and how best to handle the guards. When my mind could hold no more and my eyes felt the heaviness I could no longer resist, I fell asleep, exhausted on one of the beds, the voices of the men fading into the distance. When I awoke, only Obersius was there.

"Good morning, my queen. May I get you some water? Would you like some bread?" he asked.

"Yes, thank you. Where are the others?"

"My brother has taken your friends to see the location of the tunnel so that they can understand what the challenge is first-hand. They should be back soon. They left at first light and the tunnel entrance is not far from here, but it must be approached by water," said Obersius as he set the bread and water on the table.

"Do you think this is foolishness?" I said as I tore a piece of bread off.

"Cleopatra has done some good in Alexandria, and beyond. Under her leadership, we have managed economically, and we have now enjoyed some years of peace. But she is still tied to Rome in ways that most Egyptians do not like. Even with Caesar's passing, she continues to court the newly named Augustus Octavian and Marc Antony much as she did with Julius Caesar. Even though she could maintain Egypt on her own without any Roman interference, she seems to feel the need to have their... I do not know. Protection? Support? It is unclear what motivates her."

I leaned back in my chair. My father had said to carefully consider any action against another of my family. He wrote that it should not be driven simply by my own need for power and control, but by what was in the best interest of our people. Was it possible that Cleopatra was a good ruler and that she should be allowed to continue?

"Are you happy to have Cleopatra as Pharaoh?"

"Ah, happiness is an interesting choice of emotion. We accept her. I will say there have been some who are wary, as we have endured several years of poor crops. The Nile has not risen much for the last few years and without the annual flooding, we can grow much less. Some think the gods are angry with her for her alliance with Caesar and that this is their way of punishing her. Unfortunately, they are punishing all of us for her indiscretion, if that is the case. We all firmly believe that given the opportunity she will once again align herself with Rome. She wants to see Caesarion rise to rule both Egypt and Rome. That is very clear to all around her as she makes no secret of it."

"How is the boy?" I asked.

"He is a fine child of more than four years now. He is bright and well-mannered. His mother dotes on him and denies him little, but she also expects him to work hard at his studies, I am told. I seldom see him when I am in the palace."

Just then, the door opened, and in came Darius and Watenatie.

"So, what do you think?" I said hopefully.

"I think it will work your Highness. We believe we have a good plan for how to get inside the tunnel and deal with the guards on the other end as well. Gallenus has gone to make some arrangements. Khonsu will be small in the sky tomorrow night as the cycle comes to its natural end. It should give us the extra cloak of darkness we will need to be successful," said Darius as he sat down at the table, helping himself to a large hunk of bread which he devoured rapidly, washing it down with the large cup of wine that Obersius sat in front of him.

"Tomorrow?" I said with more hesitation than I probably should have.

"Is there a reason we should wait?" said Darius looking rather puzzled.

"No," I said with a bit of a nervous laugh. "No reason at all. It is just so sudden."

"The gods are with us; the darkness will be fleeting and

Khonsu's light will grow brighter with each passing day. If we do not go tomorrow, we will have to wait weeks for the end of the cycle again. The longer we wait, the greater the chance that we will be discovered," he said, placing his hand on mine.

I quickly pulled my hand away, hoping Obersius had not noticed this affection between us. For whatever reason, I felt it best not to bring attention to it. Gallenus knew, and now possibly Obersius. I did not think it was wise for our feelings for each other to be known. I did not want anyone to believe that my decisions were unduly influenced by him, or to have concerns about what my feelings for him might mean should I regain the throne.

"Of course. I am in agreement with your plan," I replied confidently, sitting up a bit straighter in my chair.

I could see a glint of pain flicker in Darius' eyes. He knew this barrier between us must always be present when others were near and that he must be seen as deferent. I sincerely wished it did not have to be, but there seemed to be no way around our circumstances. The day went quickly in preparation for nightfall and after we finished our evening meal, a fine meat and vegetable stew, the last of the preparations had been made.

"Since the queen is no longer necessary to show you the way to Cleopatra's quarters, wouldn't it be best if she stayed here until the deed is done?" asked Watenatie.

"No, she must take the throne immediately. There can be no delay. We cannot risk that someone else already inside the palace will try to claim the throne," replied Gallenus.

"But there are no other family members within the palace as far as I know. Who else might make a claim?" I asked with surprise.

"As much as you like to think otherwise, Caesarion is a Ptolemy. I would imagine someone who would support Caesarion succeeding his mother would try to establish rule as a Vizier on his behalf until he reaches the age of maturity."

"He is not a Ptolemy! He is the bastard child of a hemar! He will never sit on the throne of Egypt if I have breath in my body," I said, slamming my hand on the table.

"Of course, my queen, as you say," replied Gallenus, surprised by my outburst.

We gathered up the last of the things we needed and prepared to leave. We would board the boat at the agreed upon meeting place.

"I will pray for your safety, and it will be my honor to be one of the first to call upon you when you are on the throne," said Obersius, bowing low as he kissed the top of each of my hands.

"It will be my honor to receive you," I replied squeezing his hands in mine.

His hands were old and frail. I could feel the years of work flowing through his fingers into mine. But I also felt something else. A calmness came over me as if the act of holding this old man's hands in mine was a sign from the gods themselves. He looked into my eyes, and I could see sadness in them. Years of loss, perhaps? I saw no sign of a wife or children having ever been in this home. Perhaps he had been too busy working for my father to pursue such things. Yet in his eyes, there was an optimism for the future... and for me.

As we turned to go, I couldn't help but look back to see Obersius already kneeling in front of his altar, to which he had added Osiris just today. I was grateful for his prayers. We would need them.

We walked quietly but quickly through the fading light saying nothing to each other as we passed a few men on the streets. We ducked in and out of doorways when people passed too closely. Indeed, it was dark, except for the lights coming from the modest houses we passed on our way to the river. I was still dressed as Amin, but this time underneath the masculine clothes, I wore my own tunic and a bag holding my jewels and bracelets so that I could quickly assume the role of Pharaoh. Of course, I anticipated also being able to avail myself of those things I might find in Cleopatra's quarters, but I did not want to appear simply dressed as her. I wanted to be dressed in my own clothes. I wanted to be Queen Arsinoe, not a version of my sister.

"Stay close to me now. We have to go down a steep hill here. There are two small skiffs waiting for us," said Darius quietly.

"Why two? Certainly, we could fit in one?" I asked.

"Yes. One for us and one for a… diversion," he replied.

I could almost see him smiling in the darkness. I did not know what they had come up with, but I have no doubt they have thought it through carefully.

The hill was indeed slippery, and we half-walked, half-slid down the side of it till we arrived at the water's edge. There, among the reeds, was a man sitting in a skiff holding onto a second to keep it from drifting away.

"Let me help you," said Darius as he picked me up and waded into the knee-deep water before setting me down in the empty boat. Gallenus quickly joined me while Darius spoke to the other man before also hopping into the boat.

"Quiet, now. Our voices will carry easily across the water.

There must be no sound or they will know we are coming," said Gallenus as he pushed off the shore with his paddle.

The man in the other boat turned and went ahead of us as we glided silently through the water. Croaking from the frogs and the sounds of the crickets were the only noises, save a little trickle of water each time the paddles were pulled from the water. We pulled up to a cluster of reeds and Gallenus planted his paddle into the soft mud to anchor us in place, holding his finger to his lips to remind me there could be no talking. The other skiff was already there, and the man got out, sliding into the water which was just below his shoulders. He reached into the skiff and pulled the lid off a small jar, and I realized there was a flame inside. Quickly he knocked the jar over and then he and Gallenus pushed the skiff downriver as hard as they could. The current picked up the small boat just as the flames began to spread, and the man disappeared into the reeds.

I could hear some voices nearby, but I could not see them. Some men were shouting, and a small boat came out of the darkness and began following the skiff. It stopped in the middle of the river as the flames raged, licking the sides of the boat in every direction.

"Now," said Darius.

The two of them began quickly paddling along the shore when out of the darkness hidden in a cluster of trees appeared a waterway which we quickly turned into. The guards had left in their own boat leaving the opening unattended as they went to see about the burning skiff, and we slid in completely undetected. In just a short distance there was a small sandy landing and Darius jumped from the boat to guide us into it, before turning back to lift me out of the boat.

"We must hide this. Quickly! I think they are coming back," said Gallenus breathlessly as he and Darius struggled to grasp the skiff so they could carry it into the tunnel to hide it from view.

"This way," said Darius as he led me into the darkness. Gallenus fell in behind me, keeping very close.

There was no light to be seen, just the inky darkness. We were barely able to even see each other. We moved slowly, feeling our way with our hands and sliding our feet along the rocky path. At one point we could hear distant men's laughter. The guards must have returned to their post but were none the wiser that we had entered while their attention was diverted. The path had changed. It was more like a floor which meant we were getting closer to the palace. Even the sides of the tunnel had become smoother, and it was easier to move faster. Darius suddenly stopped. There was now a bit of light outlining what must be a door. We had reached the palace. If Obersius was correct, Cleopatra's chambers lie just on the other side.

Gallenus stepped around me and he and Darius whispered to each other as they tried to peer between the small cracks to see if there were guards on the other side. But with their limited view, they could see little.

"Surely the guards must be there. They would never risk leaving this entrance unguarded," I heard Darius say.

"Agreed," replied Gallenus as each man drew his knife.

"Wait here in the darkness. If we are killed, you will be on your own to get yourself out of the palace and back to Obersius. Can you do that?"

"Yes, but you cannot die. I need you here with me. Please, be careful," I whispered back.

Gallenus nodded and they both went quickly through the door as I stood back in the shadows. There was very little noise, just a loud thud, before Gallenus reappeared at the doorway dragging the body of a palace guard. His throat had been slit nearly from ear to ear.

"Come," he said as he roughly grabbed my hand and pulled me out into the light.

I could barely see. My eyes were still adjusting to the brightness, but I quickly realized we were indeed in what appeared to be Cleopatra's bed chamber. But she was not here. Near the bed lay a body of what looked to be a servant girl. Her throat had been cut to prevent her from crying out, I was sure.

"Where is Darius?"

"Just outside in the hallway. He is trying to see if he can determine where in the palace Cleopatra might be," replied Gallenus.

It felt so strange to be back in the palace. It seemed so familiar, but at the same time so different and new. There was a garden just off this room with flowering plants of all kinds, and an enormous pool for bathing which I did not recall.

"Step back," said Gallenus as he pushed me back behind the door to the tunnel.

The door to the bed chamber opened. It was Darius.

"I haven't seen or heard anyone nearby. I can hear some voices in the distance, but I say we wait until she returns. To go any farther means risking an encounter with the guards and we can ill afford to do that."

"Perhaps we could hide in the garden? If this door is open, they will know there has been a breach. We are blind behind it, unable to see who is in the room," I replied as I stepped out from behind the door.

"Yes, that is a good idea," replied Gallenus as he led me toward the garden. Darius was keeping a close watch on the main door.

"Here, behind these statutes. There is a small alcove in the wall. I do not think we could be easily seen here in this darkness," I said as I motioned for the men to follow.

"You stay here," said Darius as he and Gallenus went and retrieved the body of the servant girl and brought it into the garden, hiding it behind some rushes. I saw Darius was also cleaning up some blood from the floor by the bed and near where the guard had been standing. It was best not to trigger an alert if someone came in and saw that something had occurred.

There was a small ledge at the back of the alcove, and I was able to sit there and peer out between the statues and hedges to watch the men work. Suddenly, they both ran back to the alcove and crouched down in front of me as the door to the bed chamber opened. I held my breath. A servant girl, carrying what looked like bathing cloths, came in and walked over to the bathing pool. She set them down, then looked around quizzically, perhaps wondering why there was no guard, but she said nothing and left as quickly as she had come. I could hear the men sigh with relief. She had not sounded the alarm, yet we still did not have Cleopatra.

Just a few moments later, the door opened again, and two women appeared, one dressed in a fine tunic and the other the girl who had brought the cloths. They chatted as they approached the bath, and the servant helped the other woman to undress before she walked into the bath and settled on one of the benches.

"Arsinoe, is that her?" whispered Darius.

"I cannot be sure. I did not see her face well, but who else would it be inside her chamber in her bath?" I whispered back.

The two men nodded at each other before they silently worked their way through the garden. They reached the area just beyond the bathing pool and then they pounced. Gallenus leapt out at the woman in the pool who let out a scream before he could grab her by the hair and hold her under the water. Her arms and legs flailed about for a minute before she went limp. Darius had killed the servant girl, and a small trickle of blood had seeped into the pool, turning it from clear blue-green to a muddy shade of reddish brown as her blood mixed with the water. It was done.

"Come Arsinoe. We must hurry," said Darius as he motioned me forward while he wiped his blade on a nearby cloth.

I scrambled out of my clothes and quickly opened the bag that I was wearing around my neck to put on my adornments. Cleopatra's body floated face down in the pool. She had not been wearing the crown when she came in, so it must be here somewhere. The three of us quickly searched the room but the crown was not there.

"It is not here. It must be in the throne room. We have to get there before her body is discovered," I said vehemently before I ran toward the main door with Darius and Gallenus following closely behind.

There was no hesitation on my part. I knew this section of the palace as if I had just walked its colonnaded halls yesterday. I ran quickly but quietly. I saw a few people out of the corner of my eye carrying fruits and meats on a platter, but they paid me no mind. We kept moving. The throne room was just around the corner, and I could hear voices coming from that direction. We slowed our pace and moved more cautiously now until we could see the back of the throne room. There appeared to be a five or six men and women gathered there. I didn't understand why they were here if Cleopatra was not, but I could not worry about that. All I needed to do was get to the front of that room and sit down on the throne. The gods would take care of the rest.

We moved closer, inching our way slowly, till an opportunity to run forward could present itself. I was so close now. Our plan had worked. I was going to be the Queen of Egypt again. From the shadow of a column at the back of the room, I peered around its smooth edges to see what was happening. To my shock and surprise, a woman wearing the neme, the crown of Egypt, was sitting on the throne. It was Cleopatra.

RUN

I audibly gasped before Darius clamped his hand over my mouth. A few people turned in my direction, but no one made any moves although I could see a guard now looking this way.

"We have to get out of here, now," he growled in my ear.

Gallenus smiled, trying to blend into the crowd, and I couldn't help but think that it was the first time I had seen a smile on his face. Darius pulled a scarf from his shoulder and handed it to me.

"Here, cover your head. Your hair will draw attention to you… attention we cannot now afford," he said quietly.

"We have to go back out the way we came," said Gallenus still smiling, nodding his head as if in agreement with what was being said at the front of the room.

The three of us eased our way out of the throne room and turned to go down the hallway when a guard stopped us.

"What is your business here?" he said with a skeptical air as he looked us up and down.

"Oh, it is nothing for you to be concerned about. I work

for the Pharaoh… teaching her son. I just wanted to show my brother the throne room. I am sorry. We will return to my quarters," I said with a smile as I pushed Darius before me, not pausing to see if the guard accepted my story. I was afraid my clothes and jewelry would give me away, it was not how a servant would dress, and the men were certainly not dressed in Egyptian clothing. We should have thought about that, but here we were. It was too late now.

Darius had his knife in hand, as I am sure Gallenus did too, but a battle here would quickly be lost. The guard shrugged and gestured down the hallway before turning his attention back to the dais. We continued to walk, trying not to draw attention and doing our best not to panic.

"Run, Arsinoe, now," said Darius as he looked over his shoulder. The guards talked it over and did not buy our unlikely story. They were coming for us.

"Go! I will do my best," exclaimed Gallenus as he held up his knife and turned to face them.

We didn't hesitate, running as fast as we could back toward Cleopatra's bed chamber. My heart pounded as I heard the scuffle and cry behind us, but I dared not look back. Surely Gallenus was dead already, having stood no chance as he fought alone against multiple guards. We reached our destination, and Darius blocked the door behind us with a dresser, hoping to slow them down for a moment. I opened the door to the tunnel.

"No, come this way quickly. Leave the door open," he said as he ran toward the garden.

The body of the woman we killed still floated in the pool and the body of the servant lay beside it. Blood no longer oozed from her. I followed Darius deep into the garden to a corner up against the wall that separated this area from another part of the palace.

"Why are we hiding? We should go now to the river," I whispered.

"No, we can't risk getting trapped in the tunnel with soldiers on each end. They will think we have gone that way, and it will take them a few minutes to realize we have not. Once they are in the tunnel, we try another route," said Darius. He panted as he tried to catch his breath.

"If we can get over this wall, I think I can get us out," I replied.

Only a few moments passed before the guards pushed the dresser away from the door and entered the room. There were at least six of them. One ran to the pool, but realizing the women were both dead, he quickly turned his attention to the rest of the room.

"This way! They are trying to escape through the tunnel!" shouted one of the soldiers.

Most of the men went through the door into the tunnel but one remained behind, continuing to look around the room. He even began opening some of the drawers on the dressing table. Perhaps he was thinking this was an opportunity to steal something of value when it would be blamed on the intruders. We watched as he pocketed several pieces of silver.

"We must go before the rest of them return. They will surely place a watch here," whispered Darius.

"I think we can climb over the wall at the alcove. There is a ledge there. If you stand on it, you should be able to boost me over and then climb up behind me."

"Go, softly," he replied.

We crawled on our hands and knees quietly through the garden, doing our best not to brush against anything that might make noise or draw attention. The guard continued to rummage through the room with his back to the garden. At last, we reached the safety of the alcove, but now we had no choice but to stand and hope we would not be seen. Darius stepped up onto the ledge and I jumped up beside him.

"Go to Obersius if we become separated," he said as he lifted me to the top of the wall.

I grabbed onto it and pulled myself up and as I did the guard stopped and looked in our direction. He did not see us at first but when Darius hoisted himself up, he ran toward us. He was a young man, not much older than me, and he looked frightened. I wasn't sure if that was because he feared being attacked or if it was because he knew we had seen him stealing from the dressing table. The scarf I had covered my hair with had fallen away. As he looked at me, I could see that he had a moment of recognition. Between the jewelry and the amulets, he realized who I was. I held my gaze, not taking my eyes off his while Darius jumped down on the other side of the wall. I held my finger up to my lips. He nodded. I was not sure why, but apparently, he was not going to sound the alarm.

"Go quickly before they return," he said before turning away.

"Thank you," I replied. I jumped down into Darius's waiting arms.

On the other side of the wall was another colonnaded hallway. This one led to the servants' quarters and the cooking areas. We ran quickly toward the path that would lead us down to the street, and now I could hear the alarm being raised behind us. Everyone would be looking for us straight away. Suddenly I had an idea.

"In here," I said as I grabbed Darius's hand and pulled him after me into one of the servants' quarters. Thankfully it was empty. It appeared to be the quarters of two men which would be perfect for what we needed to do.

"We need to change out of these clothes," I said, quickly fumbling through the few possessions of these men to gather enough for the two of us to wear.

Thankfully there was a turban, which I desperately needed. I removed all my jewelry and Darius wrapped everything in a cloth that he tucked inside his tunic. We hid our things under the bed with the hope that they would not be found and trigger a search for two men dressed in servants' clothes. When we stepped out in the colonnade. We were just two of many male servants and we walked along unbothered by the soldiers who were running in every direction. Darius grabbed an empty basket and put it up on his shoulder so we could say we were going to the market should anyone ask. By the time we reached the gate to the street, the soldiers had spilled out into town. They searched the nearby buildings. We kept moving, trying to get as far away from the palace as we could, but would it be enough?

"Is it safe to go back to Obersius?" I asked, as I stopped and leaned against the wall. The emotion of the day and the running had exhausted me, and I desperately needed to lie down.

"Yes, I think it will be alright. I can see you are tired. Can you go a bit longer? I don't think we have much farther to go," said Darius, clearly concerned.

"With the help of the gods," I replied.

"I must say, they do not seem to have been of much help so far," replied Darius with a wry smirk.

"This is my fault. I should have known that woman was not Cleopatra," I said with tears welling up in my eyes.

"It is not your fault. How could you have known that someone would take the liberty to use her bath, perhaps without her knowledge? It is a conclusion any of us would have reached."

"Now Gallenus is dead, on his journey to the underworld, because of me," I replied flatly.

"He was your loyal servant and so he will be rewarded and not judged harshly. You need not worry yourself over his fate. For now, we must focus on getting you to safety. Are you ready? Come now, we must keep moving," said Darius as he took my hand.

We continued to walk. Soon I could see we were on the street where Obersius and Watenatie lived. My feet were bleeding from cuts and sores from the ill-fitting shoes. Every part of my being ached, but the end was in sight as I stumbled my way behind Darius to the door. He knocked and to my relief, it opened at once.

"My queen, Darius, are you alright? What has happened?" asked Watenatie, clearly shocked to see us again and in this state.

"We have heard the soldiers in the streets. Come in quickly," added Obersius as he peered out into the darkness before closing the door behind us and dropping the bolt into place.

"Things did not quite go as planned," said Darius as he explained to our hosts what had happened.

"Truly, my queen, I am sorry for what has happened to you. You should take refuge here for a few days until things quiet enough for you to try to escape back to the Temple."

"They are searching houses. We do not want to endanger you," I said hesitantly.

"Not to worry," said Obersius with a nod toward his brother.

He and Watenatie scrambled to quickly move the table and chairs, revealing under the rug a door that led to a chamber underneath the house.

"When we built this house, we made sure we had a… safe place we could go should we ever need it. You will have everything you need to sustain you for a few days. There is a vent leading to the street behind the house so you can cook and there is fresh water in the barrel. I will get some extra food which we will bring down to you, but for now, go quickly inside."

"Thank you," I replied, stopping to kiss Obersius on the cheek as he helped me down the ladder.

Once inside, Darius lit a small lamp. We heard the furniture being placed back over the door.

"We are safe?"

"Yes, for now," said Darius as he pulled me into his arms and held me tightly.

I do not know why but I began to cry. Sobs bubbled up from me in wave after wave like the sea crashing against the shore. Darius picked me up and sat down on the edge of the bed, holding me in his arms like one holds a child who has fallen and hurt themselves. He wiped the tears from my face with the back of his hand.

"Do not cry, my queen. As long as you are alive there is hope," he said as I gulped at the air in an attempt to get control of my tears.

I wrapped my arms around his neck, burying my face in his shoulder, and cried until I could not cry any longer. Darius finally laid me on the bed, covering me with a blanket and I fell into a dream-filled sleep. Visions of being chased from the palace and a woman's body floating in the water haunted my rest and I tossed and turned despite my profound weariness. How could I have made such a mistake? It may have cost us everything. Cleopatra now knew of my intentions and outside of the safety of the Temple of Artemis, everyone presented a threat.

We spent nearly three days in our underground shelter, although it was hard to mark the passage of time as no light from the sun reached us. Obersius brought food to us every day and updated us on what was happening. The house-to-house searches seemed to have stopped as their focus turned towards the docks and the roads that led out of Alexandria.

"How can we possibly go to the ship with so many soldiers searching the docks?" I asked as the four of us gathered at the table. Thankfully there was no longer a need for us to be underground.

"It is a dilemma to be sure. I do not think just disguising you as a boy is effective any longer. They will be looking for a man and a boy, or a man and a small woman. Either way, you will not pass," said Watenatie.

"You are right," agreed Darius.

"We cannot stay here, I am grateful we asked the ship to stay but I must get back to the Temple. She would not dare harm me there, away from Egypt, where Rome still exercises their control. Whether I am captive there now or not, it is still a sacred place, and one that no one would breach. Besides, we must now gather an army. My presence is needed," I said, feeling my frustration rising.

"Obersius, have you any ideas?" asked Darius.

"I think I might. What if we hid the Queen inside a wine cask, hidden among other wine barrels?"

"For a change, it seems as if my small stature may be helpful. What do you think Darius? Can it work?"

"I think it might. Obersius, can you get us a barrel to try out? If we can make her comfortable in there long enough to get her back onboard Lucius's ship, then we can get her safely back to Ephesus."

Sure enough, I fit easily into the barrel, although the pungent smell was a bit nauseating. Thankfully I would not be in it for long. We would leave first thing in the morning. Watenatie arranged for a wagon full of similar wine barrels to stop here in the morning to pick up one more… one I would be hidden inside. Darius would accompany the wagon to the dock and unload my barrel as well as several others, so it seems consistent with a simple gathering of supplies for a journey.

"My dearest friends I cannot thank you enough for all you have done for us," I said to Obersius and Watenatie as we sat down to eat our final meal together.

"My heart is broken that you were not successful, but I know that you will find a way. You are a Ptolemy. Your family has ruled Egypt for hundreds of years and your time will come. Be patient yet persistent and you will find that things turn in your favor," said Obersius with a genuine smile.

"Thank you," I said as I took his hand in mine.

He reminded me of my father in some way. Not just his age, although they were probably similar, but in his demeanor. It was the way he spoke to me. It had a familiarity about it that made me feel safe. It also made me realize I had no one, no family to join me in this fight. Loyal friends and believers? Yes, but it was not the same as having those who shared your blood and your history on your side. But that thought also made me laugh a bit, as it was against blood and family that this fight was waged.

When morning dawned, I climbed into the barrel and Darius hammed the lid on. It was a bit disconcerting, but I knew he would let no harm come to me. When the wagon pulled up, the three men worked carefully to load the barrel with me inside. Obersius and Watenatie each patted the lid, signaling their final goodbye. I could not see out between the staves, but that also meant no one could see in. While it was not terribly comfortable at least I felt safe that I would not be detected.

As we rattled along the street, I used my arms to steady myself inside the barrel. Even so, it was not a comfortable ride. I could hear Darius talking to the cart driver about the weather and a recent storm. It appeared our subterfuge was working; we should be at the dock in no time.

"Stop," I heard a loud man's voice ring out.

"Whoa," said the driver as the wagon clattered to a stop.

"Why have you stopped us?" I heard the driver say.

"We are searching all the carts going in and out of the dock," replied another man who sounded very close.

"It is just wine, my fine young man, just wine. Do you wish to take a look?" said Darius with a hearty laugh.

My heart skipped a beat. Would he make them open all the casks?

I felt the cart sway as Darius climbed down. The barrel I was in sat in the middle of the wagon to make sure there was no chance that it would fall out.

"Here, let me give you a sample," said Darius.

I could tell he had climbed up into the back and he was prying the lid off a cask.

"Hand me your flask, young man," said Darius.

"All of these are wine?" asked a man.

"Yes. We are taking it to the dock to load on a ship leaving today. If you have no more concerns, we need to be on our way."

Suddenly I could hear someone knocking on the casks, first on my right, then the cask just next to me. If he thumped on my cask, he would be able to tell it was hollow. I held my breath trying to be as still as possible.

"All right, be on your way then," I heard the man say.

"Thank you," replied Darius and the cart rocked once again as we continued our way to the dock.

"It is a beautiful day, is it not?" said the driver.

"It is now," Darius replied.

He was smiling. I could tell just by the sound of his voice, and it reassured me. It took only a few more minutes before we stopped again, and I could hear many men's voices and then the sound of barrels being offloaded. Without warning, my barrel was slid along the cart to the back and then hoisted into the air. I banged my head against the side of the barrel and quickly covered my mouth to stifle my outcry.

"Sorry," I heard Darius say. I assumed that his apology was directed at me.

The men were on an incline and so I was sure we were going up the gangplank. I was almost safe. Suddenly the barrel was unceremoniously dropped onto the deck. It was all I could do to not cry out.

"Just a bit longer," he said, bending down next to where he thought my head might be.

I knocked lightly to let him know I understood. It was warm

now and so I was grateful to have a little water. The irony was I had no wine! Obersius had packed a bit of bread and some fruit for me wrapped in cloth and so I ate, waiting as patiently as I could. I needed to relieve myself so I hoped it would not be much longer. To my surprise, I must have nodded off because the movement of the cask startled me awake. Someone was removing the lid.

"Are you ready to get out?" asked Darius as he lifted the lid, freeing me from my wooden prison.

I shielded my eyes from what was left of the sun. It took me a moment to make out Darius's face peering into the barrel at me.

"Yes, is it safe?"

"It is. Let me help you," he said as he reached in and lifted me up. My legs were cramped and sore from crouching in such a small space for so long.

The barrel had been moved to a place at the back of the ship, away from the dock. There was a very tall young man holding up a cloth to make a curtain of sorts to shield me from view. I was dressed as Amin, but still, it was best not to be seen climbing out of a wine barrel.

It took me a moment to get my legs moving again. Finally, I was able to walk to the ladder and down to the cabin below. It seemed surreal that I was back here again, instead of in the palace and on the throne where I belonged. This time, I stayed below as the ship set sail and waited until we could not be seen before going up on deck. The sun was already below the water's edge, but its glow could still be seen in the sky. We would not go far this evening, just far enough to be out of the grasp of the Egyptian fleet. Far enough to see any ship that may be headed in our direction with enough time to set sail ourselves and keep a distance.

"We have stopped for the night," said Darius as he came and stood beside me as I gazed out on the glass sea.

"Thank you," I said reflectively.

"I know you are sad, my Queen. We will yet prevail, you will see," said Darius as he nudged me with his shoulder.

"Will we? I do not think that is a given. Just look at where we are! We have made no progress and now Cleopatra knows we are coming for her. That will make this even harder," I whined.

"That may be true, but harder does not mean impossible. Besides, you do now have Lucius and Cyprus on your side. Do you still want to try or are you saying you just want to give up and let your half-sister and her bastard son rule the throne of Egypt?"

"No, I am not saying that. I am just… discouraged," I replied.

"Understandable."

"Do you think we should continue this fight?" I asked hesitantly.

"I think we should do whatever your heart and the gods tell you is the way forward. You know I am with you no matter what you do or where you go," he replied with a warm smile.

"I am so fortunate to have you by my side. I would never have managed this long without you," I said as I looked at him, brushing the hair from his eyes.

"My only concern right now is getting you back to the Temple where you will be safe. We should be there in a couple of weeks. Until then, rest and clear your mind so that you know what it is you want to do when we arrive. Bennu has been preparing for war but if that is no longer your desire, he will understand."

I wrapped my arms around his neck and pulled him close to me, breathing deeply of his musky smell. There must be a way for me to be Queen and have this man too. My love for him was deeper than any I had ever known. I could not imagine my life without him by my side. Perhaps Lira could do some digging to see if there was in fact some royal blood in his family line. Anything that could help me to justify my decision to the gods and my people. At least he was Egyptian. That alone set him far above Cleopatra and her bastard son.

The weeks passed quickly, and I did as Darius had suggested, spending my time sleeping, watching the sea for hours on end, and praying for an answer. My cause was still a just one but if the gods were on my side, why were we not successful in our coup? In my heart of hearts, I felt that we were right. Surely the people of Egypt would rather be ruled by me than by Cleopatra's son. I would have a son of my own someday and he should be the rightful Ptolemy ruler. Land had appeared on the horizon, signaling that within another day we would be back in Ephesus. It had been nearly eight months since we left, and I was anxious to see Lira. I also knew that I must have a conversation with Bennu, and hastily. He must know what I desired to do, but was it clear even to me? At that moment, I must admit it was not.

Once again in the disguise of Amin, for what I hoped was the last time, I waited at the bow as the ship was moored. Finally secured to the dock, I spied Bennu, Cente, Amon, and Lira waiting for us. I was so happy to see Lira it was all I could do to wait while they dropped the gangplank. As soon as they did, I ran down into her waiting arms and embraced her. The two of us laughed gleefully as the others showered their welcome and greetings on me.

"My queen, I am so happy and relieved that you have returned, although I wish your trip to Egypt had turned out differently," whispered Lira as she held me tight.

"It is my true happiness to be reunited with you, my dear friend. Although as you say, I wish it had been in Egypt," I replied.

"Amin," cried Bennu as he also embraced me before whispering in my ear, "My queen, we are glad to see you are safe."

It was an odd moment as if we were celebrating something, but there was little to celebrate. Lucius had reconfirmed his commitment to the cause, but our unsuccessful coup was certainly not a triumph, and it was my fault. Perhaps they did not know that yet, hence the warm welcome.

"Amon will get your trunk. Let us get you back to the temple so you can get out of these clothes and bathe," said Bennu, motioning at Amon to go on to the ship to get my things.

"Where is Darius?" I asked looking around in a bit of a panic, unable to locate him on the ship or the dock.

"I do not know, but I am sure he will join us later. Ziyad and Masduse are waiting at the house as well. They will join us for dinner," said Bennu as we began our walk toward the Temple. The streets were full of people, and we blended into the crowd easily. Maybe this would be a better life. One where I was just part of the crowd, not standing out. Lira linked her arm through mine the entire walk as if she needed to secure my body to her own, preventing me from leaving again. We talked amiably about all the things that had happened since we left but mostly about what was happening in Rome. Tempers seem to have cooled now after months of unrest immediately following Caesar's death. Still, it was unclear how this three-headed monster, the newly formed trio of leaders may prevail.

"This timing works to our advantage, I feel," said Bennu as we reached the gates of the Temple.

"Why so?"

"Now that things have quieted in Rome, I think the last thing they will want is to get involved in a conflict in Egypt," Bennu replied.

"Oh, yes. I had not considered that."

As we walked through the Temple gates I turned to look back out into the street. If I declared war on Cleopatra, I would once again be captive here as she would surely have me murdered were I not under the protection of the goddess Artemis. For as long as the war may take, I would be safe only inside these walls. Is that what I really wanted? It felt like no life at all sometimes. While everyone else got to live, coming and going as they pleased, I was once again in a gilded cage.

"Are you coming?" asked Lira, staring at me intently.

"Yes, of course," I said trying to shake the thoughts from my mind. I linked my arm through hers as we began our climb up the steps.

The morning crowds were heavy as usual as the people came in droves seeking the blessing of the goddess for safe childbirth, successful crops, and fruitful hunts. They came to ask for favor in all the things the goddess was known to have dominion over. They came to pray at her feet. We walked with the crowd toward the front of the temple, caught up in the wave of the throng. I continued with them, not trying to resist the direction they were taking me.

"Amin, this way," said Bennu as he gestured toward the gate which would lead out to the courtyard and the villa.

"Go ahead. I will join you shortly," I replied as I continued forward, Lira staying right beside me.

It seemed as if the goddess was calling to me, as if she was telling me to come to her, to reach out to her. As the crowd grew denser, it required more effort on my part to find my way forward, exploiting any small opening to make it to the front where the temple guards stood next to the tall gleaming braziers. The flames flickered as they lit the area around the enormous statue of the goddess Artemis standing in the alcove at the front of the temple. Her likeness was carved in black obsidian, yet it shone as though it were lit from within, bringing her features to life. The shadows danced on the wall and ceiling like reflections of the past playing out in darkness and light. There was a sound too, like the sound the wind makes as it blows between the buildings. It was a whooshing sound that carried with it the smell of all the flowers and grasses it had blown over before arriving in this place.

When I finally reached the area, just a few hand widths from the statue, the guards would let me go no closer. If I had been dressed as Arsinoe they would have let me go as close as I wanted, but as Amin, the guards were right to stop me. I was a waif of a boy with no standing. But I sensed in this moment that I needed to touch her, to feel her power surge through me. Kneeling in front of the statue, as close as I could get, I waited patiently hoping for the guards to become distracted so I could reach out, my knees beginning to ache from the cold hard stone beneath them. It felt as if I had been there for a long time, but truly it was probably mere moments when unexpectedly someone dropped what sounded like a sword behind me. I did not turn around. The guards both moved away from the statue to see what had happened. It was my chance.

I leaned forward and stretched out my left hand to reach the statue's foot that was closest to me, closing my eyes and breathing deeply as if somehow, I could inhale her strength and wisdom. She would know what I should do, what life I should lead, but would she tell me? My fingers felt as though I were touching the edge of a burning log, but I kept them there. I could not break our bond. The heat began to creep up my hand, and then to my arm like I imagined a poison spreads through the body until I could feel the warmth in my chest. Even though the temple was protected from the elements, it felt like a gust was blowing around me, swirling like a whirlwind. Then I heard her voice being carried on the breeze. *You know what you must do.* I strained to listen to the voice… *You know what you must do* I heard it again more clearly this time. She was here she was speaking to me I was sure of it, but then my mind went blank. Now there was only the darkness enfolding me in its embrace

"Arsinoe?"

The voice sounded far away, a distant echo in my mind. Was it the goddess? I must answer her. She was calling me.

"Arsinoe, you need to wake. You cannot continue this way. You must eat."

It was Lira, I finally realized, as I struggled to open my eyes.

"Where am I? What happened?" I asked as I rubbed my eyes trying to get my bearings. I was not sure if it was day or night.

"I watched while you knelt at the foot of the goddess. I saw you lean forward and then suddenly you collapsed on the floor. You have been sleeping for nearly two days. I did not want to wake you as it seemed as though you very much needed the sleep, but you have not had anything to eat or drink now for so long and I fear for your well-being. I determined you must wake," said Lira. The concern in her voice was obvious.

"How did I get here?" I asked, still trying to comprehend what she was saying. I had been asleep for two days, but it seemed only a moment ago that I had been kneeling at the statue.

"One of the guards carried you here. Cente and I settled you in your bed and bandaged your hand, which looks much better now," said Lira with a sigh of relief.

"My hand? What is wrong with my hand?" I asked as I realized I now wore a piece of linen wrapped tightly around my left hand and wrist.

"I do not know what happened. When we brought you here, we found your fingers red and raw as if they had been burned," said Lira as she knitted her brow.

I stared at her for a moment, trying to clear the debris from my mind. What had happened?

"It was the goddess. When I touched her foot, I felt heat like from a burning piece of wood," I said as I turned my hand back and forth with a look of astonishment. It wasn't just in my mind that the statue had felt hot to the touch. It had burned me.

"It is a sign from the goddess!" exclaimed Lira as she looked to the sky.

"Lira, go find Bennu and tell him to bring Megabyzos, then return here quickly with Cente. Go, hurry," I instructed as I gingerly climbed out of bed.

"Arsinoe, please. You must be careful. You have not eaten," said Lira as she helped me to get to the chair at the dressing table.

"I will, I promise. Bring the wine and food over here before you go, and I will eat. I give you my word, but this cannot wait. Go at once," I said urgently.

While I waited for Lira to return with Cente, I did as I promised, eating some of the fruit. I quickly gulped down two glasses of wine. The words were echoing through my mind, over and over. *"You know what you must do,"* she had said.

I did not know for sure what I wanted to do before the goddess spoke to me, but now there was no doubt in my mind. I did know what I must do. When Lira returned, I had her and Cente dress me in the finest clothes and jewels that I owned. Then we added a makeshift headdress we had fashioned out of some reeds and fine cloth. Once I was ready, I joined Bennu and Megabyzos who were patiently waiting in the garden.

"Thank you both," I said as I joined them.

"We are at your service, Princess Arsinoe," said Bennu as he and Megabyzos each made a slight bow.

"Megabyzos, you are the high priest of this temple are you not?" I asked.

"I am. I have been in this esteemed position many, many years now," he replied as he stroked his long white beard.

His robes were simple without much adornment, but from his neck hung a blue lapis lazuli the size of which I had never seen before. It reflected the light as if it had been stolen from the night sky by the gods themselves. As he looked at me his eyes were nearly the same shade of blue. They were soft and kind and I liked him at once.

"Megabyzos, I am Arsinoe, daughter of Ptolemy XII, daughter of Egypt and my birthright is its throne. I am anointed by Isis and Osiris and the goddess Artemis has spoken to me. I need your help, your affirmation," I said confidently.

"I believe I understand. I will prepare for what needs to be done. Come to the statue at sunset. I will be ready," he replied with a low bow before shuffling away.

The villa was a frenzy of activity for the next few hours, but I quickly realized someone was still missing. "Where is Darius?" I asked no one in particular.

"He said he had some business to take care of," said Bennu.

"I am sure he will be back soon," added Lira.

His absence made me uneasy. We had been through so much together and apart so little that it seemed so odd to me to be separated. Stranger still, he left with no explanation and with no word as to when he would return. But for now, I could not contemplate it. There were too many other things that would need my attention. Bennu and Amon were preparing the house while Cente and Lira worked to make platter after platter of food. There were sweets and wine for those that would come. There were workmen of all kinds coming in, as well as women from the local market with flowers and food. They came and went in a flurry. All I could do was sit, and wait, never an easy thing for me to do. To pass the time, I retreated to the library and spent a few hours reading through some of the many scrolls Bennu kept there. It made the hours move more quickly and it was not long before the time drew nigh.

Once the sun nearly reached the horizon, we gathered in a procession to walk to the great statue together. This time was very different from my visit just two days ago. Crowds of people stood on either side of an isle of sorts that had been strewn with petals and greenery. Dozens of oil lamps lined the path. As we drew near, I could see Megabyzos standing in front of the great statue of Artemis. Her face seemed almost alive in the glow from the lamps. He was wearing a white linen robe with a single leopard skin draped over both his shoulders. The contrast between him and the statue could not have been more profound. The darkness and the light were coming together as one.

"You must go the rest of the way by yourself, but we will be here, waiting for you," said Lira.

"I will as well," I heard a familiar voice say.

It was Darius. Somewhere along our walk through the temple he had joined the procession, and it did my heart good to see him.

"I am happy to see you, but where have you been?" I asked.

"I will explain everything later, but for now, your destiny is waiting, my queen."

As I continued my walk toward the high priest, I felt calm. I had been here before, years ago on a hilltop on the side of the river Nile, with Gany. But this time was different. I was no longer a girl relying on the men around me to make decisions. Now, I was a woman and a leader in my own right. I did not need to wait on others to determine my way forward. As I knelt before Megabyzos and removed my headdress, the words of the rituals rang in my ears, familiar and comforting. When he placed a golden crown on my head obtained from the temple treasure room, it fit... perfectly.

"Now in the name of Ra and Serapis, I name you Queen Arsinoe IV, anointed by Isis and Osiris, ruler of all Egypt," proclaimed Megabyzos.

As I rose and turned to look back on the crowd gathered in

the temple a large cheer rose, taking me by surprise. The noise echoed through the temple like the thunderous roar of a lion. In the front of the crowd, Lira, Bennu, Cente, Amon, and of course Darius, who was now on one knee with his closed fist over his heart, as were many of the other men. Once the noise faded, I stepped forward to speak.

"I am Arsinoe IV the rightful Queen of Egypt, anointed by Isis and blessed by Serapis. With your support, I will reclaim the throne that is rightfully mine. The blood of the ruler of Egypt has been tainted by the blood of the Romans and it is now longer pure and therefore no longer blessed by the gods. The goddess Artemis has spoken to me. She has encouraged me in this endeavor and with her protection we cannot fail."

The crowd cheered again and as I walked back through the Temple toward the villa, I had never felt more confident. Lira was smiling broadly as she fell in line behind me, taking Darius's arm. Flower petals rained down on me, being thrown by the crowd as I passed. When we arrived back at the villa, I went at once to the throne room that Bennu had constructed in a room near the gardens so that I could receive visitors. With such a short time to prepare they had done magnificently. The room was decorated in shades of blue and gold. As I climbed the steps of the dais up to the throne they had made, I felt a sense of peace come over me. It was a certainty that soon I would be sitting on the throne in the palace of Alexandria. Egypt would be mine.

Chapter Eight

NO TIME FOR PRETENDERS

There were several days of celebrations after my proclamation, and it did my heart good to see how much support we had among the citizens of Ephesus. Bennu had been preparing to raise an army for months now. I have made Masduse, the most experienced fighter among the men, General over all our forces. Unlike General Achillas, I find him most agreeable, and more importantly, most trustworthy. I would not risk being betrayed again. While I'd given Darius no title, it was clear to all that he spoke with my voice and my blessing.

"So, you never did tell me where you went when we returned?" I asked when Darius and I were alone at last.

"No. I did not want to concern you until I knew more," he said hesitantly.

"What is it?" I asked.

"I am not sure, I went to investigate before speaking to you," he said with consternation.

"Do not spare me. What is it, Darius?" I demanded.

"A man in Syria is claiming to be your brother, Ptolemy XIII. He says he survived and did not drown in the Nile as was reported by Cleopatra and Julius Caesar," he said reluctantly.

I was caught so off guard by this revelation all I could do was stare at Darius. I was unable to speak, struggling to gather my wits.

"No. No!" I finally screamed as my anger rose, pushing everything on my desk onto the floor with a sweep of my hand. My fists were balled up tightly and my jaw was clenched. The clattering brought Lira immediately into the room and without so much as a word she quickly began cleaning up the mess I had just created. The gods had promised me. My destiny was the throne! How could this be happening?

"This cannot be true, can it? If he had survived, why had he not made himself known before now? He has been dead for several years! If he was in hiding, why come forward now? Surely this must be a pretender," I said as I finally gained control of my anger. My cheeks were still flushed and red with the fury I was barely keeping under control.

"There are some who seem to support his claim, but as you suggest, many others who feel this man must be a pretender. The challenge is that there are only a few who had ever met him and so no one can determine the voracity of his claim."

"I could!" I replied at once.

"Yes, of course you could. Needless to say, this man does not support your claim and so for you to travel to Syria to validate or invalidate him is not welcome. You would be putting yourself at risk to do so," said Darius with a shake of his head.

"Is he raising an army?" I asked incredulously.

"It sounds like he is trying, but whether he will be successful is yet to be seen. It does not sound like he has been able to garner much support."

"So not only do we need to fight Cleopatra… we may need to battle this usurper as well?" I murmured. I could not believe what was happening.

"I am afraid that may be the case. The best course of action may be to wait for a period to see what happens before we have General Masduse move forward with an invasion of Alexandria," replied Darius with a shrug of his shoulders.

"No, I will wait no longer. I can feel the breath of war on my neck. I have waited too long, and I will not continue to sit while others try to take what is mine. We have the support of Cyprus, we have much encouragement here in Ephesus, and what does this interloper have?"

"It seems he may have the backing of a few wealthy Egyptians who would like to see him on the throne," said Darius slowly.

"But are they aware of my claim and pronouncement?" I asked with a shrill in my voice.

"We made sure to send messengers far and wide. There is no one, in Egypt at least, that would not know by now," replied Darius, sensing my frustration.

"How are we for debens? Does the General have what he needs to enlist the men we will require?"

"He does, and he has continued to hire mercenaries to establish an elite force as well as foot soldiers for an invasion. We need more ships, though, as it is the only reliable way to get these men to Alexandria. Building ships takes time." Darius stroked his beard as he looked at me tentatively.

"We do not have time; can we not buy ships?" I asked incredulously.

"We have tried, my queen, but few merchants have been willing to sell to us. Without their ships, they have no way to buy and transport their wares and they will compromise their own living while they build another."

I could hear in his voice that tone of exasperation he often got when he felt I did not understand the challenges we faced in attempting to raise the army. But I did understand, I knew how difficult this was, but we could not be easily deterred. If Ganymedes were still with me I wonder if he too would be irritated with me, or if he would better understand my frustration. Darius is devoted to me, there was no doubt. He was loyal without question, but sometimes I thought he felt I was out of my depth. He never criticized but it was there, an undertone in unasked questions and silent reproachments. Having never lived in the palace in Alexandria as Gany did, perhaps he just did not truly understand what was at stake, what could be ours, the life we could have.

"What if we were to pay the merchants for the use of their boats to transport our forces rather than buying the boats outright? They would then have their ships to continue their trade after just a few months," I said as Lira set the last book on the desk.

"I think that is a brilliant idea," said Darius with surprise.

"I think so too," said Lira with a smile of her own.

"Let us make it so, but in the meantime, we still need to decide what to do about this pretender," I said.

Lira looked back and forth at our faces in confusion.

"A man is claiming to be my brother, Ptolemy XIII," I said with a venom in my voice that could not be hidden.

"That cannot be. Surely were it truly your brother he would have come forward as soon as Julius Caesar was murdered, and Cleopatra was without her benefactor."

"My thoughts exactly, but it will matter little if the men in power believe he is the rightful heir to the crown of the Pharaoh? I will lose my support in his favor, and I can ill afford to do that. We must find a way to discredit him."

"We need someone in a position of power to speak against him and his claim," said Lira thoughtfully.

"That might work," replied Darius as he nodded his head in agreement.

"But who?" responded Lira.

"We need Marcus Aemilius Scaurus…" I said at last.

"He is the Praetor of Syria, is he not?" asked Darius.

"Yes, and he is aligned with Marc Antony who continues to haggle with Octavian and others in Rome, but he is of significant power. If this pretender has taken refuge there, perhaps he can speak against him. If he refuted his claim, then many would believe it."

"But why would he want to help us?" asked Lira.

"If this man, this pretender, were to successfully take the throne of Egypt from Cleopatra she would surely turn her attention to Rome on behalf of her bastard son. This could prove to be very disruptive for a country already dealing with its own issues. If Cleopatra has Egypt, she will be content to have her bastard son replace her as Pharaoh. That leaves Antony, Lepidus, and Octavius to go about their business in Rome without the specter of Caesarion hanging over them," I replied as I gazed out toward the garden.

This could be our chance to not only discredit this man, whose claim I gave no credence to, but perhaps we could even convince Antony and Marcus Aemilius to support us with troops or funds. Surely, they would understand that I did not, and never would, have designs on Rome. My goal was the throne of Egypt and Egypt alone. While I recognized the need to have friendly relations with the Romans, I wanted them at arms-length and not involved in the day-to-day workings of Egypt or my rule there.

"We need to send an emissary to Syria, but I do not know who might best serve us, and I dare not go myself," I said at last.

"You know I will gladly go on your behalf," replied Darius with a slight bow and a flourish of the hand.

"Perhaps you and Bennu could go together?"

"I will speak to him at once," said Darius, quickly taking his leave.

"I am relieved you did not want to go yourself," said Lira as she sat down on the edge of the bed.

"If Darius and Bennu are going to be gone for some months it will fall to me with General Masduse and Ziyad to continue our efforts to expand our army. Besides, I have no doubt that Cleopatra watches our every move since our effort to assassinate her. She would like nothing more than for me to leave the safety of the Temple so that she can take her revenge. I have no intention of making myself an easy target for her," I replied with a weary sigh.

"Are you well, my queen?" asked Lira with a tilt of her head.

"Tired and frustrated. It seems at every turn someone attempts to thwart my efforts, and it is exhausting me. I spend every free moment on my knees but to no avail. At times I feel as if the gods have designed to test me beyond my limits."

"You need to rest. If you fall ill your efforts will be for naught," said Lira as she patted the bed beside her.

"I know. You are right, but it feels as if there is so much to do, I dare not stop. Petitioners come all day to speak with me to make a plea for some assistance or to intervene with the gods on their behalf. While the recognition of my status is appreciated it can also be… overwhelming," I admitted.

"You push yourself too hard, my queen."

"Dear Lira, you are so kind," I said as I rose and wrapped my arms around her, kissing her on the top of her head.

"I want only for your health and happiness," she replied as she lay her head on my chest with her arms around my waist.

"You have my word I will try to rest more, but not right now, as there is much to do," I said with a smile.

We all gathered. Masduse, Zayid, Darius, Bennu, Lira, and I talked about the envoy, and the consensus was it would be wise for Bennu and Darius to go together. Everyone knows that Darius speaks for me in my absence and our dearest Bennu is well known in Syria as some of his ancestors are from its soil. They would leave at once as we had no time to waste. If we were going to attack, we must do so soon. If the pretender was still sowing doubts about my claim, our men would desert us, taking their debens with them. Zayid would stay here in the house in their absence to ensure our safety.

Darius had been staying here since we returned from Egypt, forever watchful, to ensure I was never in danger. It saddened me to think that he would be gone for several weeks. We had not been apart for more than a few weeks since we first met. My heart rested easy when he was near, so I would be on edge until he returned. I was glad though that he was going though as he could be very persuasive when he wanted to be and I was sure he and Bennu would be successful in this endeavor.

In Bennu's absence, it fell on me to check the secret vault where our coins and jewels were kept. He did it every few days, but only at night, after the crowds had gone and the Temple had been closed for the night. I would normally have taken Darius with me when I performed this task but, in his absence, Lira would have to do. Zayid was unaware of the storerooms, and it was best if he did not know just yet at least. Our footsteps echoed through the cavernous temple as the light from our torch flickered, casting shadows upon the walls.

"The temple is so different at night. It feels so restful and calm after all the people leave," said Lira as she glanced around admiring the many frescos.

"I agree. The quiet is soothing… reassuring somehow."

"Have you heard from Darius?" asked Lira as we reached our destination.

"No, not yet. Here, hold my torch," I said as I handed it off to her. It would take both hands to work the hidden door.

Just as I was about to open the door, I heard a faint noise. It was almost like a cough, but we had seen no one. Normally the priests were in their quarters by now and did not reemerge until dawn. I held my finger to my lips. It was clear Lira had heard it too. We moved away from the door and hid behind a column. If someone had followed us with the intent of robbing us, it would be best not to reveal where our treasures were hidden. Again, we heard the noise, this time a bit closer.

"My queen, we should go back to the villa," whispered Lira, clearly beginning to panic.

"If someone is lying in wait for us, we would be better to hide. We know this temple very well. Come follow me, but quietly," I whispered back, keeping my eyes straight ahead.

I doused our torch, plunging us into darkness, but in a few moments, our eyes had adjusted. We could see enough to find our way to a small alcove which held a statue of Ra just off to our right and we took shelter there. I heard nothing, just the sound of our breathing.

"Perhaps it was just an animal. A stray cat, maybe?" murmured Lira.

"You may be right, but we will wait a bit longer," I replied as I peered around the corner of the alcove.

"Get back. A man is walking this way," I said as I pushed Lira up against the back wall of the alcove.

Even in this relative darkness, I could see the fear in Lira's eyes. I suspected mine reflected that fear as well. What was a man doing in the temple at night? If he had good intent, he would be carrying a torch with him no doubt. Had he followed us? I saw no one nearby when we left the villa. Other than one priest we had passed who was dousing the torches, we had passed no one else. While the gates were closed at night, they were not guarded. The Temple was a sacred place, and no one would dare violate its sanctity. But then how did we explain this man's presence? He was moving slowly, searching the darkness with his eyes. He was dressed in typical Turkish clothing, but he had a cloth wrapped around the lower part of his face, making his appearance partially obscured. I could see he held a dagger in his hand. Was he afraid of something, or more ominously, was he here to harm someone? Me?

I always had a dagger with me, as did Lira, and I nodded to her as I pulled mine from the strap that held it to my leg. She immediately did the same. It felt as though our very breath echoed through the darkness. I motioned for Lira to go to the other side of the alcove. If he discovered us, we could attack him from each side, improving our odds of at least disabling him long enough for us to get away. My mind was reeling. Who would dare to come for me inside the Temple? Surely even Cleopatra would not be so brazen. The goddess would certainly not let any harm come to us, would she? No, I could not believe that her benefice would desert me now.

I peered around the corner of the alcove. He was standing near the entrance to our secret rooms, but he did not seem to be trying to access them. He appeared to be looking for something… or someone. He let out another small cough. Was he sick? Had he come to the Temple seeking refuge of some sort and become frightened by the noise we had made earlier? But then why would he have a dagger?

"I know you are here. Show yourself and I will not hurt you," said the man, his voice echoing off the marble and granite walls.

I inhaled sharply. He was here for me, and I had no doubt that he intended to hurt me, kill me even. Perhaps he preferred to take me outside the temple walls first. While his clothing looked Turkish, his accent was without a doubt Egyptian. Cleopatra had come for me at last. I waited until his back was turned before I crossed over to the other side of the alcove next to Lira.

"We need to attack first. If he finds us in here we may not be able to fend him off," I said, my voice so low I was not sure Lira could even hear me.

"I am ready, my queen," she said, although her voice quivered.

"Give me your bracelet," I said holding out my hand.

She quickly took it off and handed it to me. This would work perfectly.

"I am going to throw this near him. When he bends down to retrieve it, we must attack. Aim for his heart or his face," I said.

"May the gods protect us," replied Lira as she nodded her head.

I watched for another moment, waiting until he was only ten or so paces away. He would discover us soon I was sure. We must act. I threw the bracelet. It landed just a few feet from him with a jarring noise that filled the darkness. Sure enough, he stopped and moved toward it, bending down to retrieve it.

"Ahhhhh!" I screamed out as loudly as I could as I lunged toward him with my dagger held high.

He looked up just as I plunged my knife toward him. It landed in his arm as he raised it to protect himself. Lira swung her blade toward his chest, and he cried out as she hit her target. Pulling my dagger from his arm I lunged at him again, striking him over and over as our screams filled the air. He swung his blade wildly, trying his best to strike us. Lira stabbed him again in the belly. Blood was spurting from his chest as he dropped to his knees, but he was still trying to attack. He tried desperately to reach me, but his knife only grazed my arm as he fell to the floor. Without hesitation, I stabbed him again. He dropped the dagger, and a pool of blood began forming around him as he stared at me with glassy eyes. He was trying with his hands to stem the red tide flowing from his body, but it was like trying to stop the Nile.

"It is not done. There will be others," he said as he gasped for breath, blood gurgling from the side of his mouth.

"I will be ready," I said defiantly as he drew his last breath.

The screams had drawn the priests from their quarters, and I could hear people coming. Their torches illuminated the ghastly scene. My tunic was covered in so much blood. His blood, my blood… and Lira's blood, who now lay motionless on the floor behind me.

"Lira! Lira, are you hurt?" I gasped as I knelt beside her, desperately trying to see if she had been wounded. There was so much blood that it was impossible to tell where it had come from.

"My leg," she managed to croak out just as the priests arrived.

I lifted her tunic and found a huge gash running across the entire width of her leg.

"Help me! Please, help me, quickly!" I screamed out as one of the priests finally arrived kneeling beside us.

He quickly tore off the bottom of Lira's tunic and wrapped it around her leg just above the gash, tying it tightly. The river of blood slowed to a trickle, but I knew this was just a temporary measure. One of the priests ran to get a litter while I continued to kneel on the floor next to Lira.

"You cannot die. I forbid it. I am the Queen of Egypt. You will do as I say," I said to her, my voice quaking as the tears streamed down my face. I held tightly on to her hand which felt lifeless in mine.

As the priests placed her on the litter and started toward the villa, I turned and ran through the darkness, leaving bloody footprints in my wake. I ran as fast as I could to the base of the statue of Artemis, an imposing spectacle in the near darkness. I threw myself at her feet. My voice cried out into the void.

"I have given you my complete devotion and I have asked little of you in return but please I beg of you, do not let my friend cross the river. She is my dearest companion and like a sister to me. I need her. Please hear my prayer and spare her life. Please, please," I said crying out in anguish and despair.

But the goddess did not respond. She stood there in the darkness, the silence deafening. I heard nothing. I felt nothing. I committed to staying there the whole night on the floor praying for Lira. Behind me, the priests removed the body of the man who had come for me and cleaned up the blood-stained floor so that all would be well when the gates opened. When the sun finally streamed in through the open doors, I managed to get to my feet. My body was stiff and cold after a night laying on the floor at the goddesses' feet. Although I cried out to her over and over, she did not grace me with a reply as she had done before. The silence had been deafening only my own agony echoed through the chambers.

My tunic remained covered in blood, as were my face, arms, and hands. As I walked past the visitors who had come to the temple, they stared and audibly gasped as I moved past them. I did not care. What they thought meant nothing to me and I barely noticed them. Would Lira still be alive when I reached the villa? Surely my prayers had to be answered. I have so fervently prayed for the gods to help, they must hear my pleas.

As I reached the gate to the villa I could feel my head spinning, and the tears began to flow again. Lira was my only family and my dearest companion. I would be lost without her.

"My queen, are you hurt?" asked Cente as she rushed to meet me at the gate.

"No, not really. There is a wound on my arm but one of the priests dressed it for me. It is fine," I replied as I stumbled forward, suddenly realizing how weak I felt.

"Sit down my queen. The priests told us that you would stay at the altar all night, but you should have come home," chastised Amon as he guided me toward a nearby chair and handed me a glass of wine. I drained it in one swallow.

"Lira?"

"She lives, my queen, but she has lost a lot of blood," said Cente softly.

"It is up to the gods now," added Amon.

"Please, let me get you cleaned up then you can go and see her. She has been sleeping since the priests brought her in," said Cente as she helped me from the chair.

I did not resist as she walked me to my room and then worked to remove my tunic which was caked in dried blood. The strap that had held my dagger had been used to hold the linen on my arm and I was relieved to see that when we removed it, the wound did not bleed profusely, oozing just a bit. One of the other girls who worked in the house had begun filling the bath and I was grateful to get into it, washing the blood from my face and hair. Cente helped me and I appreciated her presence. My whole body ached, and it was difficult to even raise my arms.

"Throw it away," I said as Cente dried my hair.

"My queen?"

"Throw it away. The tunic... I do not want to ever see it again," I said wearily.

"As you wish," she replied.

"I need to see Lira," I said, rising tentatively from the chair.

Cente bowed slightly as I made my way past her and into Lira's room. There were several men there tending to her who bowed and excused themselves as I pulled up a chair next to her bed. She was pale. Her breathing was shallow and ragged, and a very large dressing covered the wound on her leg. Several pillows had been placed under her leg and the parts that were uncovered were bruised and swollen. I could see she also had a small cut on her face across her cheek, which I was sure would leave a scar. Her skin was warm as I took her limp hand in mine, closing my fingers tightly around it.

"I am here, and so are you. The gods have not taken you across the river and I do not believe that they will. I need you; you must stay with me. Please, Lira."

There was no response or reaction of any kind. All I could do was sit there quietly. Finally, I leaned forward, resting my head on the bed next to her, and slept. My dreams were filled with the sound of screams echoing through my head, blood flowing like a river, and visions of Cleopatra laughing as she plotted her next move.

It had been two weeks since the attack, and while Lira still lived, she was very weak. She had been able to sip broth and wine, but beyond that, she had consumed little. Cente made some juice from fruit to mix with the wine and she patiently sat with Lira, feeding her small sips throughout the day. The physician comes every day to check on her and the wound continues to seep blood, although in smaller and smaller amounts. Now the dressings were changed only twice a day, which was a significant improvement from the six or seven dressing changes she needed at the beginning.

My days were filled with meetings with General Masduse, but whenever I could I sat with Lira, talking to her and keeping her up to date on what was happening. She had mumbled some words from time to time, but there was no real response. The General had placed guards at the gate of the temple at night and more guards at the villa. We especially needed the extra protection until Darius and Bennu returned. I asked that word of this attack not be sent to them. I was afraid Darius would abandon the mission and return if he thought I was in danger, and we could ill afford that. We needed to address the interloper before we could be confident in our plans going forward. Sifting through various communications at my desk, I was pleased to find a letter from Darius who said he and Bennu had safely reached Damascus. Hopefully, there might be positive news soon.

"My queen, you should come," said Cente poking her head into the library, motioning for me to follow her.

My heart leaped into my throat. Was this it? Was Lira dying? I hurried after her. Indeed, she was headed to Lira's room, and I nearly ran ahead of her. When I entered Lira's room, I was stunned by what I saw.

"My queen," said Lira as I came through the doorway. She was awake, her eyes fully open, propped up on the pillows.

"Thank the gods! Lira, you are awake!"

"It seems so," she said as she weakly rubbed her eyes.

"I cannot express how happy this makes me," I said as I took her hand in mine, leaning over to kiss her on the forehead.

"You were not injured?"

"No, not really. The assassin just barely cut me with his dagger on my arm, but it has fully healed. I hope we can say the same for you very soon," I said smiling broadly.

"Thankfully I remember very little of what happened and nothing of the last few weeks other than occasional glimpses of Cente, but she has told me of your regular visits. I am most grateful," said Lira, her voice cracking with emotion.

"She has tended to you most ardently for which I have been very thankful. It is no less than you deserve. We have all been so very worried about you."

"Darius? Bennu?"

"They are safely in Damascus, but I have had no word yet as to whether he and Bennu have been successful in getting to Marcus Aemilius. No more questions now. You need to rest," I said at last.

"Indeed. Thank you for your care," said Lira as she gently squeezed my hand.

"We need you to recover. I need you by my side. Your only task is to heal and be well. I continue to pray every night for your well-being. If you should need anything at all, you need only ask."

But my words fell on deaf ears. She was already asleep but my joy in her apparent improvement could not be understated. As we gathered around the table that evening, it felt like a bit of a celebration. Now if Darius were to be successful, we would truly have something to celebrate.

"My queen, I do not wish to disturb you, but may we speak?" Zayid said as he poked his head into the library, where I could usually be found unless I was in the throne room hearing petitions and taking callers.

"Of course, Zayid you are always welcome. What is it?" I replied as I motioned for him to come in.

"May I sit?" he asked with a serious tone.

"Certainly. What troubles you Zayid?"

"It is General Masduse, my queen. I believe he is… I do not know how to say this diplomatically, but I have a concern," he replied knitting his brow.

"Speak plainly, Zayid. You are a trusted advisor, and you need not watch your words with me. Say what you will."

"He is, I believe, stealing debens meant for securing the men who will fight for you when the time comes," he said bluntly.

I leaned back in my chair, knitting my fingers together as I looked at Zayid's face, contemplating what he had just said. He seemed sincere and concerned. My level of apprehension was rising but I tried to maintain my composure.

"And what has brought you to this conclusion?" I asked skeptically.

"Some time ago, Bennu had set in place a system whereby two people are required for each large financial transaction. When the General comes to withdraw funds from the coins we keep here in the villa, Amon and I sit with him and note in the ledger how much has been given to him. We note the money's intended use. Sometimes it is for supplies or weapons. In many cases, it is to pay retainers to men who will fight when they are called upon to do so."

"But you do not think he is using the funds to secure fighters? Perhaps he just misspoke as to the intended use. Could it have gone to purchase spears or secure boats instead?" I inquired.

"No. He was very clear that the last two times he has withdrawn money it was for payments to soldiers, but one of the Viziers who works closely with him came to me in confidence to say that for every one coin the General pays out, he keeps one for himself. This means not only is he stealing, but it also means we have fewer men at our disposal than he has led us to believe," he said flatly.

"This is a most serious charge Zayid, and of great concern. He has said that we have nearly ten thousand men at the ready. What is the truth of the matter?"

"Perhaps half that my queen. It is hard to say for certain, but I have spoken to two other men who confirm the number is far less than it ought to be. I do not know how long this has been happening," he replied.

"But this makes no sense. If he is to lead us into battle, why would he want fewer men at his disposal? This feels like he would be assuring his own defeat. Why would he do that?" I said incredulously while shaking my head in disbelief.

"My queen, as General he would be safely behind the lines of fighting. His Viziers and Lieutenants would be in the forward ranks. If the engagements are unsuccessful, he would blame it on other issues while he remains safely behind the front lines, knowing he will have debens hidden away for his use if in fact the battle is lost. I do not believe he cares one way or another about the outcome if he enriches himself in the process," Zayid said, clearly despondent over this situation.

I stared at Zayid in disbelief. Once again it seemed a man I thought I could trust, who was committed to my cause, had betrayed me. While part of me wanted to break down in tears, another wanted to take my dagger to him and make him an example to deter anyone else who may consider betraying me.

"Give him no more debens. The next time he comes for funds, tell him I have asked to review all expenditures and bring him to me."

"What will you do my queen?" asked Zayid hesitantly.

"I am not sure yet, but this cannot stand. Reward the Vizier who brought this to your attention but do so quietly. Pay whatever amount you feel is appropriate, and of course, keep some for yourself," I replied as I took a handful of debens from the desk drawer and handed them to him.

"Of course, my queen and thank you. I am sorry that this has happened, but at least now we have time to address it before we fail in battle," he said as he put the coins in the small leather bag he had on a strap inside his tunic.

"Indeed. I am most grateful for the Vizier who brought this to you and for your bringing this to me. Your loyalty and support for me and my cause has been most appreciated and when we are successful in this endeavor, I will see that you are rewarded."

After Zayid's departure, I contemplated what to do with General Masduse. My father would certainly have fed him to the alligators. Cleopatra would have him beheaded in front of the entire court. This betrayal needs to be punished, there was no doubt, but it pained me. This man had broken bread with us and spoken of his commitment to my cause at every opportunity. How could we all have been so wrong about him? Would it be smarter to wait till Darius returned to act?

No, waiting was not an option. I had no idea when Darius may return, and it felt as if this were very urgent. Every day that Masduse was in charge was another day in which our needs were not being met. Zayid could perhaps take over from him until

Darius and Bennu returned. Unfortunately, he had confessed to a lack of experience in military matters in the past, which is why we had chosen Masduse. I could not do it myself while confined within these walls, and it was clear I was at risk even within the Temple, I was certainly more vulnerable outside their protection. Amon was trustworthy no doubt, but he did not strike me as a man who would instill confidence in other men in this regard. He was kind, soft-spoken, and good with numbers, but those were not qualities one looks for in a general.

It was clear I could not just let Masduse squander our money. Things were tight as it was. Even if it meant our efforts to put out retainers are stalled, that would be better than monies going into the pocket of a traitor to the cause. I needed to be sure all the guards that Masduse had placed within the villa and at the gates of the Temple were loyal to the cause... and loyalty comes with debens. I was beginning to wonder if we would have enough to fund our fight. It felt like our money was like grains of sand just slipping through my fingers. But now, my time for deliberation had quickly come to an end. Zayid said that General Masduse is expected in the morning with a request to withdraw more funds. I needed to decide what to do, and soon.

My sleep was sporadic. I tossed and turned all night. I wanted to seek Lira's counsel, but she was still so weak and tired that I felt I could not burden her with this issue. This would have to fall on me and me alone. I sought out Zayid as soon as I was dressed and told him of my decision and how I thought it best to proceed. He was in full agreement and put his part of the plan into action. All that was left now was to wait for Masduse to arrive.

"He is here, my queen," said Cente, shaking me from my

thoughts as I gazed out the window with my hands clasped behind my back.

"Thank you. I will see him in the throne room as Zayid and I agreed."

"Of course, my queen, at once," she replied before scurrying away.

I thought it best to see him there. There were always two soldiers present whenever I was in the room, so he would not be alarmed by their presence. Zayid made sure that those men were paid an additional sum which would hopefully ensure their loyalty when the moment arrived. As I settled myself onto the throne and placed the atef on my head, a calm came over me. The goddess was by my side once again. When Zayid and Masduse entered the room, I was ready.

"Queen Arsinoe, it is wonderful to see you," said Masduse as both men bowed before me.

"General, I am told you have come to withdraw more debens," I said my tone emotionless.

"Yes, my queen. We need to pay additional retainers to the men who will be joining your fight, hopefully very soon," he said with a broad smile.

"Of course, and how have those efforts gone? Have you secured the promise of many men?"

"Yes, I am very pleased with the number of men we have been able to secure," he replied, still smiling.

"Good, and how many men would you say that you have received commitments from?" I asked, my voice still cool and calm.

"It is hard to say for sure but many, many thousands. We will be ready when the time comes," Masduse replied, still smiling.

"I have done some reconciliation, and it appears that you have taken over ten thousand deben for the purpose of paying retainers. You would agree we have the promise of that many men to fight for our cause?" my voice now taking a more serious tone. Masduse was suddenly no longer smiling.

"Ah, well yes, if that is what I have withdrawn for that purpose then, hmm… Yes, I would say that is an accurate estimate," he replied, glancing between me and Zayid, but we both remained expressionless.

"So, you would be surprised if I were to tell you that I believe that the number is much smaller than you suggest?"

"I would my queen, I… it is unclear to me why the number would be less than that which corresponds to the deben I have withdrawn," he said as small beads of sweat began to form on his forehead, despite the coolness of the morning air.

"It would not be because you have held a portion of the deben for yourself that was meant for the purpose of securing men?" I replied as I motioned for the guards by the door to move closer to him.

"No! No, my queen, I do not know where you have received this information from, but I have done no such thing. I am loyal to your cause, and I have spent the monies only on those things on which we have agreed. I do not know who would cast such dispersions on me! I am not a common thief," he replied angrily as he began to reach for his sword.

"I would not…"

He sheathed his weapon but kept his hand on the hilt.

"What do you know of this?" Masduse said lashing out angrily at Zayid.

"I know what several men, including one of your own Viziers, told me of your misbehavior. I have no reason to doubt their truthfulness. They are clearly concerned about going into battle with less than an optimal number of men as a suicide operation is not what they have signed up for," replied Zayid.

"This is a plot that is driven by jealousy and greed by those who wish to be in my position, nothing more. I beg you see this for what this is, my queen," demanded Masduse as he moved toward me.

The guards behind me immediately stepped forward until they were standing on either side of me. They crossed their bronze-tipped spears in front of me so that he could come no closer.

"My queen, this is unnecessary! I would never harm you. I am committed to your cause, truly," replied Masduse striking his fist on his breastplate.

"That remains to be seen, but for now I am relieving you of command of our forces and the guards will be taking you to a holding cell until the outcome of my investigation is fully known," I said firmly as I motioned for the guards to take him.

Masduse immediately began struggling against the attempts of the guards to seize him and Zayid drew his own dagger and joined the guards who were protecting me. The two men and Masduse continued to scuffle until they were finally able to disarm him and subdue him before dragging him away, all the while shouting for all to hear of his innocence. The echoes of his cries were still ringing in my ears when the guards finally felt secure enough to retreat to their normal spot behind the throne.

"So, are you satisfied with what I have done?" I asked Zayid.

"Yes, I think it is both fair and right. I will have the Vizier and the other men I spoke with come to talk with you as we agreed. If others have something to say either in his defense or to further support the allegations of his thievery, I will bring them as well. Also, as we discussed, I will at least oversee the Viziers until Darius has returned and can assume the role of General," he said with a slight nod.

"Thank you again, Zayid. You may go."

"My queen," he replied with a bow before turning to depart.

I could only hope that Darius would be willing to take on this role. He always tried to stay so close to me, and this would take him away from the villa much of the time. Now, there was no one else I trusted. Like Ganymedes before him, he was truly devoted to me in a way that no other man has been since then. I can only hope and pray he will do as I ask. Now all I can do is wait until he returns.

Nearly a month had passed since Zayid and I confronted Masduse, and I learned that he had taken his own life in prison. He hung himself with a rope made from his tunic. I felt both relieved and saddened, but his actions only served to confirm the voracity of the claims made against him. At least I was relieved from having to decide whether he should be put to death or not. He would instead be judged by the forty-two and not by me. More importantly, word came from Darius and Bennu. They were on their way back to Ephesus, but they were not coming alone. Marc Antony was coming with them.

CHAPTER NINE

DIONYSUS INCARNATE

We worked for weeks to prepare for Marc Antony's visit, knowing everything must be perfect. Darius's letter said that before Marcus Aemilius Scaurus could lend us any support for our cause, his benefactor, Marc Antony wanted to meet me. He is well known throughout many kingdoms, having been the right hand of Julius Caesar for many years. Despite having been in and out of favor in Rome since Caesar's passing, he was still a powerful man. He had begun to style himself as the incarnation of Dionysus and he had a reputation for heavy drinking and carousing. This would be an entertaining endeavor to be sure.

I did not know what he expected to gain from meeting me in person, but if that is what it required for him to allow Marcus Aemilius to support me in this effort, so be it… Meet him I will.

"Lira, is there something we could do differently with my hair?" I asked as I gazed at my reflection thoughtfully.

"You are beautiful, my queen. You need not worry about what Marc Antony might think, but I am sure we can think of something to do that you will be happy with. I saw some beautiful shell combs at the market. I will buy one when I am in the market next," she said smiling as she brushed through my hair.

It had finally grown back to the length it was before Darius cut it off to hide it under the turban when Amin was my disguise. It was still not quite as long as it had been at its peak. It was silly of me to be concerned about my appearance, I knew. I was not meeting Antony to find a consort but rather to find a supporter, or perhaps even a benefactor. But for women, it was always true that our attractiveness mattered, even when it should not.

"Perhaps have the seamstress come too, Lira. A new tunic might be in order as well."

"Of course, my queen, I will go now," replied Lira smiling as she set down my brush on the table.

"You are a true friend," I said reaching up to squeeze her hand before she departed.

As I sat at my dressing table, I could not help but think of the events to come. If we did not get support from Syria to counteract the pretender, we would have to take more aggressive action of our own. That would further delay turning our focus to Egypt. I picked up my brush, feeling the weight of the black obsidian handle. It was shaped like an ibis and the bristles of animal hair were stiff as I ran my fingers across them. There was a melancholy hanging over me and I did not know why. Perhaps it was the absence of Darius that was wearing on me, or perhaps just the endless delays and obstacles we had faced. Sometimes I felt as if we had made no progress at all.

A messenger arrived to herald the arrival of Atony and his entourage, including Bennu and Darius. They would arrive in just a few hours. Everything was finally ready. We added more statues to the throne room, including one of Dionysus in honor of Antony, and gold leaf to the decorations on my throne. My new tunic was beautiful. Eranie, the seamstress, had truly outdone herself with the beautiful beadwork and intricate designs embroidered along the hem. It depicted scenes of gardens with birds and symbols of the gods. Even Lira was complimentary of Eranie's work and she assured me I looked more beautiful than I ever had.

Why did I feel so insecure? My insides were all a flutter, and my hands shook as I applied the kohl to my eyes. In the mirror, the dark brown eyes that were staring back at me were those of a girl, one who should be thinking about finding a husband and having children, not one who seeks to be the leader of one of the greatest countries in the world. I continued to stare deeply into the mirror, hoping to see something else. Perhaps a great ruler would stare back at me. But nothing else came, and the image remained the same. Did I really think I could convince one of the most sophisticated and worldly Romans I would ever encounter that I would be the Pharaoh of Egypt? I wondered what my father would say if he were here. Would he support me in this effort, or would he laugh and mock me for being foolish?

In the distance, I could hear the horns blowing and the cheers of the crowd. It would not be long before the entourage arrived here. This was it. There was no more time to question myself or our efforts to prepare. What was done was done.

"They are coming, my queen," said Lira as she entered my room with a broad smile.

"So they are," I replied with a sigh.

"Come now. You will be wonderful. You are the rightful Queen of Egypt. Remember that and the gods will shine down upon you. There is no need to fear," said Lira as she took one last brush through the back of my hair.

"Come. I want to see what is happening," I said grabbing her hand as I raced toward the garden wall, hopping up onto a large bench to peer over the fence.

"Be careful, my queen. The tunic might tear," said Lira as she looked at me disapprovingly.

"I need to see him before he sees me," I said, craning my neck to peer over the fence.

The streets were lined with men and women, although far more women I must say. There was a festive atmosphere. Large feathery stalks of papyrus were being waived by many people, making the crowd look like a large bird in flight. Many of the women were dressed in their finest clothes and jewels in hopes of catching Antony's eye no doubt. There were men carrying platters of fruit and nuts, holding them up high so the men on horseback could help themselves to their bounty.

At the front of the procession was a man with a trumpet and one with a drum, the beat reverberating between the walls. As the procession wound its way toward me like a snake, I craned my neck trying to find the face of the man I was about to meet. Finally, Darius and Bennu came into view, riding on either side of a man I could only assume was Marc Antony.

Darius looked as handsome as ever, even if a bit of gray was now showing up in his beard and along his temples. It made him even more alluring than I remembered, and my heart skipped a beat. Bennu looked tired and a bit overwhelmed by all of the attention. The man in the middle was clearly reveling in the spectacle. His armor of red and black dazzled in the sun and he wore on his head a wreath made of vines, much like the gold crown worn by Julius Caesar when I last saw him. A reminder to all who saw him of his closeness to the throne of Rome no doubt. He was a handsome man, in a more rugged way than Darius, although he sat lower in his saddle. It appeared that he was of smaller stature. He was stocky and well-muscled with a strong chin with his famously dark and curly hair extending to his shoulders. "Dionysus!" they cried as they hailed him, the crowds cheering. Women threw flowers at the feet of their horses.

"My queen, you must get to the throne room. They are almost at the gate," said Lira as she tugged on my sleeve.

I jumped down carefully and hurried to the throne room. She was right. It would be a misstep to appear to keep Antony waiting. I doubted he had ever waited for a woman in his life. I heard the drumbeat and trumpet just outside the gate and those waiting with me in the throne room parted to make way for those who were about to join us. As I took my place on the dais in front of the throne, I could feel my heart pounding. I still failed to comprehend why the thought of meeting this man had me so flustered, but whatever it was, I was about to face it head-on.

"All hail Marcus Antonius," I heard a man ring out from the entrance of the villa and a trumpet blow a long note which echoed through the halls.

A bit of laughter tried to bubble up as I worked to maintain my composure. All this pomp and circumstance for a mere man entering a villa. As the rightful Queen of Egypt, I did not put so much into my arrivals and departures as this man seemed to do. It said a great deal about him and his ego. Out of the corner of my eye, I could see Lira thinking the same thing. We dare not make eye contact as we could both dissolve into a fit of laughter if we were not careful. The last thing I desired was for this man to see me as a mere girl, one not capable of controlling herself, let alone a powerful country. I dug my fingernails sharply into my palm. The momentary discomfort helped me to set my countenance to one more befitting this occasion.

Darius and Bennu entered first and each paid his tribute before stepping to either side of the throne, turning to face the entrance. There, at last, the figure of Marc Antony appeared. As I had suspected, he was of shorter stature than Darius, but still cut an imposing figure. His armor was so highly polished it practically emanated its own light, and his features were chiseled. His Roman nose and strong chin formed a handsome face, and his thick black curly hair was shiny and carefully arranged. It was clear he was a warrior with his arms and calves heavily muscled. His skin was dark brown from months on end in the field of battle. But he was also something else… vain. As he walked toward me, there was no hint of an expression on his face. As he drew closer, I could see a bit of a sparkle in his eyes. Rather than reassuring me, it sharpened my skepticism.

"Princess Arsinoe," he said with a slight bow.

"Queen Arsinoe," Lira responded before I could.

"Not yet…" he replied with a wry smile.

"The High Priest of this Temple, on whose grounds you now stand, declared me the rightful Queen of Egypt and I have been blessed by the goddess Artemis. You will address me as Queen," I replied with a sardonic smile of my own.

"As you say," he replied with a deferential nod.

"I am pleased to welcome you to Ephesus, and I hope your journey was a pleasant one. It is my honor to receive you," I said as I sat down upon the throne.

"After being regaled as to your beauty and accomplishments by your emissaries I felt it was best if I came to see you for myself. I believe I am a very good judge of character," he said as he looked me up and down.

I was acutely aware it was not my character that Antony was assessing, but rather my appearance. I could feel the heat rising in my cheeks. Darius peeked over at me to gauge my response, and I could see him stand up a bit straighter as if to further reinforce the height difference between himself and Antony. Was he feeling jealous? He had no need. Despite Antony's proximity to the power of Rome, he was no more of royal blood than Darius. I had no intention of being seduced by what many claimed to be his considerable charm.

"I am sure you will not find my character lacking. I am a Ptolemy, and we have ruled Egypt for hundreds of years. Successfully, I might add."

"Of course. I meant no offense," he replied, looking a bit defensive.

"We have planned a banquet tonight in your honor. In the meantime, I will have you shown to your quarters as I am sure that you would like to recover from your long journey," I said gesturing to one of my aides who appeared quickly at his side.

"Yes, thank you. I look forward to the banquet tonight,

and to getting to talk with you privately," he said looking at me intently.

This man was a rouge no doubt, but I knew I must tread carefully. If I appeared to rebuke him, it may well spell the failure of my efforts to discredit the pretender. I needed his support, but there was a limit to what I was willing to pay to get it. My journey to this place had not been an easy one, but my virtue had never been in question. I would not let it be now.

"Of course. We will have plenty of time to talk," I said as I gestured toward the door.

With a slight bow, he was gone, along with the dozen or so men in his entourage. The throne room quickly cleared as servants and aides moved on to the next challenge at hand. Hosting a banquet of this size was no easy feat.

"Bennu! It is so good to see you again," I said as I rose to embrace him.

"It is good to be home, my queen, and it pleases me to see that you are well. I was disheartened to learn of the attack on you and Lira in our absence, but I am relieved to see that you are both well. Also, the unpleasantness with General Masduse brought me much sadness. I thought of him as a friend, a true and loyal compatriot, and for his betrayal, my sincerest apology."

"Bennu, you have nothing to apologize for. The actions of General Masduse were his and his alone. I am most grateful for Zayid, and his loyalty to the cause saved us from further difficulty. What damage he has done can still be overcome, but it will take us some time to recover. Zayid is doing very well in his efforts to recruit more soldiers, and I do not doubt with your return our success is assured."

"You flatter me, my queen, but know that my commitment to your ascendency has never wavered. I will continue to be of service to you in any way that I can," Bennu replied before excusing himself, leaving me at last alone with Darius.

"Come with me," I said, leading Darius by the hand to my bed chamber where I knew we would not be seen or overheard by others.

Once we were alone, I embraced him. It was a joy and a relief to have him back with me once again. He held on to me tightly and stroked my hair as I lay my head on his chest.

"You should have sent word about the attack on you and Lira I learned of it only after we were already on our way back. I am glad there were others here to attend to you and that we were able focus on the task you had set for us, but still . My relief at learning you were relatively unharmed was profound, but I know how much anguish Lira's injuries must have caused you. I am sorry I was not here to protect you," he said as he kissed me on top of my head.

"I have not prayed that hard since you were washed overboard, and we nearly lost you. The gods have been good to me on more than one occasion. Lira and I were both very lucky to have escaped with our lives. It was a surprise to me that Cleopatra did not respect the sanctity of the Temple. It was something for which I was not prepared. I did not believe she would attack me inside the Temple walls but would instead try to find a way to lure me out of its protection. It speaks to how low she will stoop," I said shaking my head, still in disbelief of the events of that day.

"It speaks to how much of a threat she believes you are as well," added Darius.

"True. If she thought that I was of no consequence to her, she would never have sent someone into the Temple to assassinate me. I am sure she rues the day Caesar decided to send me here rather than execute me as she wanted."

"She will not stop, you know," he said as he finally released me from his embrace.

"I know. Even the assassin said as much with his final breath. But it cannot cause me to falter in my endeavors. If she is successful, then it is as the gods wish it to be, but if I have breath I must continue. But tell me of Antony. He seemed to be mocking me in some way. Why did he want to come here?"

"No, he was not mocking you, my queen, it is simply his way. He is rather full of himself, and he always wants to be the most important person in the room, I am afraid. It is his stated intention to get to know you to determine if you are worthy of his support. He is, if anything, intimidated by you and is hoping it does not show," replied Darius with a smirk.

"It does not feel that way. If he questions my right to rule, why did he even come here? If we do not counter the claims of the pretender soon, I fear his support will grow and our momentum will be lost. The deceit of General Masduse has already cost us dearly and I genuinely fear we can endure no more," I said, my voice cracking under the strain of the emotion that suddenly washed over me.

"My queen, you have come so far, and we have already endured so much. Please do not give up hope now," replied Darius. His voice was concerned.

"Why does it matter to you? If I gave up my designs on the throne, perhaps we could…" I dare not say what I was thinking.

"We could, yes… but could you be happy? Would being my wife, the mother of my children, be enough for you? Truly could you say that it would?" said Darius a hint of anger, or perhaps it was frustration coloring his words.

I could feel his eyes boring into me, but I stared at the floor, unable or unwilling to meet his gaze. Why did I even suggest that I might be able to give up on my cause? I knew deep down nothing short of taking the throne would fulfill me. Surely it was just my insecurity that caused me to speak in this way, but I could see the suggestion of it gave hurt him deeply. It was if I was offering him a prize only to snatch it away should he try to reach for it.

"I am sorry," I replied finally meeting his gaze. I could see the pain in his eyes. It was pain I had caused him with my careless words, and there was no way to undo what I had just done.

"Please do not suggest to me that which you are unwilling to do. It only serves to pain my heart, and it is a pain I do not know if I can continue to bear. I am loyal to you now and always but…," he replied before simply turning and walking away. He left me stunned into silence.

The tears slid slowly down my cheeks, hot on my skin, as I wiped them away one by one. He was right. I had been cruel to even suggest that I would abandon my quest for the throne. Now my heedlessness caused him great suffering, and he was hurt by my words, having not been back in the villa for a single day. I wanted desperately to run after him, but the banquet would be starting at any moment, and I could not let myself be distracted. If my plea failed to impress Antony, then we would likely be done. I could not let that happen.

As Ra's bright glow disappeared below the garden wall, I

finished applying the final touches to my face. Lira helped place the beautiful gold and white double crown upon my head. It was called the pschent sekhemty. It symbolized the unification of Upper and Lower Egypt. It was a regal headpiece, and I sincerely hoped that when Antony saw me wearing it, he would recognize at once that I was the rightful and crowned Queen of Egypt. I could feel both the weight of the crown and of this moment bearing down on me, but I was ready.

"You are beautiful, my queen," said Lira as she stepped back to admire her work.

"Thank you," I replied, forcing a smile.

"Is something wrong?"

"Ah, Lira, you know me too well! I had an unpleasant conversation with Darius, of my own making I am afraid. I am afraid I have hurt him deeply, and it weighs on me," I said with a sigh.

"I am sure you did not mean to be hurtful. He will calm down and come to understand, as he always does," replied Lira soothingly.

"Maybe not. He is feeling very wounded, and it should not be assumed that he will continue to simply recover each time I say something insensitive to him."

"He is devoted to you beyond measure. There is no doubt of that, but now you must turn your attention to Antony. Darius will have to wait," said Lira in that motherly tone she often took with me despite being my junior.

"Yes, you are right. Is everything ready?"

"It is. Cente has outdone herself. The banquet has been set up in the garden and it is resplendent beyond imagination," said Lira with a huge grin.

"I am sure that cost a great deal. Let us hope it will be a good investment," I replied rising from my chair.

Lira was right. Cente had created a magical place that I was sure would impress the worldly Antony. Lanterns hung from every tree and the light of a hundred candles danced across the scene, painting everything in their glow. A large quantity of brightly covered pillows created seating around a large low table that was overflowing with delicacies of every kind. Fruits, nuts, and sweetmeats were piled high on bronze platters that gleamed in the candlelight. Flowers of bright pink and ruby red spilled out of vases, perfuming the cool evening air. It was magnificent to be sure. In the corner, a woman was playing a lyre. The notes of the music wafted through the air and echoed off the garden wall. Ten or fifteen servants were putting the final touches on the scene. They finished just in time, as the sound of Antony and his entourage arriving whispered out into the night.

This time their approach was heralded not by the sound of clinking armor, but instead by the soft leather of their sandals padding on the tile floor. Bennu was at the front of the group and dressed in his finest robe. It was one I had only seen him wear once before, at my coronation. Zayid was on his left and Antony was on his right, along with his aide who was a man named Vionenza. All the men seemed to have dressed in their finest tunics, and it was a sight to behold indeed. There were also a few of the more important men of Ephesus and their wives that Bennu had invited to join us. They lit up the night in their brightly colored tunics and shimmering golden jewels. I purposely asked Bennu not to include any single women as I did not want Antony's attention elsewhere. I waited with Lira at the entrance of the garden to greet our guests, the tableau behind me forming a perfect backdrop that was sure to impress.

"My queen, you look especially beautiful tonight," said Bennu as he bowed in front of me.

"My queen," Zayid said, adding his military salute.

"Princess Arsinoe. Ah, rather, Queen Arsinoe, should I say," said Antony, although he did not bow or offer his tribute.

"Good evening. Welcome Consul Antony and all our esteemed guests. It is our pleasure to have you join us," I said with a slight nod.

"You wear the crown well, I must say," said Antony with what felt like a genuine smile.

"It is my destiny. The Ptolemies have worn the crown of Egypt for over three hundred years, and we will continue to rule Egypt for a thousand more," I replied with a demure smile.

"I had the pleasure of knowing your father. He was a learned and respected man, and someone that Caesar thought highly of," he replied.

"It was mutual. My father spoke often of his admiration for Caesar and all he had accomplished in Rome, and of course of his support when my sister Bereneice tried to usurp him on the throne."

"Yes, you Ptolemies do seem to fight among yourselves, do you not?" remarked Antony, surely not expecting a reply.

"Please come. Let us sit," I said, gesturing to the area at the center of the table that had been reserved for Antony and me.

"May I?" asked Antony as he held out his arm.

I rested my hand lightly on his forearm as he led me to the cushions. I could feel how muscular his arms were, and as he helped me down to the pillow, his strength became even more obvious. Lira gently removed my crown, replacing it with a circlet of beautiful gold leaves set with emeralds. It was the stone only allowed to be worn by the pharaoh. It did not escape my attention that he looked at it intently, perhaps studying its worth… or maybe mine? As the other men and women settled in, I realized Darius was not here but there was nothing to be done about that now.

A line of men appeared from the villa carrying jug after jug of wine. As they poured, the conversation and laughter commenced. Voices rang out through the air, intertwining with the music of the lyre. We would not talk business now. First, we would drink and then we would eat. Once the pleasantries were done, we could talk of more serious things. There was a celebratory atmosphere with plenty of wine and even some exotic animals were brought in to be paraded around from guest to guest. Antony regaled us with stories of his many military victories. I found myself relaxing and even enjoying his company. He was attentive and polite, nothing like the roguish brute I was expecting. He was not as well-read as me, but an educated man who had learned a great deal through his travels and his limited formal studies.

"So, all they could do was take off their clothes as we had ordered and walk naked back to their village," roared Antony draining his goblet of wine… again.

Everyone laughed and applauded after yet another story of prowess and conquest, where Antony was always the star. It was clear he was charming my guests as well as me. Zayid seemed the least impressed, seldom smiling or laughing at his jokes. He seemed to always have a watchful eye on Antony as if waiting for him to do something that might require his intervention. Without Darius here, Zayid took it upon himself to see my safety. Perhaps that is why he was so watchful. Thankfully no one inquired as to Darius's whereabouts which saved me from the embarrassment of having to say that I did not know why he was not here. Only Lira noted his absence. Beyond that, she said nothing. I am sure she assumed his absence was related to our earlier disagreement.

"Consul, how are your children and your wife, Fulvia? Are they well?"

"They are indeed. Rome is a wonderful city with much to do, and magnificent food and wine," replied Antony.

"I did not find it so… welcoming," I said sardonically.

"Ah, yes. I suppose that is true. My apologies for what you endured, but Caesar was under the spell of your sister Cleopatra. You are very fortunate that he did not execute you as she had asked but acquiesced instead to the wishes of the Senate. Clearly, he would regret that decision were he alive today."

"Please take no offense in my next remark, but Egypt is to be ruled by Egyptians, not by Romans. We have ruled ourselves for centuries. Had my sister not entered into this forbidden liaison with Julius Caesar, there would be no reason for me to object to her rule, but it is unmistakably written in our laws. Her bastard son Caesarion cannot ascend to the throne of Egypt, yet it is clear his ascension is what she intends."

"Yet you have no children to succeed you should you become Queen," said Antony, cocking his head to one side as he looked at me questioningly.

"It is true. I have not married and have no children, but that will be remedied as soon as I am seated on the throne in

Alexandria. You need not fear for our line of succession if that is your concern," I replied reassuringly.

"Rome would not want to see unrest in Egypt as we rely on your grain as much as you do. Civil war could disrupt farming and shipping, and the region could ill afford that," he replied, moving a bit closer so our conversation would not be easily heard by others.

"War is coming to Alexandria. I have no choice but to take the throne by force, but I assure you we will do our best to limit its impact on the citizens of Egypt, who by most accounts, would prefer me on the throne instead of my sister," I said quietly.

"I have met your sister on several occasions. The first time when she was only fourteen, and of course many times in Caesar's company. Cleopatra has done an admirable job of leading Egypt by all accounts, and without a man by her side," replied Antony.

"She and Caesar's forces chased my older brother Ptolemy XIII into the Nile where he drowned. She has outright murdered my youngest brother with poison feigning it as illness. Now she pretends that her son is the rightful heir, and she has even named him Ptolemy XV. It is by her own hand that she lacks a Ptolemy male to rule with her."

"This man in Syria who claims to be your older brother. You do not believe it is him?"

"No. I know my brother. Had he survived our first attempt to remove Cleopatra from the throne, he would not have given up so easily. He would never hide for years with no word of his survival. If he had lived, we would have learned of it long before now, I do not doubt it," I replied vehemently.

"Some seem to believe it," Antony replied with a shrug.

"It is a lie. If they are willing to believe it, it is for their own nefarious ambitions. To put a pretender, a lackey, on the throne of Egypt to be controlled by those who have put him there would be unwise. Our coffers are full of coins, precious gems, and grain. I am sure many men of ambition would do anything to have control over such riches."

"And you will not be a pawn of the men who help to put you on the throne?" he whispered in my ear.

I looked at him. Our faces were only a hands width apart. His eyes were dark, a window into his ka through which one could clearly see. This was a man of ambition who lusted for power. Perhaps we were not so different from each other after all, I suddenly realized.

"I am the pawn of no man or woman. Those who help me to take what is rightfully mine will be rewarded, as is right, but do not think for one moment that if you help me I will do your bidding in the future. A good relationship with Rome is a priority and I hope we will find once again the days of mutual respect and support for one another. But be clear, Egypt will bend its knee to no one. Nor will I."

Antony leaned back a bit, studying my face as if trying to judge for himself the voracity of my words. I remained motionless, my face revealing nothing to him of what I was thinking. Unexpectedly, he leaned in so close to me that his lips were touching my ear as he spoke.

"Well then, Queen Arsinoe, what would my reward for helping you be?" he said huskily.

I tried not to wince. I had anticipated that this moment would come. Antony was a notorious philanderer and Bennu and Lira had both warned me that he would try to take my honor. My sister had made a grave mistake by giving herself to Julius Caesar and I did not intend to make the same one. Still, I must choose my words carefully. A sip or two of wine gave me a moment to think.

"What is the reward you would seek in exchange for helping me to discredit the pretender?"

"Well, you said it yourself. You will find a husband to rule alongside you. Perhaps that could be me?"

"And what would your wife think of that?"

"Those… complications, if you will, can be easily managed," he replied with a slightly sinister tone.

"You flatter me Antony, but as we have already discussed it is the Roman intrusion that I am railing against. To take a Roman husband and make him Pharaoh with me would make me no better than Cleopatra. It would surely start the civil war you yourself said should be avoided," I replied.

"Ah, well, there was no harm in trying," responded Antony as he leaned back and took a long drink of his wine before slamming his goblet on the table. He leaned in again, his voice now nearly a low growl in my ear, his breath hot on my face. His eyes were beginning to glaze over.

"I cannot help but notice you speak of war so easily for one who has not experienced it firsthand. Taking the life of another is a heady potion to be sure. You have never heard the cracking of bones and wails of pain and fear filling the air. The blood sticks to everything it touches and then becomes covered with sand, caking itself to your skin. When you are fighting hand-to-hand, each of you on the brink of death… one feels oddly alive as though time stands still. You do not yet know which way you will fall. War is not something you should be in a hurry to bring to Egypt, even for your own benefit," he rasped before leaning back into his cushion.

I motioned for one of the servants to bring more wine.

"War is inevitable, but the thought of it is not something I relish. I hope that with the right preparations, it will be swift and merciful. But I will not hesitate to do what must be done. Surely you must see that by now," I said, looking at him thoughtfully.

"Yes. It is clear to me that you will do as you must. I see a bit of myself in you, especially my younger self when what I craved was the glory and honor of fighting and winning. But also like me, the thing you crave the most is respect. I cannot help but admire that, especially in a woman as young and beautiful as yourself," he replied as he raised his glass to me.

"So, we understand each other?"

"I think we do," he replied.

Finally, the moment had passed. We settled back into more casual conversation, and I breathed a sigh of relief. Still, Antony had not actually committed to helping me discredit the pretender. It was a discussion that still must be had, but not tonight.

"You knew my sister Berenice?" I asked, trying to delicately change the subject.

"No, I never had the pleasure. Her last husband, Archelaus, was a man I counted among my friends, having met him during my time in Antioch. I once did him a favor, getting him an audience with Proconsul Gabinius, when I led his calvary against Alexander in Judaea."

"You were with Gabinius when he marched to Egypt to restore my father after Berenice's failed attempt to keep him off the throne that was his birthright?" I asked.

"I was, but I spent little time in Alexandria and none in the palace. I hear it is a beautiful place," replied Antony as he leaned toward me, spilling a bit of his wine.

It was becoming more and more obvious that Antony was drunk. His stories, which had been a staple of the evening, became more vulgar and boisterous as the night wore on. It was all I could do to put on a pleasant face as Antony frequently leaned his head on my shoulder or put his arm around me in a much too familiar way. Zayid was watching intently but I shook my head no when it appeared he might intervene. This I could bear.

Finally, our guests began excusing themselves and eventually, two of Antony's men steered him toward his room and off to bed. Only Bennu, Lira, and Zayid lingered with me.

"So, are you satisfied that Antony will help you?" asked Zayid.

I sighed.

"To be honest I am not wholly sure. He seems amenable, but he did not say directly that he would, nor did he say he would not. He proposed that I consider marrying him when I get on the throne."

"That is not a surprise. I must say, he is a man who seeks out power and wealth at every opportunity. He was very much wounded by Caesar's failure to name him successor and he has been trying to best Octavian ever since," said Bennu.

"That is a laughable proposal," said Lira bitterly. "He would ask you to do the very thing that has caused you to seek to take the crown from Cleopatra. He has no understanding of Egypt or her people."

"No, I do not suppose that he does," I replied reluctantly.

"So, what shall we do now?" asked Bennu.

"When is he planning on leaving?"

"He had said he would only stay for a short time as he stopped here only on his way to another destination, so it could be as early as the day after tomorrow. He will need at least a full day to get his retinue together," replied Zayid.

"I will speak to him directly before he leaves, but for now I am exhausted as I suspect all of you are as well. We should retire for the night. Bennu, please express my sincere appreciation to Cente and Amon. The evening could not have been more resplendent. If Antony decides he will not support my cause, it will not be because of any failure to impress him and provide a royal welcome."

"Of course," said Bennu with a bow as he helped me up from the floor.

Lira helped me remove my jewels and the kohl from around my eyes before retiring to her room. I lay in bed for only a few minutes before easily drifting off to sleep. The cool breeze helped to soothe my weary body.

What was that? Suddenly, I found myself startled awake. A noise had awakened me, but in my slumber, I could not identify the sound or where it had come from. I sat up in my bed peering out into the inky darkness. As my eyes adjusted to the dimness, I looked carefully around my room for the source of the noise, but seeing nothing, laid back down to try and sleep once again. I heard the noise once again. This time, I bolted upright next to my bed, reaching for the dagger that I kept under my pillow. There was someone nearby. I was sure of it, but I still saw nothing. My heart was pounding in my chest, and it was all I could do to keep my breath quiet.

I thought about calling out, but Lira was the only person close enough to hear me. The last thing I wanted to do was subject her to another attack. I would have to manage this alone. The dagger felt heavy in my hand, the hilt smooth and cool to the touch as I moved quietly along the wall, keeping my back protected so no one could come from behind. It was quiet. The only sound was the rhythmic flapping of the drapes hanging near the archway to the garden. I must have been dreaming, or perhaps one of the many Temple cats had been making his way out to the garden. I shook my head, annoyed for being so easily frightened. No one would dare make a move against me with all these people in the villa. Most of Antony's faction was staying here. You would have to be a fool to come for me with so many nearby.

Finally, I put the dagger back under the pillow and climbed back into bed, pulling the linen covers up over my shoulders. I settled back down to try and sleep once more. Based on the light from the moon and the shadows it cast into my room, I knew there were a few more hours of darkness before I would have to rise.

"You are even more beautiful when you sleep," said a man's voice in my ear as a hand clamped over my mouth.

I tried to sit up but the weight of his body against my chest held me in place. As my eyes adjusted, I made out the figure of a man sitting next to me on the bed.

"You think you are so special. The Queen of Egypt, you say," he said with a bit of a laugh as I struggled against his grip.

My mind was racing. As I looked more carefully at his face, I realized he was with Antony's retinue. He sat next to Antony at the banquet, but his name would not come to me in my panic. Had my half-sister paid him to murder me? Was this some plot on Antony's part to humiliate and subdue me?

"Do not cry out. I am warning you. If you are quiet, you might live, but should you scream, I will kill you," he whispered ominously as he pulled back the linen covers.

I realized at once that murder was not his primary objective. He was not here to kill me. He was here to defile me. I wanted to scream but the look in his eyes told me he was telling the truth when he said that he would kill me, and his hands were big and strong. Surely, he could choke the life out of me easily and quickly.

His hands were rough against my legs as he pushed my tunic up to my waist. He positioned himself on top of me, forcing his knee between my legs while keeping one hand over my mouth. He struggled to get his tunic up out of the way with just one hand and I felt his grip lessen just a bit.

I did not hesitate. I twisted my body so that I could free my hand to reach for the dagger. But before I could act he cried out and fell forward, his entire weight bearing down on me. Blood was spilling out of his mouth covering my hair and face, hot and sticky as I turned away from the ruby red river that flowed out of him.

"Are you hurt?" Antony asked as he pulled the man's body off me and onto the floor, a large dagger in his back now visible in the moonlight.

"No, I am not hurt," I replied in a voice just above a whisper.

"Lira, come at once," he called out as he helped me to pull down my tunic before lifting me from the bed and carrying me to a nearby chaise.

"Arsinoe!" screamed Lira as she came quickly into my room. She had a torch in one hand and a dagger in the other.

Lira shrieked when she saw me covered with blood and immediately turned to face Antony her dagger pointed at him.

"No, not him. He saved me," I rasped out struggling to speak.

"It is not her blood. Take her to your room and help her to bathe and to change. I will get Bennu in a moment."

Lira looked at him cautiously, but now her gaze followed the trail of blood to the man lying dead on the floor next to the bed. I could see her finally understand what had happened.

"Arsinoe, I am here. Let me help you," she said as she dropped her dagger onto my bed. She grabbed a linen cloth off my dressing table to wipe the blood from my face.

"Can you walk, or shall I carry you?" asked Antony.

"I can walk," I said quietly.

"Go then with Lira. We will take care of this. I am sorry, Arsinoe. Please know that this man, this man I trusted, was not acting at my behest but purely for his own carnal desires." He bowed slightly before he headed off to find Bennu.

I walked slowly with Lira to her room, leaving a trail of blood droplets behind me as I went. Soon the whole villa was alive with voices. While the men tried to keep their voices low, there were some angry exchanges. Their words were muffled and unclear to me. I felt like I was still sleeping, that somehow this was a nightmare from which I would soon wake. Cente joined us and between the two of them, they helped me into the small bath in Lira's room. They washed my hair over and over, trying to remove every trace of this man from my hair and skin.

They had just finished getting me out of the bath and into a chair when Amon came to the door. He motioned for Cente, then he whispered something to her and handed her a vial. She nodded. I looked past him over his shoulder to see two men carrying the body of the man who had attacked me, now wrapped in my bed linens.

"Here. Drink this, my queen," said Cente as she handed me the vial. It was a draught Bennu had prepared.

Antony appeared suddenly next to Amon in the doorway between my room and Lira's. "Put her to bed in here. It will be a few more hours before her room is as it was before," he said.

"I thank you sincerely. I do not know what would have happened had you not arrived when you did," I said as I looked up at him from the chair.

"I woke to find that he was not in his bed next to mine, and I became suspicious when he did not return within a few minutes, but I never imagined..." he trailed off.

"We are so grateful for your intervention," said Lira.

He acknowledged our thanks with a nod and left without another word. I could see that he was feeling awkward, embarrassed even. I was not sure. The draught was already starting to take effect, and my thoughts were a jumble. My head was pounding.

As I lay down in Lira's bed, I could not help but wonder if Antony was telling the truth. Had he saved me, or had he been watching and waiting to be sure the deed would be done, but when I seized my own dagger, he knew the man must be silenced so as not to reveal their plot. My mind felt as if it were underwater. Everything was muffled and distant and soon my body would follow my mind into a deep and dreamless sleep.

CHAPTER TEN

POWER UNLEASHED

The sun was high in the sky by the time I awoke. My head felt heavy as though it was filled with flax and rocks, but I managed to sit up.

"You are awake," said Lira, looking up from her embroidery.

"I do not suppose my memories of last night were fabricated in my dreams?" I asked hesitantly, already knowing the answer.

"No, sadly they were not. How are you feeling? Do you need the physician to come back? He was here to look in on you this morning, but he chose not to wake you. He left another draught should you need it."

"No, I am fine, mostly," I replied as I knit my brow, my voice tinged with worry and confusion.

Lira came and sat next to me on the bed. I drew my knees up to my chest and sat up, leaning back against the wall as she pulled the linens up around me. I could see the worry in her eyes.

"Has Darius come?"

"No, I have not seen him," Lira replied.

"And Antony, he is still here?"

"Yes, he came by with Bennu a few hours ago to see how you were doing but they did not want to wake you. He asked me to come and find him when you were awake. Would you like me to fetch him?"

"No, no not yet. I am still trying to make sense of what happened last night. I heard a noise but saw nothing, then again… still nothing. Just a while after I went back to sleep, he… that man…"

"Vionenza was his name. He was Antony's aide-de-camp," said Lira.

"Yes, Vionenza. I did not recognize him at first but he was suddenly next to me with his hand over my mouth so I could not scream. He said something about my being beautiful. I thought he had been sent by Cleopatra to kill me, but it was clear my death was not his first thought," I said wearily.

"Antony said last night that he became suspicious when he woke and the man was absent from the bed next to his and that when he did not shortly return, he went to look for him," said Lira.

"But why look for him in my room? What reason would he have to think that the man, this Vionenza, would be in my bed chamber?"

"I heard Antony talking to Bennu in the garden this morning while you slept. This man had raped and killed another woman, the sister of one of the other men in Antony's camp."

"He should have been charged with the woman's rape and murder and executed! Why did that not happen?" I said incredulously.

"Rape is not the same crime in Rome as it is in Egypt. He alleged that he merely seduced her and that her death was accidental. Her brother challenged him and was killed in the altercation. Then there were no more male members of her family to prosecute any charges and no one alive, save Vionenza himself, to say what had happened. It sounded to me like Antony was genuinely remorseful about what occurred last night, but you must judge for yourself," said Lira.

"He said if I were quiet, he would let me live. Perhaps he assumed that he would not be prosecuted for rape here either and that he could have his way with me with no consequences."

"It chills me to my very ka to think of what could have happened to you. Now there will be a guard at your door every night. Bennu told me this morning. We should have done it before, at least when strangers are here in the villa," said Lira regretfully.

"It is past. While I was genuinely fearful for both my life and my honor, no harm has been done. I agree that a guard is probably wise. We think we are protected here, safe from those who wish me harm, but you and I already know that Cleopatra will not hesitate to come for me inside these walls. The villa is not a sacred place. We must all be more careful," I said as I squeezed her hand in mine.

"Would you like to sleep a bit more or can I get you something to eat?" asked Lira as she brushed the hair out of my eyes.

"No, I can sleep no more. I need to speak with Antony. I must look into his eyes for myself to judge his truthfulness in this matter. Help me get dressed and have a Cente bring something for me to eat. As soon as I am ready, I will go to the throne room.

Then you can find Antony and have him brought to me there. Make sure that the guards are there. I no longer wish to be left alone with any man save Bennu, Amon, Zayid, or Darius."

"Of course. Would you like to stay here or return to your chamber? It has been cleaned and Bennu had a new bed brought in this morning. Cente has been working since the first light to make sure that no traces of the horror of last night remain, but if you prefer, you can stay in here with me," said Lira.

"You are dear to me, and Cente too. Please be sure to thank her for her efforts, but I will return to my own chamber. This man will not impact me any more than he already has.

As I dressed and brushed through my hair, I could not help but play the events of last night over and over in my mind. What had seemed so sharp in my mind a few hours ago was now hazier, but still. How long had Vionenza been in my room? Was he the noise that had first awakened me? It must have been him, just waiting for the right time to pounce on me like the cat does to the mouse.

In a short time, I had finished dressing and eaten. Lira walked with me to the throne room, leaving me there with the guards before going off to find Antony.

I felt as though everyone we passed was staring at me, wondering perhaps what had really happened last night. Presumably, only those close to me were aware of what occurred, but anyone in the villa last night must surely have known that there was a commotion of some sort. The guards, when not on duty, sleep in the villa next door. Bennu had rented it out for them some time ago. Conceivably they would not be aware, but still. Perhaps it was my discomfort with the events of last night that made me feel as though people were staring and not because of some knowledge as to what might have occurred.

I sat on the throne waiting patiently for Antony to arrive. My anxiousness at that moment made it seem like a long time, but it was probably only a few minutes.

"Consul Antony, my queen," said Lira as she entered the throne room with Antony following closely behind her.

"Thank you, Lira. You may leave us," I said, trying to sound in control of my thoughts and emotions. Inside my head it felt like leaves swirling in the wind, tumbling across the ground and I could not get them to stop.

"Queen Arsinoe, I am very pleased to see you up and looking well," said Antony with an uncharacteristically shy smile.

"I have you to thank for that. I was very fortunate that you came into my bed chamber when you did. I still do not understand why you considered looking for your man Vionenza in my room."

"After the banquet, several of my men and I sat up drinking and talking in our room for a bit longer. Vionenza went on and on about how beautiful you are. Given his proclivities, I thought maybe he may try to seduce you when he was not in our quarters," said Antony.

"I would not call what he did seduction," I replied sardonically.

"No, you are right. For that, you have my sincere apology," he replied with a deep bow.

"Why did you kill him? You could have simply pulled him off of me," I observed as I looked at him closely, trying to gauge his thoughts.

"It is true, I could have. Even if he had not... completed his act, his attempt at doing so to someone in your position and of your status… it was obvious to me that the most severe punishment was warranted. I acted quickly but without regret."

He never blinked, which my father always said was a tell-tale sign someone was lying. His words seemed sincere, and his explanation made sense, but still in my mind flowed this underlying current of suspicion that I could not quash.

"I did not want to spoil the banquet with business, but we did not conclude our conversation as to whether I can expect your help in putting down this pretender in Syria. Is it your intention to do so?"

"I will. My travels take me farther afield, but I will send one of my men back with a message to Marcus Aemilius. I will tell him to begin immediately to discredit the pretender and to discourage others from supporting his efforts. They will risk my ire if they do, which they know can be quite dangerous."

"You have my sincere appreciation. When I am on the throne of Egypt, I hope that we can be allies," I replied with a faint smile.

"I am hopeful we can be more than allies. Partners, perhaps?"

"What business might that be?" I asked warily.

"I know a very wealthy Roman benefactor. His name is Consus Planidus he is a senior member of the Senate, a patrician, and a major landholder. He would like to expand his ability to import gold to Rome, which is something Egypt has a great deal of. Perhaps he could partner with you to increase your exports to Rome?" asked Antony.

"Why would I be interested in increasing Egypt's exports to Rome?"

"Because you need money to fund your war to regain the throne. Consus has money to spend. If he helps you, then you help him, and he helps me with the Senate. It works to everyone's benefit. I could make the introduction if you are interested."

I leaned back on the throne, contemplating his proposal for a moment. Egypt already traded with Rome, so there would be nothing objectionable there. Perhaps it would not be as much gold as they would like, but I could do something to increase exportation. We could certainly use more debens. After General Masduse's betrayal, we were woefully behind in our conscription efforts and more coins would certainly help. My father sought financial help from the Romans during his life, so I thought he would have supported this alliance.

"Yes, I believe that would be beneficial for all of us indeed," I replied at last.

"Good. I will send a messenger to him to see how he would like to proceed. Undoubtedly, he would also like to come to meet you as I have. He will be impressed by you. I certainly have been," said Antony with a broad smile.

"It has been my pleasure to meet you, and I thank you again for your support. I assume you are leaving soon?"

"Yes, we will leave at first light. I have more business to attend to, but I do hope our paths will cross again, Queen Arsinoe."

"I am sure that they will," I said with a nod of my head.

The next few days passed in a bustle of activity. Feeding the number of people now in the villas was a monumental task and it seemed like there were always many people around with whom I was not familiar. This made me wary. Zayid himself had chosen a man to be with me whenever I desired to walk to the temple to pray, or just to be nearby when I was in the garden. This was in addition to the men always in the throne room when I received visitors. There was a man now stationed at my bed chamber door each night, also chosen by Zayid. These were men he would trust with his own life and now with mine.

Antony has finally departed, and I did not see him again after our discussion in the throne room. He was a man who would put his own interests above those of anyone else, always. It would be wise to keep him at arm's length and to always be watchful. Just as the few bruises I sustained during Vionenza's attack have faded, so has my concern that Antony was involved. He was ambitious to be sure, but he is not a fool and only a fool would have suborned that attack.

Darius had not returned to the villa for many days, and Zayid has told me that he has taken on the task of traveling throughout the small villages and towns to enlist soldiers. He is not likely to return any time soon. He did send a letter expressing his thankfulness that I was not harmed in the attack and he offered to return from his duties in the field but I assured him he should continue his efforts as they are crucial I knew our relationship must change as the throne drew more and more within my reach. I would soon have to turn my attention to finding a royal husband. Lira did try to find some royal blood in Darius's family, but to no avail, as I had suspected. While he is high born, he is not noble, and as the Pharaoh only royal blood would suffice.

For centuries, the Ptolemies have married within the family but as there were no remaining brothers for me to marry, I would have to widen my search to consider royal men from other, smaller countries. It would have to be those countries that were subservient to Egypt, rather than those who would try to exert power over it. There were some branches of the Ptolemy family still in

Macedonia. Perhaps there would be a man there who would make a reasonable match. Possibly, as Cleopatra had done, I could rule on my own, but then there is the issue of an heir. She has the advantage of already having a son, but would the citizens accept a half-Roman half-Egyptian ruler? I did not know for certain, but I believed in my heart that they would accept me. Welcome me even.

The weeks seemed to pass quickly in an endless parade of petitions, all wanting their complaints and wishes to be heard. Some were Egyptians living here in Turkey who wished for me to restore land or property taken from them when Caesar worked to quash the rebellion I led against Cleopatra. Many of the elite who supported my brother or me had their properties seized, forcing them to flee to safer shores. They hoped that my return to rule would also restore their wealth and position. The list was a long one. There were many more than I imagined. I knew it would be no small task to set those things right, but I promised to do my best once I was on the throne.

"Good morning, my queen," said Bennu as he startled me from my daydream.

"Oh, Bennu, good morning," I replied cheerfully.

"I have received this morning a letter addressed to you from the aide of one Consus Planidus. He says that the Senator would like to meet with you at the Temple of Apollo in Klaros. He will be there in about two weeks according to his aide's letter," said Bennu as he handed me the parchment scroll.

"Where is Klaros?" I asked.

"It is a beautiful little village by the sea to the south of here. I suspect he is arriving by ship, and this is an out-of-the-way location where you are unlikely to encounter other high-ranking Romans. It seems he wishes to keep his meeting with you a secret, which I think is wise for both of you," Bennu replied.

"I can certainly understand him wanting to keep our meeting hidden from others, but why do you think I should do so?" I asked quizzically.

"My sources tell me Senator Planidus is a very powerful man. If it becomes widely known that he has become your benefactor, it could both hurt and help you. His support could bolster your cause and perhaps result in additional support from others in Rome, but it could also be interpreted as a betrayal… much as your half-sister did with Julius Caesar," he said plainly.

"It is not the same. My father sought financial support from Rome without criticism. Why should I not do the same?"

"Before Cleopatra's treason, I would have said the same. Now, your people will be suspicious. If they come to see you as no different than her, it begs the question why they would endure a war to replace one traitor with another."

"Ah, you are saying that because I am a woman, the assumption is that he would only support me if he were receiving my honor in return."

"Sadly, it is so. Men may choose to copulate with whomever they please and it usually has little or no political consequence, but for women, it is not so. A child born of a liaison between a powerful man and a powerful woman becomes a liability. The child is a potential problem for both sides," replied Bennu frankly.

"Like Caesarion?"

"Exactly. He is not fully Egyptian so he may not be accepted as heir to the throne of Egypt. That is a problem for her. But, if

Cleopatra were to take up with another powerful Roman, she could be seen as trying to put him on the throne of both countries. Then it becomes a problem for Rome. Do you see what I am saying?" asked Bennu, cocking his head to one side as he often did when making an important point.

"Yes, I do. But I have no intention of giving myself to this man Planidus. I have held onto my virtue this long. I will not trade it now for a few coins," I responded wryly.

"You know that, and now I know that. But, your followers and the citizens of Rome will not know that. They know only what they see. Their sight is limited, and half of what they hear is propaganda generated by one side or the other, or worse yet is an outright lie to discredit you and your cause. Much was said about Cleopatra in Roman circles that was both inaccurate and unflattering. You do not want to suffer that same fate."

"I see. Yes, you are right. We must maintain a veil of secrecy around this meeting. How long will it take to travel there?" I inquired.

"If you go by litter, it will be nearly two weeks. That means you must leave at once if you wish to arrive before him. If you go by horse, you could arrive in three or four days. Both of those things assume that the weather presents no challenges, as rain could slow your journey further."

"Going by horse would draw less attention to my travels. I would not want Cleopatra to get wind of my departure from the Temple. Please make those arrangements. I should leave in a few days to be sure that I will arrive before the Senator, as you suggest. Do you know of a place that we might stay in Klaros?" I asked.

"No, my queen. I am afraid it is a town I have never visited but

I will speak with General Zayid. We will send an advance party to make some arrangements for you. Between here and there, a tent will have to do," said Bennu with a glint in his eye.

"I have stayed in a tent before, my dear friend. This will not be as much of a hardship as you might think. Lira is less fond of them than I am. She abhors the spiders that are often found in the desert, and they do seem to have a way of creeping into our tent at night much to her dismay," I replied with a tinkling laugh.

"Well, I am not sure there is much we can do about the spiders, but we will assure your safety as much as we possibly can I assure you," said Bennu as he turned to go.

"Before you leave, have you word of Darius? Does he intend to return to the villa anytime soon?"

"No, he has told the General he will be traveling for many months trying to fill the ranks of your soldiers, but he reinforces his commitment to your cause, and you should never doubt him. He knows we need to make up for the time and money that were wasted by General Masduse's treachery. But he is well, and I am sure he will return as soon as he is able. You do not need to worry."

"No, I was not worried. I just… thank you, Bennu," I said as he left in the direction of the kitchen. No doubt he would be giving Cente and Amon instructions to begin packing for the trip.

My heart felt a pang of regret and sorrow thinking of Darius, but I also knew this was for the best. Nothing could ever come of our feelings for one another, so it was best to let the embers simply die rather than continually fanning the flames that we could not allow to consume us. Surely, he would soon find someone to marry at some point as I knew he desired children very much.

"Lira," I called out hoping she was nearby, but there was no answer. Perhaps she was in the garden. Sure enough, I found her sitting on a bench under the large cyprus tree. She seemed to be crying.

"Lira! What is wrong, my dearest?" I said as I sat down beside her.

She wiped at her tears with a small cloth and brushed the hair from her eyes which were red and swollen.

"It is nothing, my queen, do not concern yourself," she said with a feeble attempt at a smile.

"Come now, Lira. We have known each other too long and too well for us to keep secrets from each other now. What troubles you so?"

"You need not burden yourself with the small worries of others that are of no consequence in this world. Truly, it is nothing," she replied once again forcing a smile.

"Then I will sit here with you quietly to comfort you, even if you choose not to speak," I said, taking her hand in mine.

We sat there in silence for a few minutes until finally, she unburdened herself.

"A letter came for me today. It is from my brother," she said at last.

"I did not realize you have a brother. We talk so little about your family. I remember that your father died during the fighting, but we have never really spoken of the rest of your family. Where do they live?"

"Just outside Alexandria in a small village there. My mother, brother, and younger sister," said Lira looking down at her hands that were now folded together in her lap. I sensed her tears were about to flow again so I said nothing, waiting for her to gain her composure.

"Has something happened to them?" I asked quietly.

"Ianmani, my brother writes to say that my mother and sister have died from a sickness which has spread through the village. Also… a man, his name was Peterus, he was…".

Her voice choked with emotion. There was a pain in it I had never heard before, and it hurt me just to listen as it was clear this news had shaken her profoundly.

"Was Peterus kin to you also?"

"No, he was the man I was to marry, someday. When my father brought me to serve you, I always believed that you would prevail. I thought that soon we would be in Alexandria and that I would see my family and Peterus again. I hoped that once you were on the throne you would permit us to marry. We were betrothed before my father brought me to you, but he said we were too young to be married. Peterus promised to wait for me until I reached my maturity, which I did not long after I joined you," said Lira wistfully.

"Lira, why did you not tell me? You could have gone home. I would not have kept you from your family and this man whom you loved," I replied with a lump in my throat.

"Once I came with you to the Temple, I knew I could not leave you. The gods had called on me to serve you. Peterus understood and he promised to wait until we returned. I loved him very much. We have known each other since we were children, and we always knew we would spend our lives together. We wrote to each other often. But now…"

"I am sorry, Lira. My prayers tonight will be for the safe

travels of your loved ones through the river and to the afterlife beyond. You will see them again one day, I am sure of it," I said as I wrapped my arms around her, holding her close to me.

Her sobs could no longer be contained. They oozed from her very soul and out into the world, the tears spilling out onto her cheeks, sliding down her face and onto her tunic and mine. I did not let go. My arms wrapped around her even more tightly as her body heaved under the weight of her grief and even though I did not know her loved ones, I could not help but grieve with her. My own tears soon mixed with her own. We sat there for some time, the sun passing from one side of the garden to the other. Finally, she was quiet again.

"Lira, would you like to leave? You could go to your brother back to your village?" I asked with no small amount of trepidation.

I had come to think of Lira as a sister, not just a friend. She was one of a handful of people I could trust without hesitation. Should she depart, I would miss her terribly. But she has already sacrificed so much for me, and I felt no more could be expected of her.

"No, I will stay with you, my queen. You have been my family now for these last years and while I will grieve my loss there is nothing for me now in Egypt. But my brother, he will come here now that my mother and sister are gone. He wishes to take up arms on your behalf if you will have him," said Lira proudly.

"Of course, he would be most welcome. Surely there must be a position on General Zayid's staff which would suit him," I said lifting her chin to look at her.

Her tears had left a trail on her face but in her eyes I could see a thankfulness and gratitude that I was not sure I deserved. After all, her family had already given so much in my service. Finding a position for her brother was the very least I could do.

"Thank you, thank you," she repeated as she kissed me on the top of each of my hands in turn.

"Write to Ianmani. Tell him to come and I will tell the General to anticipate his arrival. It will be good for you to have your brother here," I said confidently.

"Yes, he will be a most welcome sight," she said as she managed a genuine smile.

"I came to find you to tell you that we are leaving in a couple of days. We will meet with Senator Planidus in Klaros and will travel there by horse. It will be you and I with just a small contingent of guards, and perhaps Bennu. We need to begin to prepare for our departure. I am confident that Bennu has already spoken to Cente and Amon to begin their preparations, but I will need you to help pack my clothes."

"Of course. I will start right away," said Lira as she stood, smoothing her tunic which was still spotted and streaked with the stain of her tears. She gave a slight bow before leaving me alone in the garden.

For these past many months, I have bemoaned my unfulfilled desire for Darius, never once imagining that Lira, my dearest Lira, was pining away for someone she could have been with, had she chosen not to be with me. There was a pang of guilt, of sorrow, for the future I had stolen from her. Had she not come with me to Ephesus, she could have returned to Alexandria to be with her family and Peterus. She would be a mother by now. Instead, she was alone in her service to me with no one to call her own. The gods had blessed me with Lira, Bennu, Darius, Zayid, and so many loyal and dear supporters and friends… but none more than her. Her reward will surely come in the afterlife, but I could only hope that having her brother here with her will be some small comfort to her that I cannot be. Her family was a real family which is more than I could claim. Until I married and had children of my own, I was a family of one.

Our preparations took only three days. We hurried to ensure we would arrive before the Senator, and we decided to go on to Klaros now even if it meant we must wait for several days. As I anticipated, Lira was less than thrilled about the idea of staying in tents, but she knew we must maintain a degree of secrecy and control. Keeping our own company was the best way to ensure both. Finally, we were ready to go, and the horses were brought into the courtyard, loaded up, and ready to go. A dappled mare would be my mount. I was glad to see a horse I was familiar with, having seen her many times. Lira mounted a black mare that was slightly smaller than my own. Bennu sat astride his gelding and two men Zayid had chosen, Wassius and Clodiousas, joined us. They were fully armored in the Roman fashion and even Bennu wore a sword in a scabbard and a dagger in his belt.

Lira and I had hidden small daggers under our tunics. I hoped we would not ever have need of them. We were going and there was no turning back now. The five of us set out just as the sun was peeking out from behind the horizon, bathing our path in shades of gold and yellow. We would ride for six or seven hours each day, stopping to make camp before we lost the light of Ra. At this pace, we would arrive in Klaros in four days, well before the Senator.

Our ride was quiet, encountering only a few merchants along our path. The terrain was easy and the weather pleasant. The gods had smiled on us, and it made the journey an easy one. We rode in formation with Wassius in front, Bennu next to me, Lira behind us, and Clodiousas behind her by a few lengths. Despite the ease of our travels, my legs were very sore by the time we stopped for the night. I had not ridden this long in quite some time. Perhaps I would need to ask Bennu for an additional blanket for my saddle for tomorrow to provide a bit more cushioning. I need not wonder how Lira was doing. When she dismounted it was obvious she was as sore as I was, although she would never complain.

I dreamed of a hot bath, but unfortunately, a small river had to do. She and I washed our arms and faces, sweeping away the dust of the road, while the men set up our little camp. There was a small tent for Lira and me. The men planned to sleep outside so that they could take turns keeping watch. The horses were hobbled on a hill near the few trees we had found a small distance from us. Bennu had seen to their welfare. Lira and I warmed up some of the stew that Cente had sent with us for our first meal. After tonight, we would have to eat what we could catch as there was only beer and some bread in our packs, and nothing for the horses who must be content to graze on what they could find.

The stars burned brightly in the sky as we sat communally around the fire sharing the stew. Here, in this place, I was no Queen of Egypt. We all sat on the ground sharing the same food and drink with no rank or privilege for anyone. Wassius was a wonderful storyteller, as was Bennu, and between the two of them, we were entertained for our whole meal. By the time Lira and I entered the tent for the night, I was as sore from laughing as I was from riding.

"I hate tents," said Lira, huffing as she lay down on her blanket next to mine.

"It could not be helped," I said, settling in beside her.

"Spiders. There will be spiders," she said as she gave a furtive glance around our little tent.

"If there are I will handle it," I said reassuringly as I pulled the blanket up to my chin.

I need not have worried. Lira was asleep in an instant and her rhythmic breathing soon lulled me to sleep as well. The night air was cool and fresh as we slept soundly. I had just turned over, bemoaning the fact that I could see the light beginning to filter through the tent when a sound caught my attention.

"Lira," I said shaking her gently.

"Hmm," she said.

"Wake up!" I shouted as I jumped up pushing back the tent flap and stepping outside.

The men were tending to the horses and preparing to saddle them up, laughing and talking amongst themselves. I listened again. It was a sound I recognized, a slight roaring in the distance. When I was a child, my nanny and I had been at the Sothy River. It was a branch of the Nile that ran through the southern part of Alexandria. We were there with my younger brother, having a picnic. We had simply been enjoying our day when a roaring sound filled the air. At first, it was very distant, but it came closer and closer.

"Children, come with me! Hurry! Gather up your things. We must go at once," she said as she quickly gathered up what she could.

"Why? We are having such a good time," I whined.

"Now! There is a flood coming downstream. We must go now," she replied sternly as I recall.

"Lira! Grab what you can. Hurry, the stream is flooding. There is a wall of water coming this way. Hurry!" I screamed into the tent before turning in the direction of the horses.

"Bennu! Bennu!" I called to him, waving my arms.

The men stopped and turned to look in my direction. The stream that had flowed quietly behind the tent was now beginning to expand out of its banks. The men instantly realized what was happening. Somewhere upstream there had been a storm or maybe even a dam break. A wall of water was now rushing toward us. Instantly the men began running in our direction as fast as they could.

"Arsinoe, run! Come this way!" yelled Bennu gesturing in his direction. The horses had been hobbled on a hill that was probably high enough ground to protect them. Lira and I were at the tent which we had pitched not far from the river, providing us easy access to the water. Lira scrambled out of the tent with all our belongings in the satchel.

"Go! Run toward Bennu," I said, pushing her in that direction. As I began to follow her, something held me in place. I tried my best but I could not move forward. My sandal was caught in the rope holding the tent to the ground and my foot would not budge.

Lira stumbled but regained her footing and took off toward the horses. Bennu passed her on his way to me. Wassius grabbed Lira, taking her uphill as the water licked at their feet.

"Arsinoe, go now!" said Bennu gasping for breath as he and Clodiousas reached me.

Pulling with all my might was of no use. My foot would not come free, and I could not get my sandal off. The water was already swirling above my ankles and rising.

"My foot is caught on the rope," I said, looking at Bennu and Clodiousas. Their eyes instantly filled with horror.

They were now both on their knees struggling to untie the rope or to free my shoe, but as they could not see under the rising water, the task was difficult at best. With each moment the conditions were getting worse. The water began spinning around us, threatening to grab the tent and pull it downstream in the torrent, and me with it. There were also branches and tree trunks in the water. They became weapons as they were swung around by the force of the water.

"Bennu, please hurry," I gasped, as the panic rose into my throat making it hard to breathe.

"Let me try," said Clodiousas as he disappeared under the water that now rose to above my knees.

Bennu did his best to hold onto me against the tremendous force of the water, but his grip was slipping. Suddenly I could feel my foot was free, but Clodiousas did not remerge.

"Go," said Bennu, pushing me toward Wassius, who was standing now at the edge of the water, as close as he dared come without risking being swept away himself.

Bennu continued pushing me from behind as the water rose higher and higher now nearly to our waist. Our movement was slow but steady and finally, I was able to grab onto a rope that Wassius had thrown to us. Hearing a loud groan behind me, I turned to see Bennu struck in the back by one of the large logs. He teetered and then fell backward, his hands reaching out for me as the raging tide tore him away, his arms failing before he disappeared beneath the foaming, dirty water.

"Bennu!" I screamed out over the roar of the rushing water.

In an instant, he was gone.

"Hang on, Arsinoe! Do not let go!" screamed Lira from the safety of the hill as she paced back and forth frantically.

The water tugged at my clothes. My legs felt like lead and my shoes had disappeared. I could feel my feet sinking into the rapidly developing mud. My hands were burning from the roughness of the rope and the fierceness of my grip, but I dared not loosen it. Wassius was groaning under the stress of pulling and Lira now joined him, both of them pulling the rope with all their might. Slowly I began to make progress again, and I could feel my feet coming free from the mud as I reached less saturated ground.

"A bit more Arsinoe! Hold on, hold on!" yelled Lira.

I was close enough to see her eyes, filled with pure terror. She did not think I was going to make it. The water was now up to my chest, and it would have been so easy to just let go and float away as Bennu had. To disappear under the foaming waves like Clodiousas, never to be seen again. But deep within me was a voice, a force. *Keep going, you must keep going…*

I looked up at Lira and Wassius, both pulling, and forced myself to take a step, then another. The ground was starting to slope upward now and with each step the water got more and more shallow. My progress became easier. Finally, when the water was knee high, Wassius dropped the rope and waded in to grab me by the arm, half walking and half dragging me the rest of the way.

"Arsinoe," cried Lira as she dropped the rope and scurried toward us, helping Wassius get me the remainder of the way up the hill.

Exhausted, the three of us collapsed in a heap next to the horses as the sound of the rushing water filled the air. It drowned out every other noise. My mind was swirling very much like the water, trying to grasp what had just happened.

"Bennu!" I screamed scrambling to my feet and heading back toward the water's edge.

"No, stop. There is nothing you can do," said Lira as she grabbed onto my arm, pulling me back to safety.

"Let me go," I said trying to shake her grip, but she held firmly onto me before pulling me close to her. My tears began to flow.

"They are gone. There is nothing you can do," said Wassius as he helped Lira to walk me back up to the safety of the hilltop.

"Not Bennu," I groaned as the realization that he was gone washed over me just as the water had washed over them.

He could have stayed on the hill in safety rather than coming to my aide but instead, as he always had, he put my safety above his own and now he was gone. They had risked their lives to save me, and the gods had chosen to take them while sparing me. It was so unfair.

"Wassius, was the man Clodiousas your friend? Did he have a family?" I asked when I was finally able to catch my breath.

"He was the son of my mother's brother. He has a wife and three small children in Ephesus," he replied stoically.

My heart was bursting. There, in the dirt, I dropped to my knees and began to pray. I prayed for the souls of these men, my friend, Wassius' family, and their journey to the afterlife that was just beginning. They would need all the intercession for their safe and swift passage that we could muster, and Lira quickly joined me kneeling next to me to pray. Wassius stood quietly by, keeping an eye on the river to make sure we were not in any further danger. Finally, he spoke, interrupting our prayers.

"Queen Arsinoe, we should go. We need to keep moving if you are to make it to Klaros in time," said Wassius firmly.

"Yes, of course," I said reluctantly.

I wiped the tears from my eyes as I scanned the scene below us. The water had slowed but was still quite deep. There was no sign of what our encampment had been, or of the men who once stood there. By now, their bodies would be very far away, having been carried off by the force of the river. It pained me to know they would not be buried with the honors they deserved.

With a heavy heart, I finally turned away from the water and set about readying myself to go. Lira helped me change out of my wet tunic and into dry clothes. She retrieved the other pair of shoes she had brought with us. They were a bit ill-suited to horseback riding, but they would have to do. Riding barefoot would leave me blistered and sore.

As Wassius helped me to mount. He tied Bennu's horse up behind me and Clodiousas's horse behind Lira. I couldn't help but feel despair. Bennu was a dear friend one of a few men who had supported me consistently and with genuine admiration. He had become almost like a father to me. I had depended on him for so much and his encouragement had sustained me on more than one occasion when I doubted myself.

He welcomed me into his home when I had no one and treated

me almost as a daughter, the daughter he had lost who had not grown to adulthood. I trusted him. There was no man I trusted more, and it grieved me beyond measure to think of telling Cente and Amon that was gone. He was the only family that they had, both like a father and a benefactor. This loss would be felt by them most profoundly. Surely, he had provided for them in his will, and I would ensure that the widow and children of Clodiousas were also well cared for. I could only hope my prayers would be answered and that he and Clodiousas would be well judged.

We plodded along together quietly. Only the nickering of the horses and the occasional cawing of a bird broke our silence. We rode next to each other now, with no one to guard our front and rear. We simply had to stay together and be as watchful as we could. Bennu's horse knew something was amiss. As he reluctantly walked behind my mare, he occasionally came forward to nudge my knee with his nose. His liquid eyes were full of worry that his master had not rejoined us.

"It was not your fault," said Lira, looking straight ahead.

"I know."

"If you had not heard the water when you did, you and I might both be dead. All the men would likely be taken as well, as they would have tried to rescue us. Their loss is a painful one to be sure, but it could have been worse. It could have been all of us," she said quietly.

"Maybe, but it also could have been none of us," I spat back, much more rudely than I probably should have. My grief was giving way to anger.

"It is as the gods wish it to be," Lira replied matter-of-factly.

She was right of course, as she frequently was. The rising river could have swept all of us away had I not recognized the sound for what it was. Lira and I certainly would have been drowned and it is true that had all the men come to our rescue, it is quite likely all would have joined us in a watery grave. As we plodded on throughout the day, my sorrow rose and fell just like the tides. There were moments when I thought I might be overcome, and others when I felt as though Lira was speaking the truth. It was simply as the gods wished it to be and not under my control.

That night, we slept under the stars. It was just the three of us and the absence of the tent was a constant reminder of all that we had lost. It was a restless night. Wassius and Lira took turns keeping watch over our small encampment, but sleep would not come to me. No matter how much I tried, my dreams were filled with the sound of rushing water and the silence of absent voices. The morning came as a relief. Ra chased the darkness away along with my dreams. We had bread and beer as well as a small rabbit that Wassius had been able to catch for our meal, but I found I had no appetite. The day became cloudy as it wore on and I began to fear it would rain. Would the desert flood again? Wassius reassured me we were on high enough ground and need not be concerned but agreed to avoid dry creek beds and ravines just to be on the safe side.

A pallor hung over us and we spoke little as our journey wore on. In two more days of travel, we could see Klaros on the horizon and I was greatly relieved. I was desperately in need of a bath, a change of clothes, and a glass of wine. As soon as I could, I needed to send word to Cente, Amon, and Clodiousas's wife telling them what had happened. Complicating matters further, Bennu had sent the advance party. Without him, we did not know where we were to go. We would need to find someone who might know what arrangements had been made.

When we reached the center of the village, I looked at the faces carefully, hoping to see someone I recognized who might be able to help us. I knew no one. Spotting an inn, Wassius stopped nearby and helped us dismount. My legs trembled, having ridden for so long and they felt unsteady beneath me.

"I'll go inside and see if you and Queen Arsinoe might be able to get a meal and rest while I ask around to see if I can determine what arrangements Bennu had made," said Wassius.

"You should eat too," said Lira with a hesitant smile.

"I have some bread. I will get some beer to take with me, but thank you for your concern," he said gratefully.

While there had been little conversation on my part, Lira and Wassius were frequently talking each night as I drifted off to sleep. I wondered if she had an interest in him. She seemed to be shy when talking with him, almost demure. It was very different from her normally very confident and assertive demeanor. The thought of it made me smile. With the loss of Peterus, perhaps she would consider other suitors. She could certainly do worse. He was, from what I had seen, a kind and thoughtful man. He was clearly loyal to Zayid and our cause.

My bones were weary, my stomach growled, and I was hopeful that we might find a good meal here. I was relieved when Wassius returned from the inn with word that we would find some comfort here.

We settled in to eat at a small table near the door. I was very grateful for the warm stew and wine. I ate more heartily than I had in many days. The inn was small, and the innkeeper was a large, hearty man who seemed to have a smile painted on his face, never changing no matter what he was doing or whom he was talking to. There were just a few men inside and thankfully they seemed to pay us no mind. The village saw some level of wayfarers coming to visit the Temple of Apollo, so our presence was not entirely unexpected. Wassius had spoken with the innkeeper before departing and I was sure I saw a few coins slipped into his hand. Whatever the reason, we were being well cared for and it was a relief just to sit in a chair and have a table to eat from.

It was nearly dark before Wassius returned. I had begun to worry that he had abandoned us, but Lira had no such concerns, and she was right to have faith in him. We were waiting outside to keep an eye on the horses when he returned.

"Were you successful?" asked Lira as she grabbed the reins of his horse as he dismounted.

"It took some effort, but yes. There is a small villa just near the temple that Bennu had arranged for your use, and they are ready to receive you," said Wassius smiling.

"Is it close enough to walk?" I asked.

"Yes, my queen, it is not far. If you would like to walk, we can lead the horses."

"I think I have ridden enough for now. The walk will do me good," I said with a faint smile.

The three of us walked along in companionable silence. Out of the corner of my eye, I could see Lira and Wassius occasionally smiling at one another, and it lifted my spirits. Our walk through the village was a pleasant one, and people nodded and smiled as we walked past the small houses and shops. Finally, we reached the place Wassius had been told about and sure enough, several people were waiting outside to greet us. One of them was a servant from the villa who I recognized, and that was reassuring. The villa was small, but it would serve our needs. As usual, Bennu had done well. I already missed him so much.

This meeting with Senator Planidus was still a few days away. We would be well settled before he arrived. I hoped I would have an opportunity to replenish my clothes and shoes. This meeting was an important next step, hopefully, one that will move us closer to the goal of returning to the throne of Egypt. I was looking forward to it. Sadly, Bennu would not be by my side, but I promised the gods I would do everything I could to honor his memory by securing the support of Planidus. I had no intention of letting him, or myself down.

TOO HIGH A COST

We had been in Klaros for three days and my mood had lifted somewhat as we settled in. I did my best to put the tragedy of the past week behind me. The sadness was still there, but it was no longer the overwhelming grief I felt just a few days ago. There were far fewer shops than in Ephesus, but Lira was able to find a lovely new tunic to replace the one I had been wearing when the water overtook us. It had been torn and stained beyond salvaging, thankfully, as I did not want to wear it again. It was a reminder of what had happened and what had been lost. In many ways, we were fortunate that most of our belongings had already been loaded onto the horses when the river overflowed. The debens we had brought with us to fund our trip were safe.

Every morning and afternoon the man called Hespus went to the Temple of Apollo to see if there was any word from Planidus. While we waited, Lira, a young girl named Cyntheris, and I planned a banquet to be held in Planidus' honor. We would need a few more women and men to help with preparations and serving but Cyntheris has assured us that she could bring in additional help as it was needed. It was fun to sit with them, laughing and scribbling as we worked through the details. This mundane task helped to take my mind off my grief and the meeting to come. Flowers, meat, nuts, fruit of all kinds, and copious amounts of wine had begun arriving at the villa. Thankfully there was no parade of petitioners as I had feared when my presence became known.

There was a small library, and I spent most of my time reading. I stayed within the safety of the villa rather than venturing out into town. With only Wassius to rely on for our safety, his job would be made easier if I were to stay within the relative safety of these walls. He was always nearby, discreet but watchful, and the door to the villa was never opened to admit people or goods until he had a chance to inspect the contents and search for weapons. Bennu would have been my personal protector, but in his absence and with the loss of the other man Clodiousas, it all fell to Wassius. He knew no one here and trusted only those who had already been arranged. They were servants, not soldiers, so the task of keeping us safe fell to him alone. He even slept in a chair just outside the room that Lira and I shared, but I sometimes wondered to myself if he would choose Lira over me should trouble break out.

"Hespus?" I asked sticking my head into the kitchen.

"He is still at the Temple, my queen," replied Cyntheris, looking up from the chicken she was plucking.

"Of course. Thank you," I replied with a smile.

"Would you like me to send him to you in the library when he returns?"

"Yes, thank you."

We were still a bit early in Klaros based on the initial reports, and yet my mind could not help but wonder why we had not heard anything. Planidus would be unable to send a messenger if he were still at sea and had not docked anywhere else along his journey. I was being paranoid for nothing. Surely there were no issues. His letter was clear and we must simply be patient. But still, this trip had already cost me dearly. There was nothing more I wanted now than for it to be worth the sacrifices that had been made. When Hespus returned, he confirmed there had been no word and that no ship had been sighted.

Three days became five days. Then five days became nine. We continued to wait in Klaros. My patience had worn thin, having now been nearly three weeks since we left Ephesus to come to Klaros.

"He should have been here by now," I said angrily.

"Yes. I agree, my queen, but perhaps he has simply been delayed by weather or perhaps his departure was not on time. Should we continue to wait here for a few more days, just in case?" asked Lira as the frown on her face revealed all too well that she also thought something was amiss.

At this moment more than any other, I missed Bennu's council. Without him, only Zayid or Darius would have been able to advise me but of course, they were not here. Had Antony led me astray? Was this just some sort of ruse to get me away from the Temple so that Cleopatra could attack? He seemed genuine, but we had no way of knowing that the letter we received was truly from this Planidus, if he even existed at all!

"Have we been played for fools, Lira?" I asked thoughtfully.

"What do you mean, my queen?" she replied, cocking her head to one side.

"Is this meeting some sort of hoax? Was this arrangement just a way to lure me away from the safety of the Temple, or perhaps just a way to humiliate me?" I said, wringing my hands as I paced back and forth in the small library.

"Why would Antony do that? What does he stand to gain? It sounded like he was all for this alliance between you and the Senator. He seemed to feel it would be beneficial for everyone."

"I agree. A motive for subterfuge has not come to me, but at the same time, I have no explanation for why we have not heard anything from Planidus. How much longer should we wait here?" I asked tersely.

"My suggestion would be to wait two more days. It will take us that long to gather supplies and pack for the return trip anyway, so nothing is lost. If you have had no word by the time we are packed and ready to go, then my advice would be that we return to Ephesus. But you are Queen and must make your own decisions. You know I will support whatever you decide to do," replied Lira with a nod of her head in my direction.

"Yes, that is wise council. Speak with Wassius and let him know of our intentions. He and the others can begin preparations for the trip back. I would like to take Bennu's horse with us, but he can sell the other or use it as a pack animal, whichever he would prefer. But be clear, we will leave in two days. We will wait no longer."

"Yes, my queen, I will convey the message."

My heart pounded a bit less now that a decision had been taken, but still, my mind raced with the possibilities as to why this meeting had not occurred. Was it something as simple as a weather-related delay, or was it something more nefarious? There was no way to know but lingering here would bring no value. We needed to return to Ephesus and make our own way. We still had money at our disposal, and we could continue without this man's support or support from anyone outside the circle we had already formed. Enough of these Romans! We did not need them. Assuming Antony has done as he said, he has helped by instructing his representative to discredit the man who pretends to be my brother. I am grateful, but beyond that, we needed no further help. This trip cost us so much, but now it seemed it was for naught. The anger bubbled up from me like molten gold boiled up from the jeweler's cauldron.

No word of the ship came and as the sun broke over the horizon, we mounted once again. Hespus graciously agreed to go with us, which was a great relief to Wassius. He did not hesitate to express his fear that this was a ruse to get me out of the Temple and onto a desolate road. He feared an attack on our return trip. Hespus served in the Roman army in his youth and was still good with a sword. He was also knowledgeable about field tactics, and it would be good to have him with us. We have assured him he could stay on with us in Ephesus if he wished, or I would pay for his return to Klaros.

He rode Clodiousas' horse and Bennu's mount was loaded with our supplies, including the new tent that Wassius was able to secure for us. Appreciated, but also a reminder of what having a tent with us cost us on our way here. Had my sandal not gotten caught in the rope... I could not think about it now.

Our return to Ephesus seemed to go more quickly than I

anticipated. Despite any misgivings, there were no incidents of note, save a small altercation with a beggar just outside the town that Hespus handled very tactfully. As we neared the completion of our trip, it was clear that one good thing had come from this experience. Lira was in love with Wassius, and he was in love with her. They talked every night by the fire long after Hespus and I had turned in for the night. Their hushed voices and Lira's occasional laughter could be heard in the quiet night.

It was only a few weeks ago she learned that Peterus had died. I hoped that this was a genuine affection between them, and not just something to fill what must be the hole in her heart left by his passing. Time would tell as I would insist on a period of engagement if that was the direction they chose to go. Lira's happiness was nearly as important to me as my success and I wanted to ensure that Wassius was the man he appeared to be, deserving of her love.

Finally, the Temple of Artemis could be seen on the horizon, shining in the sun like a beacon to guide us back home. Home? Odd. I had never thought of this place as my home. My ka, my ib, belonged to Egypt, to the city of Alexandria, but in many ways, this place had become a home to me. Cente and Amon had become like siblings, Bennu like a father, Zayid like an uncle, and Darius… well Darius was a true friend, and he had given up much to support my cause. It was sad, truly, that our affection for each other could go no further. But it could not be changed. Our future was written by the gods and the laws of Egypt. We could only accept it.

Finally, the gate to the villa was in front of us and I no longer needed to hold the reins, the horse would do the rest. Once inside,

I could see many familiar faces had turned out to greet us and I was grateful to see them.

"Let me help you," said Zayid as he reached up to aide me in dismounting.

After so many days of riding, I was no longer sore. My body and legs had grown more accustomed to the effort, although Lira still complained nightly of her soreness. She bought some liniment to have with her on the ride back.

"Thank you, Zayid. It is good to see you. Has there been any word from Planidus or Antony?"

"No, my queen, there has been no word. I am… I am sorry about Bennu. He was a fine man, and he will be missed. We have prayed for him and the other man who was lost each day since we received your news. I am sure his heart will be light, and Osiris will receive him," said Zayid somberly.

"Surely this is true, and we have prayed for him each night as well."

"My queen," said Cente, who had been waiting patiently nearby.

A lump developed in my throat as I approached her, taking her hands in mine.

"My dearest Cente, my heart is heavy at the loss of our precious Bennu. You should know he died as a hero. He and Clodiousas both came to my aide in a moment of great danger. Surely, I would have been lost had they not come for me," I said before embracing her.

We both gave into our tears, holding each other close and each trying to offer some comfort to the other. The rest of the assembly stood by quietly, each one feeling the weight of this moment. Amon was wiping away tears as were several of the other servants, their heads bowed. Then one by one, everyone went to the gelding, standing quietly in the courtyard of his missing master, some stroking his muzzle affectionately, before Amon led him away.

"Shall we draw you a bath, my queen?" asked Lira.

"Yes, and just a small meal," I replied as we linked arms before going inside.

As we walked to my room, we passed the painting of Bennu's wife and daughter, and I stopped once again to gaze into their eyes. The beautiful Aziz and his daughter, Feme, had stared back at me so many times as I walked these halls. Now they were together as a whole family. I was sure he was very happy to see them again and it made me smile. Perhaps I would have someone create a new painting depicting all of them, together at last. I felt a lump building in my throat, and it was all I could do to hold back my tears. This loss would be with me, with us, for a very long time.

"Still no word?" I asked Cente. It had been nearly two weeks since we returned to the villa from our trip to Klaros.

"No, I am sorry. There is no word from the Senator and Amon is talking with the men at the dock to see if there is any word of a ship sinking, but he has heard nothing. Perhaps he just changed his mind?"

"It is certainly possible, but I would have expected someone to say something by now to explain why Planidus did not come to the Temple. This has been such a frustration, and to think what we have lost for it to gain nothing."

"You know that Bennu would have done anything for you,

my queen, as would Amon and I," said Cente with her character-istically shy smile.

"I know. All of you have been nothing but welcoming and supportive of my cause, which causes my heartache to be more profound. Bennu was like a father to me in many ways, as he was to you. We will miss him for a long time to come."

"Yes, it will not be the same without him, I am afraid."

"Have you found his will? Has he provided for you and Amon?" I asked hesitantly.

Surely Bennu would have taken care of them, but I realize that whatever he wrote had implications for me as well. Would I be forced to leave the villa and find other accommodations? The villa not only provided me with a sense of safety and home, but it had been a perfect place to conduct our business. Now that we also had the villa next door, we had been able to accommodate everyone nearby. I would have hated to see that change.

"Yes, Amon knew where it was. As Bennu had told us before, he left the villa to us as well as the allowance that your father had left to him for its upkeep. Of course, that came with clear instruc-tions that you are to continue to be welcome here for as long as you need. Even if Bennu had not left those instructions in his will we would have never asked you to leave. In an odd way, you and Lira are like family to us, my queen. We will miss you both when you return to Egypt," replied Cente, her voice cracking with the emotion of the moment.

"Thank you, Cente. You and Amon would be most welcome at my court should you decide to go to Egypt with us."

"Thank you, my queen. That is very generous of you, but it was Bennu's wish that we stay here in the villa and keep it always at the ready should you ever need it again, not that I think you will," she said with a wide grin.

"You are very kind Cente, and to that end, I need to speak with General Zayid. Can you have word sent to him?"

"Of course. I will at once," she replied.

I sat at my desk, deep in thought. What could be the reason Planidus did not come? Was Antony behind it or was it as simple as Cente suggested, that he simply changed his mind? More importantly, how should I respond, if at all? We could certainly send a letter directly to the Senator, his aide, or Antony, but I was not sure what I would say. It was late in the day by the time Zayid arrived at the villa. He looked tired and gaunt.

"Zayid, thank you for coming. Are you well? You look tired," I said in greeting.

"Yes, my queen. I have not been sleeping well, but it is nothing for you to be concerned about. Cente sent word that you wanted to speak with me?" he said before settling into the chair I had indicated next to my desk.

"Yes, I wanted to hear from you as to how the recruiting is going. Do we feel like we have enough men and ships to begin our attack? Surely, we will not be able to afford to pay men to be at the ready for much longer. We need to act soon, or the moment will pass us by."

"Well, you will be pleased to know that Darius has done a wonderful job of signing up soldiers. I do believe that we have enough men now at our disposal to launch an invasion. We have arranged for the ships as well, but our money has not yet been spent. The captains who have agreed to transport soldiers for us and we will need to pay half of what we have promised to them when we depart and the other half when we arrive safely in Alexandria."

"Wonderful. We should take an inventory of what we must have to ensure we have adequate funds to make the journey, both for ships and supplies." I looked at Bennu's most recent ledger. There were roughly six thousand deben left, and in addition to that, many Roman coins. We will have to manage now with whatever money we have as there seems to be no monetary support coming from other channels," I replied.

"That should be enough. I am concerned as to the absence of any word from Planidus. I am not a politician, and I do not pretend to know the workings of things as complex as the Roman senate, but it does strike me as odd. Antony commits to you a meeting with this man, his aide sends word to you, and then he simply does not show up. It unsettles me. Perhaps that is why I am not sleeping well. It gnaws at me. What does it mean?"

"I wish I knew; the same thoughts have kept me awake more than one night in the last couple of weeks. I do not think we can dwell on it further. I have decided not to contact either Planidus or Antony. Whatever we are going to do, we will have to do with what resources we have at our disposal. We should assume no further help is coming," I said straightforwardly.

"That is wise, my queen. Once we put this plan into motion, we need to know that we can see it through on our own. I suggest we retrieve the money we need, then summon our soldiers and begin the transports. We only have a window of a few months of good weather, so we should move quickly," said Zayid, stifling a yawn.

"Agreed. You should now go with me to the vault in the temple where we have kept our monies hidden. We will take with just the household's most trusted members. Let's bring Lira, Cente, Amon, and the guards to retrieve the coins. Then we will keep them under guard while you make the necessary payments. Send word to Darius of our plan. He should return to the villa soon as well. You have your battle plan and your generals in hand?"

"Yes, I do. Darius will lead one of the legions, General Scipionus will lead one, and I will take two legions myself. Stonius has come from Cyprus he will lead the naval assault. He is a good sailor and the men respect him."

"Wonderful. Tomorrow evening after the temple closes, we will gather to retrieve the coins. I am grateful, Zayid, for all that you have done to bring us to this place," I said as I laid my hand on his.

"It has been my honor, my queen, but there is still much to do to get you back on the throne in Alexandria. We should meet here with all the generals as soon as we can gather everyone together to be sure all are fully versed in the plan and that there are no concerns. Then we can send out the call for our soldiers to go to the ports we have assigned them to in order to board their transports."

"Of course. We will be prepared. I will see you at sunset tomorrow," I said, rising from my chair. "Now, please go and get some rest."

"Yes, my queen, I promise that I will," he said as he took his leave.

Finally, we were going to do something. All these months and months of talking, while necessary, have done nothing to advance my cause. Now, we could begin to reclaim what was mine. I was exhilarated but also cautious. In the back of my mind was still the failed coup that cost the life of Gallenus, and nearly mine and Darius's as well. If we failed this time, there would not be another. The gods had given me many chances, but there was a limit to our funds and our resolve. We must give this effort everything we had and if we did, I did not doubt that we would be successful.

The next day passed quickly. Lira and Amon worked to gather up several small carts we could use to bring the coins to the villa. Zayid brought up two additional guards as well. The coins would not be here long, as Zayid needed to begin paying our ship captains and buying supplies for the journey, but we could not afford to take chances. Very few people knew about the vault or what it contained. Bennu, who took responsibility for it, was a master at keeping its location a secret.

"Follow me?" I said, looking around at the expectant faces now lit by torchlight.

Lira and I had not been back into the Temple at night since the attack on us some time ago. I was sure it was on her mind as we walked through the Temple. The clattering of our carts echoed through the chambers. We walked in silence to the alcove that hid the secret door to the vault. I could not help but shudder, knowing Lira and I hid in this very place. Thank the gods she survived the attack that occurred here.

Zayid handed me his torch so he could use both of his hands to pry open the door, which swung freely but with a loud groaning noise. We all hesitated, peering into the darkness to be sure the noise had not attracted any attention. Hearing no one, we proceed down the three steps into the chamber where our treasure was held. I lit the torch that was kept on the wall when suddenly I heard Lira gasp.

"Lira?"

"No this cannot be," she said, her voice trembling.

"What?"

"No, this is not right," said Zayid.

I turned and looked around the room. The vault was empty with not a single coin in sight. All we could do was look at each other. The realization of what was happening hit me as if someone had struck me with their fist. Our money, my money, was gone... all of it.

"There must be an explanation," I said as Zayid, Lira, Amon, Cente and I gathered in the library back at the villa.

"Bennu would not have stolen from you, my queen," said Amon defensively.

"No. Of course, he would not have stolen, Amon. I would not even consider that as a possibility," I said shaking my head.

"He must have moved everything. Maybe before we left for Klaros, knowing we would all be gone and there would be no one to see to the security in our absence?" suggested Lira with a shrug.

"He could have asked me," replied Amon with frustration.

"I am sure it was not a matter of trust, Amon. We had all agreed to keep the number of people aware of the location of our funds to a minimum," I said, wearily rubbing my eyes.

"So, assuming Bennu moved everything, where would he put it? He obviously thought he would return from Klaros and either return the treasure to the vault or monitor it in its new hiding place. But without Bennu..." my voice trailed off.

Zayid was pacing back and forth slowly as we all looked at each other helplessly. There was shock in each face, as well as consternation.

"This would not have been an easy task. If he did it alone, it would have taken him several days. We should speak to everyone in the household. Every servant and every guard. Someone had to have seen something or perhaps they helped him in the effort," said Zayid.

"Yes, I agree. The money and jewels must be here in the temple somewhere. There must be another safe space that Bennu thought would provide more protection in our absence," I replied.

"Should we speak to High Priest Megabyzos?" asked Lira.

"You think he might have taken our money?" I asked, stunned by the suggestion.

"No, not necessarily, although he would not be the first high priest to steal. I was thinking maybe he was aware of Bennu's movements. Maybe one of the priests saw something?"

"Quite possible, but I think we should limit the number of people who know of this situation," said Cente quietly.

"That is very wise council, Cente. You are right. We need to keep this to ourselves. If word gets out that we have no money with which to pay our soldiers and captains, then all will be lost. It will be the end."

"I will speak to all the household staff, and I will be sure to be discreet. I will not be specific about why I am asking about Bennu's movements," offered Amon.

"I will do the same with the guards. Let us plan on meeting again in the morning. To have all these conversations now would require rousing men from the annex and that would create suspicion," added Zayid.

"Agreed. We will act discretely and without emotion. Let no one know the real reason for our inquiries," I replied before sending everyone on their way, except for Lira who stayed behind.

"What are you thinking?" she asked, looking at me expectantly.

"Honestly, Lira, I do not know what to think. It is beyond my imagining that Bennu would betray us. The money set aside to maintain the villa was also kept there. Certainly, I could see him removing what he thought my father intended for his use, but to take the monies meant for me? I do not think he would."

My head hurt; my eyes felt raw. This man whose passing I had been mourning for the last few weeks could not be a traitor and a thief. Not this man I thought of as my father. He must have done this because he thought it was the safest option, and as we had agreed, he maintained the secrecy we had sought. It probably never occurred to him that he should have informed me, as he thought it would be of no consequence when he retrieved the coins himself. Of course, now, that was impossible.

I knew I should rest, but would sleep even find me? My insides churned. Could this be the end? Was all this for naught? I could not think about it. A draught finally lulled me to sleep but my dreams were haunted by images that were strange and disturbing. The rise of Ra was a welcome relief.

As we gathered once more in the library, I could only hope that someone had some good news or some idea as to what had happened to the money.

"Zayid, did you learn anything from the guards?" I asked as we all settled in around the table.

"Yes and no. One of the guards said he had noticed Bennu going back and forth from the Temple several times during the days leading up to your departure, but he did not notice that he was carrying anything of note. He thought he had simply gone to pray in the Temple in anticipation of the trip," replied Zayid.

"No one in the household staff noticed anything out of the ordinary either, although Jasinus made that same observation. He also noticed that Bennu had been to the altar several times to pray before he departed," said Amon looking thoughtful.

"But what does it mean?" I asked.

"Perhaps it means nothing, only that he was looking for protection for your trip?" said Lira.

"But that does not help us find the coins," I retorted with frustration.

"Maybe we should look in his room?" suggested Cente.

"It cannot hurt," I replied as I motioned for everyone to follow me.

Bennu's room was very nice. It was smaller than I had expected for the owner of this villa. It struck me that despite my years in the villa, I had never been in this room. The furnishings were old but still in good repair. It was clear a woman had decorated this room, and I suspected Bennu never changed anything after his wife had passed. There was a nearly life-size portrait of her on one wall, as well as a smaller painting of Feme. The painting of Aziz was unique in many ways. It was painted onto a hide and the hide was stretched onto a wooden frame. While you saw this type of painting in royal palaces, it was unusual to see it in a private home. Most paintings were done fresco style, directly on the walls. Perhaps this was a gift to Bennu, maybe even from my father.

This invasion of his private space made me cringe. I muttered my apologies under my breath as we each tried to be respectful while searching the room. We looked in and under everything, hoping beyond hope that the answer would reveal itself.

"This is pointless. There is nothing in here large enough for Bennu to have hidden that much coin," observed Amon.

"He is right," added Zayid, looking about in frustration.

It was true. There was a small chest of blankets and pillows, a chest of clothes, and what appeared to be mementos, but even if the monies had been divided there would need to be a lot more containers than this room could hold.

"We must find the money," I said, stating what everyone already knew.

"Could he have taken them from the Temple to a place outside the grounds?" asked Lira.

"It is possible, I suppose. I would have thought that doing so would be a real risk and Bennu was a cautious man. He was always mindful of doing what was in your best interest, my queen," added Cente.

"We must speak to the high priest; we have no choice. We must know what has happened and time is running out. If we do not pay our ship captains in the next few days and put out the call for soldiers to report, the weather will change and we will miss our chance," I said to one in particular as I stared out into the garden.

Despite myself, I was beginning to think that Bennu had betrayed me. I did not want to believe it, but would he have just moved the money for safekeeping without telling me or anyone else?

"I will summon Megabyzos," said Lira.

"Bring him to the throne room, Lira. General Zayid and I will meet with him there," I replied before she hurried off to find the high priest.

It seemed like an eternity before Lira returned with him, but truly it must have been a short time. My fear and worry had only been amplified as Zayid and I waited quietly not speaking, perhaps each afraid to say what they were thinking.

"My queen, you asked to speak to me," said Megabyzos in his deep gravelly voice.

"Yes, thank you for coming, especially on such short notice. I hope we did not disrupt your prayers," I said, motioning for him to take a seat.

"The gods understand that sometimes the needs of the living need to take precedence over prayers and ministrations for the dead. It is of no consequence. I will return to my prayers when we are done here," he said with a wry smile.

"My apologies for the interruption. We have an urgent matter we must speak with you about. It has to do with Bennu," I said hesitantly.

"Ah, yes. I have prayed for his safe passage since his death, and I will continue to do so. Did you want to make a sacrifice in his name?"

"Yes, I am happy to do so, but that is not why we summoned you. Did you know that Bennu had a secret room in the Temple where he kept… valuable items?" I asked cautiously.

"I was aware."

"Do you know what he kept there?" asked Zayid.

"No, that was of no concern to me. Bennu had spoken to my predecessor many, many years ago about the storeroom that he maintained in the Temple with our blessing. He said that it was important that he maintain a veil of secrecy about this place. The other priests were not aware. Only the high priest of the

Temple knew about the room," replied Megabyzos, his expression unchanged.

"Before Bennu traveled with me to Klaros it seems he may have moved the valuables from the room in the temple and moved them to another location, but we do not know where they might be. Would you have any idea?" I asked bluntly.

"No. I paid no mind to Bennu's comings and goings. In that regard, and to my knowledge, he had only one storeroom. I will say he did come to pray quite frequently in the days leading up to your departure. I assumed he was just seeking the blessing of the goddess, and I paid it no special attention," he said his voice devoid of emotion.

I looked at Megabyzos carefully. He did seem to be truthful in his response. There was no sense that he was hiding anything from me.

"Thank you for coming to speak with me. If you think of anything that might help us in our search for our valuables, please let me know right away," I said as I nodded in the priest's direction.

"Of course, my queen, and I will pray that you recover your possessions. I will also pray that Artemis blesses you as she always has," he replied before turning quietly to go.

I leaned back on the throne and closed my eyes. A feeling of helplessness overtook me. What would we do now? Without the money, we were doomed. Even if Planidus were to come through now it would not be enough. Even he could not make up for the loss we had suffered.

"Do not worry, my queen. We will find the coins," said Zayid, sensing my despair.

"Will we?"

"Surely, he could not have moved the money far. There is no way he could have done so without an effort that would have drawn the attention of someone."

"Maybe there is another room that the high priest is not aware of?" I asked hopefully.

"Unlikely, I think. He is responsible for the workings of the temple. Given his position, he would be ill-advised not to know all that goes on within its walls," replied Zayid.

"Do you think he is being truthful?"

"I do."

"So, what do we do now?" I asked. I was almost afraid to hear the answer.

"We do as Bennu did. We pray," replied Zayid.

"Agreed. Let us go to the altar. Maybe there is a clue there or some guidance we can glean that might tell us what to do next," I said as Zayid helped me off the dais.

Together we walked quietly through the temple. The sun had moved high in the sky and the halls were full of visitors. It was hard for me to blend in with the crowd, given that two soldiers accompanied us, but no one paid us much attention. I was a familiar sight in the Temple. The guards kept petitioners away so that we could kneel at the altar uninterrupted. While Zayid began his prayers at once, I hesitated. I looked carefully around the altar to see if Bennu had left us a clue or if there was anything that might tell us where he had taken the coins. Despite my best efforts, I saw nothing that would tell us what Bennu had done. If the goddess knew his secrets, she was guarding them, and no wisdom came to us. We knelt before the statue of Artemis for some time before we reluctantly decided to go back to the villa.

As Zayid helped me up, something caught my attention. It was on the floor near the foot of the goddess, the very same foot that I had once reached out to in a time of need. I looked at it carefully before I picked it up holding it tightly I hand.

"What is it, my queen?" murmured Zayid.

"I think I might know where Bennu moved the coins," I said as I looked at him with a smile.

The sun had passed completely across the sky by the time the five of us returned to the altar. The visitors had left, and the priests had retired for the night when Zayid, Cente, Amon, Lira, and I returned to the altar. It was now shrouded in darkness and shadow. Even our torches could do little to light the top of the statue, and her face remained hidden from us as we stood at her feet.

"My queen, what did you see earlier when we were here?" asked Zayid.

"Here, by the foot of the statue, I found something."

"What was it?" asked Amon.

"This," I said as I held up a small emerald that I had retrieved from the floor next to the foot of the statue.

I held the small stone, about the size of a pea, up to the light of the torch. It reflected the light beautifully and I could see that it was an emerald of high quality. Since emeralds were the sole purview of Egyptian royalty, I was sure it was not something that had been casually dropped by a visitor.

"This was, I believe, in a small bag that had been kept with the coins. It was part of a assortment of precious stones that my father had left in Bennu's keeping. He had them in a box in the villa, but I had asked him to move them to the vault to keep them with the coins. That means Bennu had to have dropped it when he was…"

"…moving the coins!" exclaimed Amon, finishing my sentence.

"Moving them to where?" said Cente, looking around in the darkness.

"I do not know for sure, but I believe the answer is here. We just need to find it and it was not something we could have done earlier when the Temple was full of people. Spread out. Look carefully at the statue and the floor surrounding it. There is something here we are not seeing," I said as I slipped the emerald into a bag underneath my tunic for safekeeping.

We each moved slowly and carefully around the statue, running our hands along the floor and the edges of the base of the goddess. There had to be something here, although what that something was, I could not imagine. What I did know was that the precious stones had been here. I did not know why or when, but I did not doubt that I was right.

"There is nothing here, my queen. I am sorry," said Zayid, sounding exasperated.

"Look harder. There must be something," I said as I continued crawling around the statue.

"There seems to be a small opening here on the top of the base, just there," said Cente, pointing at what looked like a small gap where two slabs met. It was just behind the foot of the goddess.

"I can get a couple of fingers in there, but I don't feel anything. It just feels like a void, not something most people would notice. It is just a small broken area, I think," I replied dejectedly.

"Do you have a knife, Amon?" asked Zayid.

"Yes, here," said Amon, pulling a small utility knife from his tunic.

"Look! Do you see, here? It looks like there is a panel on the bottom of the base of the statue. It is just there, a few feet below the space that Cente pointed out in the back of the base. The rest of the base seems to be of one continuous stone, but here it is different."

Zayid took the knife and carefully began to run it along the seams of the stone panel. I was surprised to see the knife blade going into the gaps at least a couple of fingers worth.

"It is coming loose, I think," said Amon as he knelt next to Zayid. The two men now used their fingers to try and pry the panel off when it suddenly gave way with a pop. Out from behind the panel poured our coins, hundreds and hundreds of coins.

Our laughter echoed through the Temple. Bennu had brought the coins to the goddess herself to be watched over. He must have simply been dropping them through the small opening down into the base, which was beyond brilliant.

"Well, it was ingenious for sure and probably something he accomplished very easily. I'm not sure what his plan was after he got the coins into the statue, but they would have been safe inside, certainly," Zayid said with admiration for Bennu's ingenuity in his voice.

"While this heartens me, I can see this is not everything. These are the silver coins, but the Roman gold coins and the small bag of precious stones do not seem to be here," I said cautiously.

"Then we must keep looking," said Cente as she began gathering up the coins.

Amon had gone back to the villa to retrieve two more carts

so that we could transport the coins. While we waited for him to return, we looked again around the statue, but we found nothing else. There was no indication that anything further had been hidden in or around the statue. The other coins and stones must be somewhere else. Where they were hidden, I could not imagine. It took us some time to get all the coins safely to the villa and once we were finished, everyone retired to their quarters. I laid down for a bit, but once again sleep eluded me. I found myself wandering through the villa, illuminated only by the light of Khonzu which shone brightly this night. The guard assigned to my room followed along behind me slowly, keeping a respectful distance, one hand always on the hilt of his sword. I am sure he disliked my nocturnal wanderings, but I simply could not stay in my bed any longer.

Bennu was a very smart man. He was very clever in hiding the silver coins in the statue, but the gold coins were even more valuable. Perhaps he wanted them closer to his heart, where he would be sure they were safe. Closer to his heart... what was closer to his heart? I found myself once again in front of the picture of his wife and daughter. Nothing was closer to his heart than these two, but this was a painting on a wall, and there was no place nearby where something could be hidden. I racked my brain. *His heart, his heart*, my mind kept repeating over and over. Suddenly, it occurred to me, and I ran quickly toward Bennu's room. The guard was doing his best to keep up while trying to tamp down the noise being made by his armor.

I immediately went to the painting of Aziz. She and their daughter had been his heart, but even so, this painting was large, even by Egyptian standards. The frame was very ornately carved and rather thick. This was quite a tribute by any measure one might apply. Was there a clue hidden in the painting? I studied it carefully. I observed the folds of her tunic and the carved marble of the table that she stood next to. Did the veins of the marble spell out something? Did the flowers in the vase mean the garden? I knit my brow. This was a clue; I just knew it. Or maybe I was so desperate to find the coins that I was seeing and feeling things that were not real. The guard waited patiently near the doorway but when I let out a heavy sigh, he approached.

"My queen, are you well? Do you need anything?" he asked with concern.

"No, I am fine, I just…"

And instantly I realized that it was not a clue inside the painting. It was the painting itself. I had seen something similar when I was a child, in my father's chambers in the palace. Perhaps that is where Bennu got the idea.

"Help me! We need to take the painting off the wall," I said, motioning for the guard to come closer.

We each grabbed a side and lifted. It took all my strength, the painting being heavier than I anticipated, but it was worth the effort. Behind it, recessed into the stucco walls, were shelves. The shelves held bag after bag of what I could only assume were the gold coins. On the middle shelf sat the blue velvet bag that held the precious stones. It was exactly the same as I had seen when I first arrived, minus one small emerald still safe inside my pouch.

CHAPTER TWELVE

ANOTHER ROMAN CONQUEST

It had been two months since Bennu died and we still missed his presence every day. We were free to begin our invasion once we had recovered all the missing coins. We had just started calling up our soldiers and ships when disturbing news reached us. The Triumvirate has granted official recognition to the bastard child Caesarion, recognizing his rightful position as King of Egypt. The degradation was complete with Cleopatra having fully thrown in her lot with Rome. She had made Egypt nothing more than a powerful eastern vassal. Marc Antony summoned her to Tarsus to question her allegiance to Rome, but it seemed rather than grilling her, he has been taken with her himself! How could this be happening? She had once again seduced a powerful Roman. Was this why Planidus failed to meet us in Klaros as had been proposed? Did he change his mind at Antony's behest?

"This is an unbelievable afront from this man. I thought he

was at least unopposed to my attempt to take the throne if not an outright supporter," I said angrily.

Lira, Zayid, Darius, Amon, and I gathered around the table at the villa. It was not lost on us how much smaller our trusted circle had become. Masduse took his own life when his betrayal was discovered and Bennu had been lost to the raging river. As I looked at their faces I could see the weariness, the frustration… the defeat.

"He was never to be trusted, my queen," said Lira, shaking her head.

"You could not have known that Antony would ally with your sister. I am sorry, half-sister," replied Zayid looking downcast.

Darius returned a few days ago. I had not seen him for many months, and I was grateful for his return. He expressed his sorry over the loss of our dearest Bennu and apologized for not coming to me sooner, but he needed to stay and finish our preparations which were now complete. I appreciated his commitment to our cause and because of his efforts and those of Ziyad we are now ready.

"If Antony is now supporting Cleopatra, I have my doubts as to our ability to be successful. We have received promises from nearly twenty thousand men, but that will be a far cry from what we need if his forces combine with hers," added Darius.

"I would expect that some of Cleopatra's troops would defect to support me as they did in our first efforts to overthrow her."

"Perhaps, but your prior failures will not inspire them," replied Darius softly.

His words stung as if he had taken the whip to my back, cutting through my flesh and drawing blood. I had to stifle a gasp.

My failures. My poorly executed plans. My fault. I supposed at the end of the day, it was. The men I had entrusted with these efforts let me down over and over again, and yet it was my choice to put my faith in their deeds. So truly could I lay the blame on them? Or is Darius right when he says this falls on me? Coming from him, his words were an afront and even more painful than if it had come from one of the others. I was sure Darius he had not meant to wound me so, but I could not help but feel pain. He had always been my most fervent and loyal supporter, and I am sure that has not changed, despite our current situation.

"So, are you saying that we… that I should give up this quest?" I asked. My voice was raspy and raw.

"No, not yet at least, but we are going to have to rethink our strategy given Antony's new alliance with Cleopatra. Can we secure the number of men and resources we now need with the amount of money we have left?" asked Darius cautiously.

"How many men do we even think is reasonable? Do we have the capacity to move them even if we had them?" asked Amon quizzically.

"Going by sea is the direct route. It is possible to take a land route, but I cannot even begin to understand how long that might take," added Lira.

"Taking a land route would be months of arduous marching and we risk losing men along the way to both death and desertion. Going by sea is the only strategy that makes sense, but we can barely accommodate the number of soldiers we have now. If we recruit more, we will have to build ships. There are simply not enough merchants whose boats we can engage," said Zayid with a heavy sigh.

"Building our own ships will take many, many months and we will lose some of those who have already pledged themselves to us. I am not even sure we have enough coins left to build them as we have used a great deal of what we have already. We still need to be able to supply the men and horses with rations and weapons," I replied wearily.

It was too much; it was all just too much. I had an overwhelming desire to throw myself on the floor and simply sob, much as a child does when their mother or father sends them off to bed before they feel it is time. My emotions were a cacophony of anger, frustration, and fear. It was a fear that it may simply be too late now to try to take the throne. Has this all been for naught? I missed Bennu's council dearly at that moment. Lira and Amon simply nod in agreement with anything I say, and they offer little in the way of suggestions, just encouragement and support. Zayid is rightly skeptical of my ideas. He asks challenging questions, but he also offers real solutions. Today, he has been oddly quiet. I no longer knew what role Darius played but I knew he would always be there for me. He would never do anything to actively undermine me, but he seemed less than enthusiastic about continuing our efforts. I could hardly blame him.

"So, what shall we do now?" I asked finally.

Blank faces stared back at me. Perhaps no one was willing to say what probably needed to be said… that I should abandon this effort and use the remaining coins to live on. Without the throne, I would have to sustain myself unless I find a husband who could do so, royalty or not. I did not know if Darius would still entertain such an idea, and I had been paying to support him!

"I do not see how we can move forward now without more

soldiers, more ships, more resources, and that means more coin… much more," said Zayid in his straightforward manner.

"Agreed," said Darius. He stared at the tabletop as if some other answer might be found in the grain of the wood.

"What about Lucius?" asked Lira.

"I heard he is no longer the governor of Cyprus. He is unlikely to be able to be of any further help, other than what he has already provided, which was considerable," replied Darius.

"What about Petrus? He is quite wealthy is he not? I believe you met him in Cyprus," asked Amon.

"He is dead. His widow Isiries seemed skeptical at best. I sincerely doubt she could be persuaded to lend monetary support to the cause," I said despondently.

"What about Planidus? You could try reaching out to him? Perhaps it was just a misunderstanding that he did not meet you in Klaros," proffered Darius.

"No, I am sure Antony was behind that change of heart. He is Antony's man. Either way, he would no longer be able to support me without incurring his rath to be sure."

"There are certainly some men of wealth here in Ephesus. We need to approach them," offered Lira.

"Yes, that is true. I wish that Bennu was still here. He would know who we might approach and how," I said quietly.

"Let me make some inquiries, my queen," offered Amon.

"Yes of course, please do. When you have some news, we will meet again. Until we can obtain additional monies, let us just try to hold on to what we have, the promises of the men and ship captains. Use our coins sparingly but keep everyone engaged until we know if we are moving forward."

I could not bring myself to say it out loud, but the unspoken words hung in the air like the smoke from a fire. As everyone excused themselves, I wandered into the garden seeking the solace of the plants and flowers that had so often listened to my sorrows, never chastising me for my weakness or tears.

"How are you?"

"Darius," I said, turning toward the voice I had missed so much these many months. "It pleased you have returned."

"I should have come when Bennu died. That must have been very difficult for you and the others," he said. He shuffled his feet, looking rather shy and uncertain.

"It was. I have not felt the sadness of a loss so profoundly since Ganymedes was killed. He was a true and loyal friend, and his presence has been sorely missed," I replied, gesturing to the bench next to me.

"Surely he was well judged and is enjoying his reward in the afterlife with his wife and daughter," he said with a faint smile as he sat down beside me.

"Yes, I am sure the gods smiled on him indeed."

We sat quietly, not talking, not even looking at each other. We were enjoying the light breeze, the crispness in the air, and the smell of the flowers. His hair was a bit grayer than before, and his eyes seemed more tired and haggard than I had ever seen. The light in his eyes seemed to have dimmed. They did not sparkle with the same intensity they had just a year or so ago.

"Do you think I should give up this effort?" I asked at last.

"It is not for me to say," he said without looking at me, his eyes fixated on his intertwined fingers in his lap.

"It is. I am asking you to say what you think and feel."

"Sadly, I am no longer as optimistic as I once was. Despite the support the goddess Artemis has offered, it seems that others conspire against you. This… situation with Antony," he said with a shrug of his shoulders.

"Yes. It is hard to imagine a more vexing problem than this now presents," I replied with a heavy sigh.

"You did not…. give him your honor, did you?" asked Darius, looking at me intently.

"No. Perhaps if I had we would be in a different place, but I swore to myself and the gods I would not do as my sister had done."

"It might not have changed the outcome. He is a man with a lust for women and power, and whether you like it or not, Cleopatra already sits atop the throne of Egypt. She can offer him much more than just her bed."

"True. He suggested that he could rule with me as my husband, but I am not and would never be willing to consort with a Roman. They are the very scrouge I am trying to eradicate from Egypt!" I said vehemently.

"I understand," said Darius. He was clearly relieved.

The silence enveloped us. Neither of us wanted to broach the subject which had resulted in the painful conversation we had a few months ago. What would my life be like if I were not Queen of Egypt?

"Have you thought about trying to return to the palace in Egypt under a flag of truce?" asked Darius at last.

"No. There was too much bad blood between us, and I could not simply accept her and her bastard son. Besides, I would always have to sleep with one eye open. She will see me as a threat to her rule for as long as I live, as she should," I replied bluntly.

"If you do not find a benefactor, it is doubtful you can prevail in your quest," said Darius quietly.

"I know."

"What will you do?"

"That is unclear to me as I have not yet accepted the idea that I might fail. Until I do, my thoughts can only be on success and not on what kind of life I might have if I am not," I replied as I took his hand in mine.

He did not resist but I could feel his hesitation. He was almost trembling. I knew how much I had hurt him with my prior thoughtless remarks, and I swore I would not do so again. I released his hand.

"You have been a true and loyal friend, Darius. I do not know what I would have done without your steady presence in my life. I appreciate all that you have done for me, sincerely I do. You have my undying gratitude."

"It has been my honor to be of service. I can only hope and pray that you will find the support you need. I wish I could provide it myself," he replied with a shy smile.

"Thank you."

"I am going back into the field with Zayid tomorrow. We will do our best to keep everyone in line, but I must tell you, your time is limited. If we do not move forward soon, these men will move on to the next person willing to pay for their services. You will not get them back, nor the money you have paid them."

"Yes, I understand. I can only hope that Amon's connections can be of value to get us out of this dilemma. As you say, our time is running out."

"I am sure the gods will help you find a way. You have endured so much already. It would be unfortunate to see you fail," said Darius as he rose to go.

"My best wishes go with you and Zayid. I hope to send word soon that I have been successful. May the gods watch over you both."

Amon made discreet inquiries, and he has proposed the names of two men here in Ephesus he feels may be able to help. Oceanous was a successful wine merchant, the largest in the city. More than half of all wine sold in town came from his vineyards. His wife, however, was a Roman citizen, and it was unclear if she would be willing to be associated with anyone who might incur the wrath of Marc Antony.

The other man was Evanodous. I had met him when I first came to the villa. Bennu had introduced us. I found him to be both boorish and inappropriately familiar with me. His wife had died just before we met, and I think he was foolish enough to believe that I might be interested in becoming his next wife! The thought of it made my skin crawl, but maybe I could use his interest to further my cause. Possibly a small banquet was in order, one that would allow me to speak to both men at the same time. Amon extended the invitations and they both accepted which was encouraging, but the future remained uncertain.

"Cente, we need to prepare to entertain these potential benefactors, but we cannot afford to spend more than necessary. If we do not get monetary support from them, it will just further reduce what we have left to spend on soldiers. Can you do something impressive without spending too much?" I asked hesitantly.

"There are many merchants who owe me favors or some consideration at least. I will see what I can do. My mother taught me many tricks to making simple things look elegant and I am confident you will be happy with the outcome," she replied, smiling.

"I am sure I will be impressed as I have always been. Please know how much I appreciate your efforts. Bennu would be very proud of you."

"Thank you, my queen. That makes my heart sing, and I will pray tonight for you as well as my usual attentions for Bennu," she replied with a slight bow before shuffling off to the kitchen to begin the planning and shopping.

We made the difficult decision to sell some of the furnishings we had previously purchased for the throne room to help us pay for both the banquet and some additional horses that Zayid felt were critical. It would make no difference if the throne room was less than impressive to petitioners and visitors if we could not keep our momentum. It would mean nothing in the long run. It was a small price to pay but it reinforced the precariousness of our situation. I even had Lira discreetly sell a few of my pieces of jewelry that we have purchased over the last couple of years. I would have to impress with my wit and intellect rather than my jewels.

My concerns were weighing on me as the night of the banquet drew near. There was so much at stake. If I was not successful in convincing one or both men to support me, then we may be at the end. I may be at the end. My heart ached at the very thought of it. If the blessing of the gods was upon me, I would live a long life, but live it as what? If I was not Queen of Egypt, then what was my life to be? In my mind's eye, I could not see the vision of that life. I could only see myself on the throne. There was no other life for me.

"You look lovely, my queen, but I can see you are on edge. What can I do?" asked Lira as she brushed through my hair.

"Oh, Lira. I do not know what I would do without you," I replied with a smile. "Just your presence and unfailing support is all I need. I will be fine."

"Well, you know you always have both, but perhaps another glass of wine?" she said with a mischievous giggle.

Sometimes when Lira and I were together it felt as if we were just two ordinary girls, laughing and talking about all the goings on in the house and whispering about Wassius who had become a regular visitor to the villa to call on Lira. It was wonderful to see her with a modicum of happiness and I hoped that they would marry soon. Lira kept her own council as to her feelings so that remained to be seen. Yet it was never lost on me that we were not ordinary girls; our lives were anything but.

"Your guests have arrived," said Cente, interrupting my preparations

"Wonderful. Thank you, Cente. Please show them to the garden and have Amon get them some wine. I will join them in a moment."

One last look in the mirror, and it was time. I took a deep breath and steeled myself for the gauntlet to come. Having only Lira and Amon with me made me more insecure, but Zayid and Darius were still away. It would truly fall on me to carry the day. As I walked to the garden, I stopped at the fresco of Bennu's wife and daughter. It was hard to explain but there is always something about the painting that captured my heart. Feme's eyes seemed to bore into my soul when I looked at her. It was as if she was trying to reach out to me and speak to me from the underworld. Was her message one of warning or one of hope? It was hard to say but there was no doubt in my mind she spoke to me. I ran my fingers lightly along the edge of the painting, tracing its border as I walked by.

"Good evening," I said with a genuine smile as I entered the garden.

"Queen Arsinoe, it is my pleasure to see you again. May I introduce my wife, Cassia?" said Oceanous with a slight bow.

"It is my pleasure to meet you," I replied.

Cassia was a beautiful woman, elegant and refined, with her perfectly styled hair and fine features. She looked to be in her late twenties. She was many years younger than Oceanous, but I could tell by the way she looked at him that their match was more than just a marriage of convenience.

"Thank you for your invitation. I have long looked forward to meeting you and we were very pleased," Cassia replied with a voice that reinforced her privileged upbringing.

"My apologies that it has taken me this long to arrange this meeting between us," I said a bit sheepishly.

"We are here now. Let us not dwell on how long it has taken, but instead enjoy our time together," she said with what seemed to be a genuine smile.

But there was something about her, a hint of condescension in her honeyed tones, and a dismissive air. I did not for one moment think she was genuinely happy to be here. My guard was up. Her husband, on the other hand, seemed to be unpretentious and pleasant to us all. He had struck up a conversation with Amon, regaling him with the latest in wine making techniques. He was also generous with supplying us with wine for the banquet which was very thoughtful of him and a gesture I appreciated.

"Arsinoe, how lovely you look!" exclaimed Evanodous in his always too familiar tone. He attempted to kiss me on the cheek, but I was too quick for him and dodged his embrace.

"Evanodous, it has been too long," I replied with a sardonic smile.

"You are as beautiful as ever," he said, this time taking my hand and kissing it before I could protest.

"You are too kind," I said, stifling the urge to recoil.

"I was most aggrieved to hear of Bennu's passing. He was a good friend and a kind man. I pray his trip through the River Styx was swift and that he was reunited with his family as he wished."

His praise of Bennu softened my smile. I was genuinely touched by his remembrance of the man we all missed so much. For now, at least, he seemed less objectionable. We all settled in around the table Cente had prepared, nibbling on bits of fruit and sweetmeats.

"Have you found a new wife, Evanodous?" asked Lira.

"No," he said with a hearty laugh. "Unless of course, you would be interested?" he added as he leaned closer to her, his large gut brushing up against her arm. To her immense credit, she did not visibly cringe.

"You truly flatter me, Evanodous, but I am just a humble servant to the Queen and not worthy of one such as yourself," she replied demurely.

It was all I could do to stifle a laugh. Lira was more worthy of Evanodous than he was of her, but it was typical of Lira to be self-deprecating.

"So, you have heard about Antony no doubt?" asked Oceanous.

"I have indeed, but it changes nothing. At the end of the day, I am still the rightful Queen of Egypt given Cleopatra's betrayals."

"Apparently Antony did not agree," said Cassia with an icy tone.

"What Antony thinks or does not think is really of no concern to me, and it does not change the facts," I replied trying to keep the venom out of my voice.

"No, it may not change the facts, but it does change your options. You cannot possibly still think that you can make a military assault on Alexandria with Antony now domiciled there?" asked Evanodous.

"We believe a military assault is still our best option but to ensure our success we will need more men, ships, and supplies. But General Zayid still believes it is possible. I know I still have supporters within Egypt, and I expect that many will come to our aide once the battle begins."

"I would not be so sure," replied Oceanous cautiously.

"I agree with Oceanous. Antony is not a man to be trifled with. He is battle hardened and has heroically fought with Julius Caesar and distinguished himself on the field. I think there are few who would throw their lot in with someone, even the rightful Queen of Egypt, to go up against him," added Evanodous.

"But surely there are many who will not be happy about this latest indiscretion by Cleopatra," suggested Amon.

"That may be. However, being disgruntled and being in a hurry to travel to the underworld are two very different things. It would be a fool's folly to go up against Antony. While there are fools to be found everywhere, you do not strike me as one, my dear," said Evanodous.

"If we had what we needed there is no doubt that we would prevail. I am sure of it," said Lira earnestly.

"As soon as you make a move to secure more resources, Antony will know. He does nothing now because he knows you are not truly a threat and not capable of launching an attack. But if that changes, he will bring the war to you. The odds of you making it to Alexandria are very small," said Oceanous.

"I must try, and I need your help. We need more money if we are to raise the necessary soldiers and supplies. Your investment will be repaid three-fold when I am on the throne of Egypt, I promise you," I said confidently.

"And if you fail, our investment is for naught," replied Cassia curtly.

"The goddess Artemis has assured me that she supports my cause. I believe with her support we cannot fail," I replied, looking closely into Cassia's dark brown eyes.

She disliked me, I could tell. Every gesture and word seemed to carry with it venom like that of an asp. Her husband also seemed to doubt my ability to be successful, but his concerns did not carry the same stinging tone as that of his wife. Perhaps she was a Roman simply putting her faith in another powerful Roman, but I could not help but feel this was personal to her in some way I did not quite understand.

"No investment is without its risks. Every time a galleon departs the port loaded with your wine it is a risk. Tefnut could raise a storm and drop it to the bottom of the sea while barely lifting a finger. Yet you take those risks because not doing so limits your earning potential. You take the risks because you want to do so, and you must. It is no different for me," I replied, my voice starting to crack under the pressure that is building in my chest.

"Queen Arsinoe, I know that you truly believe that you are destined for the throne of Egypt, but I for one do not see how any assistance I could offer would be enough to overcome the odds you now have before you. I am sorry. I wish my feelings were different, but there you have it," said Evanodous with a shrug.

"Oceanous, is that your opinion also?" I asked holding my breath.

He looked at me thoughtfully, before glancing at his wife. Her eyes were turned down and she did not look at him directly, but I knew she was not a supporter, and she would not permit him to be one either.

"I am afraid it is," he said finally. He did not explain his opinion, but truly it was not needed. It was clear he would not go against the wishes of his wife. There was nothing to lose now, so I could speak plainly.

"Cassia, it seems you have a great deal of sway over your husband's opinion, and I gather you do not support my efforts to regain my rightful place on the throne?"

"No, I do not. You are not the rightful Queen of Egypt. To suggest that Cleopatra's relationship with a Roman gives you the authority to remove her is ludicrous. You act as if being with a Roman taints her very soul and makes her unworthy, but it is Egypt that is subservient to Rome and not the other way around. You would do well to remember that."

"Get out…"

"My queen, please," rasped Lira quietly as she rested her hand on my arm.

"Get out!" I said more loudly as I stood up and pointed toward the gate.

"Arsinoe, we don't need to be at odds with each other. Please just calm yourself," replied Evanodous.

"Get out of my house. You are no longer welcome here, any of you. Now leave!" I shouted angrily motioning for the guards to come closer.

My heart was racing. I could see the look of surprise on the faces of my guests, but I could not help it. If they lingered any longer, I would surely resort to violence and that would not end well for any of us.

"You will regret this," said Cassia under her breath as she and her husband gathered themselves to leave.

"I am sorry, Arsinoe," said Evanodous with a slight nod as he left.

As the gate clanged shut behind them, I could feel my anger bubbling over. Egypt, subservient to Rome! How dare she.

"Leave me. Everyone. Leave me now," I stammered.

"My queen, she did not understand the weight of her words. You should not overreact to her slight," said Lira with concern.

"Without their support, I do not see how we will get the resources that we need," added Amon glumly.

"I will never accept support from someone who thinks that Egypt is less than Rome. The Ptolemy family has ruled Egypt for three hundred years, the Romans change their leaders as often as I change my tunic. For what? Because someone else wants power, someone else wants to coddle the masses of ignorant and willful citizens? It is Rome who should be looking to Egypt for its success and brilliance, and I will not stand by while this woman or anyone else tries to denigrate that. Now leave me. I wish to be alone," I said hotly.

Lira and Amon left quietly, leaving only the two guards who had retreated to their stations as I plopped back down on the pillows. My hands were shaking as I lifted the goblet and drank heartily of the wine. It was Oceanous's wine, and I drained every drop before reaching for the carafe to refill my cup. I drained it again before I felt myself starting to calm down. This was it. This had been my best chance, and perhaps my only chance, to secure the support we needed. It had failed before it had even begun. It was clear that neither of these men would support my effort. I do not know why they even bothered to come.

I stared blankly into space. *Was this what failure and resignation felt like?* The thoughts whirled around in my mind, all jumbled together. How would I face my supporters or myself after this? I should not have let Cassia goad me into anger. I was right to be angry, but those feelings were directed at myself as much as at her. Could I have been more persuasive if I had not let my emotions get the better of me? Perhaps, but it felt very much like their minds were made up long before I opened my mouth to plead our case.

"Fetch Lira," I said to the guard standing nearest to me.

"My queen," she said a few moments later.

"Send a dispatch to Zayid and Darius. Tell them to return at once."

It took nearly a month for my message to reach them, and for them to make the journey back to Ephesus. That night we sat at the table for one last time. The anger I had felt a month ago had dissolved into grief and sadness. I would not be able to save my beloved Egypt from the clutches of the Romans. There was nothing more I could do. It appeared the gods had deserted me after all, and despite my repeated earnest prayers and offerings, no other way forward had presented itself. It was over.

"I wanted to thank you, all of you, for your unwavering support and loyalty these past years. While this is not the outcome that any of us wanted, I think we are all in agreement that continuing will only result in the loss of our lives. While I am always prepared to offer mine, I no longer have any desire to risk the lives of those so dear to me."

"We could try again to assassinate Cleopatra," suggested Darius.

"There are several men in our command who could rise to that occasion," added Zayid.

"We would have to kill Antony, too. I doubt we could be successful at both, unless we poisoned them, which requires more cunning than military might," I noted.

"They have tasters for their food and wine, so even that might be difficult," said Lira.

"It is perhaps something we could find a way to accomplish, but for now it has no bearing on where we are. We must release the men and ships from their promises and settle any debts we may have. Then we can take stock of what we have left and determine if there is enough to try to mount a clandestine attack. I confess I am not confident."

"You have given it your all, my queen. You should feel no shame and bear no guilt at this outcome. I have always been proud to be of service to you and I will stay as long as you might need me," said Zayid, his voice cracking a bit.

"Thank you, Zayid but you should go. Go home to your wife and children. I know they have seen very little of you these last few years, and while I am grateful for their sacrifice, it should not continue," I said with a wistful smile.

"What will you do?" he asked.

"Most generously Amon and Cente invited me to stay here, and so I shall remain. The Temple and its grounds have become my home these many years and I will continue to seek refuge here for as long as I am welcome," I said, patting Amon on the arm.

"You are part of the family, my queen. Our home is your home always," he said squeezing my hand.

As the group dispersed, I embraced Zayid and told him I would pray for him and his family. Amon and Cente retreated to the quiet of the kitchen where they would assuage their sadness by baking as Cente always did when she was sad.

"I will speak with you later tonight. Come to my room," I whispered to Darius as he was rose from the table.

"Lira, let us take our walk," I said, cheerfully taking her arm.

These walks to the Temple steps at sunset had long been a ritual with us. Tonight, of all nights, I felt the need to have this moment with her. We linked arms as we walked out to the steps, sitting in our normal spot and enjoying the coolness of the evening air as it began to settle in around us.

"So, what will you do now?" Lira said at last.

"I am not sure, but I do know what you must do," I replied smiling.

"What is that may I ask?"

"You need to marry Wassius and have lovely children. Your brother is here now. You need to be a family, the family I have kept from you all these years," I said sincerely.

"My brother is, I believe, interested in one of the servant girls.

She seems to be returning his attention," Lira said with a bit of a laugh.

"Well, that is a pleasant surprise, but it is your happiness that concerns me more than theirs. Do you want to marry Wassius?"

"I am very fond of him, but at the same time, I do not wish to leave you, my queen. I am bound to you above all others," she replied.

"Lira, I think it is time you started calling me Arsinoe again," I said, staring out beyond the gate, watching as Ra left for the night.

"You are and will always be my queen. I will always regard you as such, regardless of what I call you," she said squeezing my arm.

"And I am forever grateful, but I want you to have your own life, the life you could have had, had your father not brought you to Ganymedes. You deserve a life of your own," I said insistently.

"Whatever the gods have in store for us, know that my loyalty and love for you is unchanged. I will always remain your humble servant in this life and the next one," she said, kissing me on the cheek.

"You are family to me Lira. I hope our lives remain intertwined always," I said, returning her embrace.

We sat in companionable silence long past the sun's departure, when only the orange glow of the horizon attested to his passing and the air began to take on a real chill as darkness fell.

"Come, Lira. Let us go. I am a bit cold," I said as I stood and extended my hand to help her up.

As we turned to go, a noise caught my attention. I looked around and saw nothing. It must have simply been a large bird, and we continued to make our way back toward the villa.

"Ah, my shoe," I muttered as I stooped to fix the strap that had come undone.

"Arsinoe!" screamed Lira.

I looked up to see a man rushing toward us from behind one of the columns. He was dressed all in black. His face was covered with a scarf, but I could see the glint of the dagger he held in his hands. Before I could reach for the dagger strapped to my thigh, he was on me, his knife piercing my leg first, then my belly. I struggled to fight him off. Lira jumped onto his back, slashing at him with her own dagger as she screamed for help, but the assailant was too much for her. He flung her to the ground and stabbed her. Her dagger clattered down the steps before he turned and ran back into the darkness.

"Help, help," I cried out weakly, trying to crawl to where Lira lay in a pool of blood that was slowly beginning to seep down the stairs.

The pain was tremendous. It was a burning, searing pain, like nothing I had ever known. Why was no one coming to our aide? I could not even call out now and as I crawled a trail of blood followed me.

"Lira, Lira," I whispered. When I reached her there was no answer.

I laid my head on her chest, and she stirred a bit. *We shall die together here on these steps, under the watchful gaze of the Temple.* I struggled to catch my breath. The cool breeze washed over me as I held my dear friend close, our blood mingling together as I waited for the darkness to take me, comforted in knowing we would travel the river together.

"Arsinoe!" Someone was calling my name. It must be my father waiting to greet me. I surrendered to the dark as I felt his arms enfold me in his embrace.

EPILOGUE

I had been laying here some ten months now, watching every day out the window as the workmen built the tomb. It would be a tomb fit for a queen. It has slowly risen from the dirt as if the gods themselves have willed it into existence. It will be a magnificent tribute when it is finished. But would the gods keep her secret?

I moved gingerly, even these many months after the attack. My body was not as it was before, and sometimes the pain was more than I could bear. I could only rest when it overcame me. My grief had lessened, and somewhat reluctantly, I had made the decision to try and move on with my life. In honor of those that we have lost.

It was clear now that Antony was behind the attack, on behalf of Cleopatra of course. Amon learned that it was Cassia who had written to him to tell him of our attempts to find more support. It turns out she was a cousin to his wife, but we did not know. It is clear the temple was not the bastion of safety we thought it was. Only a heathen would attack there, but it seemed Cleopatra and Antony had no hesitation. We were a threat, and the threat had to be eliminated. There was no way to escape it. They would not stop until we were all dead. Every one of us.

I adopted the name Feme, in honor of Bennu's daughter. Who I was, who we all were, existed no more. They faded away. It was the only way we would be safe. I married a few months ago, as soon as I was strong enough to stand. In my belly now grows a child, a blessing from the gods I often wondered if I should ever know. We have taken a small house in town, but it is an easy walk to the villa. I go and visit Amon and Cente when I feel up to it. Being with them brings me comfort and after many barren years she is also with child. We share our stories as we share this journey toward motherhood, and I am grateful to have her with me. She comes often with bread or sweetmeats, and we sit and talk, remembering and honoring those we have lost.

The curtain rustled and parted to make way for my husband, returning from his day's labors. His presence always calms me and makes me feel safe. Some days my worries overtook me, that they would come back...

"My love how was your day?" asked my husband as he leaned down to kiss me.

"As always, the workmen have made much progress today. You can see the shape of the lighthouse beginning to appear," I said, pointing out the window.

He sat down next to me on the bed, rubbing his hand along the ever-burgeoning roundness under my tunic.

"Yes, it is going to be magnificent when it is completed, I am sure. But is it good for you to watch every day?"

"It makes me feel closer to her when I watch to observe the creation of her final resting place," I said with a smile tinged with sadness

"How is the baby? Are you feeling him moving inside you?"

"What makes you so sure it is a boy?"

"Well, I am just hopeful that the gods have blessed us. If it is a girl, I will still be happy if you are both well. We have talked about a name for a boy, after my father, but what shall we name her if it is a girl?"

I looked at Darius. His eyes were twinkling.

"We will name her Lira, of course…"

AUTHOR'S NOTE

The story of Arsinoe is a fascinating one but it is poorly documented and very little is known about the time she spent in exile in Ephesus. There is evidence to suggest that she continued to raise an army to fight for her birthright, but no specific details are available. There is also no evidence to suggest that she ever met with Marc Antony while she was there. However, he was in Ephesus at the same time she was, and she was known to him, so it is certainly not out of the realm of possibility. It is rumored that Arsinoe had a wealthy Roman benefactor, but again, just whispers in history the details are unknown.

It is widely believed that Arsinoe was murdered on the steps of the Temple of Artemis by an assassin sent by Marc Antony in 41 BC. In 1926 an octagonal ruined structure was discovered in Ephesus, and some believed the remains of the woman found inside were indeed those of Arsinoe IV, but many are skeptical. The tomb did resemble the Lighthouse of Alexandria but there were no inscriptions to identify its occupant. The skull was removed for tests and was lost in Germany during World War II. A more recent revisiting of the other remains led researchers to conclude that the skeleton was that of a girl several years younger than Arsinoe would have been at the time of her supposed death. Who was in the tomb? No one knows for sure.

GLOSSARY

Amon	The king of the gods.
Ra	The sun god.
Isis	The goddess of protection, mothers, resurrection, and fertility.
Horus	The god in the form of a falcon whose right eye was the sun or morning star, representing power, and whose left eye was the moon or evening star, representing healing.
Serapis	The god of the underworld and the heavens.
Osiris	The god of the afterlife, fertility, and resurrection.
Crook and Flail	Symbol of pharaonic authority. Pharoah and the god Osiris would traditionally be depicted holding the crook and flail. Both symbols were important in religious ceremonies.
Crook (Heka)	Originated from the curved staff that shepherds use to protect and guide their sheep,

which are called awets. Awets are still used in Egypt to this day. The heka represented the pharaoh's role as a shepherd in caring for the people of Egypt.

Flail (Nekhakha)   Historians have several ideas about the actual symbolism of the nekhakha. It is possible it symbolized protection and provision, using this weapon to keep predators away from their sheep. It could also have symbolized a threat of punishment.

Vizier   A high official who served Pharoah.

Uat-ur   The god of fertility and the personification of the   Mediterranean Sea, whose name means the great green

Senet   An Egyptian board game.

Hemar   Literally a donkey, but colloquially used as an insult.

Sekhmet   The goddess of war and battle.

Shaduf   A vessel for holding water or a water pump.

Deben   A unit of weight and currency.

Khet   The physical being.

Ba   The persona.

Ka   The essence of a person.

Ib   The heart.

Faience   Ceramic glazing technique that creates a bright blue-green.

Meskhenet   The goddess of childbirth.

Tefnut   The goddess of moisture, rain, and the sea.

Nemes   A striped headcloth worn by ancient Egyptian pharaohs to symbolize their power, status, and authority

Khonsu   The god of the moon. He was also a navigator or wanderer coming from the movement of the moon across the sky

Ptah   Patron of craftsmen, and played a role in the transition from life to the underworld

Artemis   The goddess that represented many aspects of nature, the hunt, and the wilderness. She also represented childbirth, fertility, and chastity having never married herself.

Praetor   A Roman magistrate. It was a position just below the consul.

Ibis   A long-legged wading bird in the family Threskiornithidae that inhabits wetlands, forests, and plains.

ABOUT THE AUTHOR

Gail was born in the western Detroit suburbs but has lived all over the country including in California, North Carolina and Texas. She currently calls the northern Nashville suburbs her home. Working for thirty-five plus years in leadership roles in the Human Resources function she is now retired and finally living her dream of writing. Always a history geek (really how many people read history textbooks for fun) she is thrilled to be able to tell the stories of those who went before us. She is often inspired by the trials and tribulations of her ancestors especially the women whose voices are often lost to history. For over forty-years she has diligently explored her family's genealogy and it has instilled in her a tremendous appreciation for what her ancestors accomplished. Ordinary men and women whose accomplishments were anything but ordinary.

You can follow her on Amazon, at Goodreads and at https://gailoglesby.wordpress.com/

If you enjoyed this book please consider leaving a review at Amazon or at Goodreads. Your support and reviews are very much appreciated.

www.ingramcontent.com/pod-product-compliance
Lightning Source LLC
Chambersburg PA
CBHW011850300726
48970CB00009B/2725